DEEPFAKE

ALSO BY SARAH DARER LITTMAN

Backlash

Want to Go Private?

Anything But Okay

In Case You Missed It

Life, After

Purge

DEEPFAKE

SARAH DARER LITTMAN

SCHOLASTIC PRESS / NEW YORK

Library of Congress Cataloging-in-Publication Data

Names: Littman, Sarah, author.
Title: Deepfake / Sarah Darer Littman.
Description: First edition. | New York: Scholastic Press, 2020. | Audience: Ages 12 and up. | Summary: Dara Simons and Will Halpern are head of the senior class at Greenpoint High, competitors for valedictorian, but also dating each other, a fact that they kept secret until Rumor Has It, an anonymous gossip site, spilled the beans—but worse is to come because the site posts a video that seems to show Dara accusing Will of paying someone to take the SAT for him and suddenly Will is under investigation and his relationship with Dara is on the rocks, even though she denies ever having said anything of the sort, and it becomes imperative to find out who is responsible for the fake video and why they are trying to wreck two lives.
Identifiers: LCCN 2019056451 (print) | LCCN 2019056452 (ebook) | ISBN 9781338177633 (hardcover) | ISBN 9781338178258 (ebk)
Subjects: LCSH: Social media—Juvenile fiction. | Rumor—Juvenile fiction. | Cheating (Education)—Juvenile fiction. | Dating (Social customs)—Juvenile fiction. | Video recordings—Juvenile fiction. | High schools—Juvenile fiction. | CYAC: Social media—Fiction. | Rumor—Fiction. | Cheating—Fiction. | Dating (Social customs)—Fiction. | Video recordings—Fiction. | High schools—Fiction. | Schools—Fiction.
Classification: LCC PZ7.L7369 De 2020 (print) | LCC PZ7.L7369 (ebook) | DDC 813.6 [Fic]—dc23

10 9 8 7 6 5 4 3 2 1   20 21 22 23 24

Printed in the U.S.A.   23
First edition, October 2020

Book design by Maeve Norton

In memory of my mother-in-law, Phyllis Micahnik, whose love for us all was deep and real

PART ONE

DECEMBER
NOW

RUMOR HAS IT

Helloooooo, Greenpoint High Panthers! It's Monday, December 19. Only three days till Hanukkah, six days till Christmas, and a week till Kwanzaa. Have you been naughty or nice this year?

Don't worry. Rumor Has It is here with all the dirt on who has been naughty . . . You might be able to fool Santa, but you can never fool me.

Yes, I'm talking about you, Nick B and Marco G, getting detention for pulling the fire alarm to get out of a quiz. Can you spell s-e-c-u-r-i-t-y c-a-m-e-r-a-s? Santa isn't the only one who knows what you're up to when you're awake.

Jermaine K has been walking around like the star of some emo music video. I'm told that's because Mykala J dumped him for basketball center Nate A.

Some very interesting news reached Rumor Has It after a party at MJ M's house this weekend. Who knew the two top geeks in the valedictorian race, Dara S and Will H, have been dating on the down low? Even Rumor Has It was caught by surprise, and I usually know EVERYTHING that's going on at Greenpoint High.

I wonder if they compare GPAs while taking a break from making out . . . and how the fight for first place might affect their no-longer-secret relationship.

Third-place competitor—and BFF of Will—MJ is in a real funk. Is it because she's been friend-zoned by Will or because she got rejected from her first-choice school? Maybe it's a little of both? Poor MJ. Rumor Has It suggests a pint of chocolate fudge brownie ice cream.

Keep those naughty and nice lists coming—especially the naughty ones—plus any other news to rumorhasitghs@gmail.com.

WILL

Okay, I admit it: I'm *that guy*. The one who's wearing a college hoodie from Stanford that screams: *I got in early and you didn't.* In my defense, my dad bought it for me two years ago, before I'd even applied, because it's his college and he's obsessed with the place. Like, seriously obsessed. Also in my defense, I'm not the only senior walking around school with a college name splashed across their chest.

My girlfriend, Dara Simons, isn't one of those people. She's waiting for me on the school steps, wearing a skirt, green tights, and boots—looking totally hot.

The girl is first in the class, beating me by a few tenths of a percent, and she just got into Johns Hopkins. But she doesn't flaunt it.

Not my Dara.

Not that I would dare call her "mine" to her face.

It's kind of what I liked about her in the first place. Her independence and the quiet way she gets the job done—while doing it ten times better than everyone else.

We've been friends since freshman year, but it wasn't until we were both counselors at Camp Terabyte this past summer that I realized I was into her.

Luckily for me, she felt the same way.

"Will!" she exclaims as I get close, her eyes bright. "Oh my god, did you get into Stanford or something? Wow, you must be soooooooooo smart!"

"Ha-ha," I say. "Just because you're modest doesn't mean everyone else has to be."

"I'm not modest," she says. "Not all of us knew where we were going since birth. I don't even own a Hopkins hoodie."

"Okay, I guess I'll have to cut you some slack."

"I could have worn the College one my mom gave me, but *someone* got lasagna on it at MJ's party . . ." She pokes me in the shoulder.

"Oh yeah," I say, smiling as I think about what we were doing right after I got lasagna on it.

"Anyway, I haven't done laundry yet," Dara continues.

"Wouldn't have stopped me," I say.

She rolls her eyes. "That's because you're a slob."

"I'm a slob whose dad is finally happy—at least for, like, two seconds—because his son got into his alma mater," I say. "And now he's nagging me to go out for a celebration dinner. I just got another text on the way here this morning asking when I can make it.

"Why is that so bad?" Dara asks. "I mean, it's free food, right?"

"Because he also wants to bring his latest girlfriend so I can meet her."

My parents went through a long, bitter divorce, and even though it was finalized over a year ago, things haven't improved much. Or at all. Dad's been dating all these women who are like the anti-Mom—tall where Mom's short, blonde where Mom is brunette. It makes me wonder why my parents ever got married in the first place.

"He wouldn't bring a girlfriend you haven't met to a celebration dinner, would he?" Dara asks.

I shrug. "Who knows? My dad does whatever he wants. So . . . how was EMTing last night?" I ask to change the subject.

She laughs. "EMTing? That's what we're calling it now? It was good. I helped lead a triage assessment exercise with the newbie Explorers."

"How did they do?" I ask.

"Pretty well, all things considered. But obviously that's because they had such great instruction."

"Obviously," I say.

"But back to your dad. It's just one meal. It'll be over in a few hours." She goes to touch my face and then pulls back, remembering we're in school.

I put my arms around her. "Hey, we're not a secret anymore, remember?"

Dara sighs. "I know. Did you see this morning's Rumor Has It?"

I nod. Like everyone else, I have a love-hate relationship

with Rumor Has It. I hate when they write about *me*, but I can't get enough of the posts about other people. Who knew hate-reading was a thing?

"I hope MJ isn't too upset about it," Dara continues.

"Did *you* notice her being off at her party?" I ask.

Dara scrunches up her nose as she thinks back to Saturday night. "I . . . don't . . . think so. Well, except I think the fact that we've been together since August came as a total shock to her."

"Like it did to everyone else."

"But considering how tight you and MJ have always been—I think that could account for a little, you know, off-ness."

"True," I admit. I've felt weird keeping us a secret from everyone, but I hated keeping things from MJ the most. I run a hand through my unruly hair, which refuses to stay where I want it. "I'll see if I can get a chance to talk to her before Robotics."

"Good move," Dara says. "I'd hate for her to be upset about us, especially since she and I have become better friends this year." Sighing, she lays her head against my chest. She's so short she barely hits my sternum. "Just one of the many reasons I wish we'd been able to keep things under wraps."

"I know," I say, dropping a kiss on the top of her head. "But that's not an option anymore."

Dara pulls away, grabs my hand, and starts walking into school. "I wish I knew who it was."

And . . . we're back to Rumor Has It.

"Doesn't everyone?" I say. "Every year it's a new mystery—and it's one that's never been solved."

"Yeah," Dara says. "But still."

As we make our way down the hall, she says hi to Carson Taylor and his younger sister, Saffron. Their dad is engaged to her mom. I don't know how I'll feel if either of my parents marries someone else. But maybe in Dara's case it's different—her dad died in a car accident. My parents just went through the world's worst divorce. Or at least that's how it feels to my sister, Sadie, and me.

We get to the hallway where we have to part ways to get to our respective first-period classes.

"I'll see you later," Dara says, standing on tiptoe to kiss me. I tug her to me, wanting it to last longer, but after a few seconds she pulls away, her lips curved into a smile. "Hold that thought. Gotta run."

She walks purposefully down the hallway, her dark ponytail swinging in counterpoint to the sway of her hips.

Stop gawking and get to class, Halpern!

I tear my eyes away from Dara and head to computer science, my first-period class.

"Willie H, wait up!"

My friend Amir hurries to catch up with me. He's sporting a purple NYU hoodie, because he got in there early decision. I guess that makes us *those guys*. We should probably be embarrassed to be us.

"So . . . how does it feel to be Rumor Has It's latest victim?"

"Ugh! Don't remind me about that post," I say with a sigh. "Hey, did you notice MJ being kind of off at the party?"

"Well . . . yeah, especially toward the end. I thought it was because she didn't get into Carnegie Mellon, but . . . maybe it was about you and Dara." Amir hesitates. "Do you think MJ has had the secret hots for you all these years?"

"Dude, *no*!" I exclaim. "You know MJ and me . . . we're like brother and sister. There are definitely no hots involved on either side."

"Okay, okay," Amir says. "I was just asking!"

I roll my eyes. Like a straight guy and girl can't be friends without it being about "hots." "I just hope that someone else does something stupid or scandalous soon so everyone stops talking about Dara and me. Sooner rather than later."

"Don't worry. By tomorrow, people will be like 'Will and Dara who?'" Amir says.

"Man, I hope you're right. If I wanted to play out my life in the spotlight, I'd have done theater instead of track," I say. "I definitely gotta talk to MJ before Robotics, though. It sucks to have things be weird between us."

"Yeah, bad vibes between the two of you might give Karla the Killer deep psychological problems. We can't afford to pay for her therapy."

I laugh. Karla is the Robotics project we've all been working on for the county-wide Bot Battle Extravaganza that's coming up at the end of January.

"We definitely don't want that to happen," I say. "We want Karla to kick some serious butt."

"So fix it with MJ before school is over today," Amir says. "Our evil creation depends on it."

"Okay, now you're just getting weird," I say.

But I promise him I'll do it anyway.

MJ

I've spent all day trying to avoid Will. In computer science, he said something about "needing to talk." I lied and said I had to get to English early to talk to Mr. Block about my James Baldwin paper. Unfortunately, we have Robotics Club after school, which means it's going to be hard to escape that convo. I've got study hall now and would give anything to be able to zip home for it, but unlike the rich kids, I don't have a car.

So instead, here I am, stuck in school, with everyone staring and talking about me. I bet half the people think I'm upset because I've been "dumped" by Will and not because the entire school now knows that I've been rejected from Carnegie Mellon. Like I care more about some boy drama than *my entire future*. They don't realize that Will and I have only ever been friends—and despite all the dumb jokes our parents used to make about us getting married when we were in kindergarten, that's all we've ever wanted to be.

What hurts about the Will-Dara thing is that he lied to me—he started dating Dara over the summer, but I only just found out Saturday night at my party.

I thought he was my best friend.

I thought we didn't have secrets.

I thought he trusted me.

I thought I could trust him.

Apparently, I can't trust *anyone*, and that's like the worst feeling ever.

Hence, wanting to go home for study hall, but instead I'm walking into the library.

Ugh.

"Hey, MJ!" Sam waves from one of the study carrels as I head toward the bank of school computers.

"What's up?" I might not feel like talking to anyone, but I can't ignore a friend.

"Not you, from the looks of it."

"Yeah, well . . . would you be with the entire school talking about you and assuming you're in love with your best friend?" I say. "Not to mention blasting to everyone that you got flat-out rejected from your first-choice school."

"Nope, I'd be too busy planning my revenge against Rumor Has It."

"I'd be doing that, too, if I knew who they were," I say. "But no one does, so . . ."

"You're mad," Sam finishes my sentence for me. "So . . . what about the part where they say you're into Will?" He ducks his head and glances up at me from underneath his flop of straight, dark hair. "Are you?"

I stare at him. "Seriously? You know Will and I are just friends."

"Sorry," Sam says. "I didn't mean to upset you more."

I sigh. "I know," I say. "It's just . . . annoying. Like, if I'm not smiling it's because I'm a mess for a guy, as if there's nothing else in life I could be down about."

"Fair enough," he says.

I really don't want to talk about this anymore. "I better go nab a computer," I tell Sam. "See you at Robotics."

I keep walking, waving to Carly Vickers, who is sitting at a table near the computer bank with her boyfriend, Jayson Trantor, and say hi to Ada Thompson, who is working at one of the other PCs. I plop my stuff down and drop into the seat next to her.

"Are you planning to do the comp sci homework?" Ada asks. "Because this nesting loop stuff is getting me down."

"Nah, I'm down enough already," I say. "I'll tackle that when I get home."

She gives me a sympathetic glance. "You doing okay after that Rumor Has It post?"

I shrug.

"Dara's really upset about it, too," she says. "So, who do you think it is? It's so weird to look around and wonder, like, is that person Rumor Has It?"

"If it's you, our friendship is over," I say.

Ada laughs. "We're good. It's not me."

"That's probably what you'd say if you *were* Rumor Has It," I reply.

"True," Ada says with a smile. "But I'm really, really not!"

"Well, today's post pretty much proves I'm not, either."

"Or it *could* be you, trying to throw us all off by writing about yourself."

"Wow, Ada, that's dark and twisted," I say. "Like I'm not already paranoid enough?"

She laughs. "Well, I'd better get back to these nesting loops, because they're dark and twisted," she says, pulling out her headphones. "I'll see you at Robotics later."

"Yeah," I say, thinking about the giant pile of homework I have to do.

I try to get some work done, but it's really hard to concentrate. My mind keeps going back to my party on Saturday night, and to Rumor Has It's post. I find myself looking around the library, now wondering if anyone sitting here is the jerk behind that stupid website.

I finally give up about ten minutes before the period ends and log in to my personal YouTube account to watch some videos.

"Hey, MJ."

Coming from behind, Sam's voice startles me. I minimize the window of the video I was watching, yank out my earbuds, and look up at him. He looks even more shy than usual as he shifts from foot to foot. "Hey, Sam," I say back.

"I was . . . well, I was wondering if you want to go see a movie this weekend."

"Which one?" I ask. "I know Amir wants to see the latest Marvel movie."

"Oh." His face falls. "I was kind of thinking maybe just . . . you know . . . you and me."

Wait . . . is Sam asking me out on a date? Why? I mean, I like Sam a lot, and I guess he's kind of cute in his tall, gangly way. But I've never thought of him like that.

What do I say? I don't want to hurt him, but . . . no, not a date.

I glance up at the clock. Two minutes to the end of the period. "I, um . . . I don't know," I say, shoving everything in my bag and slinging it over my shoulder. "I've got to run to my next class."

"Okay . . . well, think about it," Sam says, a slow flush rising from his neck to create blotches of color on his cheeks.

"Yeah, okay," I say. "Uh, see you at Robotics later."

I race out of the library, feeling a pang in my chest because of the pained look on Sam's face.

Can this day possibly get any worse?

My plan to avoid talking to Will fails when he manages to catch me as I'm walking to Robotics.

"Hey, MJ," he says, bounding up to me. He's like a golden retriever, all energy and excitement over everything. He stops in front of me, forcing me to stop, too. But I look down to avoid eye contact because I really, really don't want to have this conversation. "Look, I know you're mad. About Dara and me. That I didn't tell you."

My chest feels like an anaconda that swallowed an

elephant. I force myself to look up to meet his gaze and see the concern in his eyes, but the elephant is going to choke me if I don't say something.

"Which part do you think hurts more? That everyone now knows I didn't get into my dream school or that my best friend has been lying to me for literally months?"

Will's hurt expression makes the elephant shrink a little, giving me room to breathe. I want him to feel as much pain as I do.

"I wasn't lying," he says. "I was just—"

"Withholding the truth," I say. "But you lied, too. There have been so many times over the last few months I've asked you to hang out and you've had something else to do. Come on, Will. You were busy with Dara, right?"

It doesn't matter what words come out of Will's mouth. The flush that spreads across his face is all the proof I need.

"Look, I didn't mean to lie to you, or withhold the truth or whatever," he says. "It's just that Dara and I agreed to keep our relationship quiet."

"But . . . *why*?"

Will picks at the sleeve of his Stanford sweatshirt.

Yeah, Will, I get it. You got in and I didn't. Ugh. I hate this feeling. I don't want to be jealous of my best friend.

"Because it was all so new, and we didn't want it to become a big deal in the valedictorian race—"

"That plan worked well," I say. "Achievement not unlocked."

"Obviously," Will says sarcastically. "But also . . ." He trails off.

"Also what?"

"We just . . . didn't want to, like, make things weird," he says. "You know, for our group."

"Well, I don't know about the rest of our friends, but as far as I'm concerned, you 'made it weird' more by lying than you would have if you'd just told me you were dating Dara back in August," I say. "You're my best friend, and now I feel like you don't trust me. Like you didn't think you could tell me because I might blab about it. And that really sucks."

"I'm sorry, MJ," he says, looking sufficiently miserable. "Really. The last thing I meant to do is hurt you. You're my best friend. And I *do* trust you." He looks me straight in the eye, and the corner of his mouth quirks into a smile. "I mean, who else would have stayed in the shallow end with me at the community pool when everyone else swam in the deep end, but I was too scared?"

"I didn't want anyone to make fun of you," I say. Although thinking of that summer makes me want to smile, too. Because even though Will was being a giant chicken, somehow he became the coolest kid in the shallow end. Like all the littler kids looked up to him, and he started organizing these massive games of Marco Polo that everyone was dying to play. Which is just so totally Will. I force the smile down.

"And I don't want anyone making fun of *you*," Will insists. "So I'm sorry you found out how you did, and I'm pissed that Rumor Has It blasted about Carnegie Mellon." He shifts from foot to foot. "So . . . are we good?" he asks.

I'm still mad at him, and I'm not ready to let him off the

hook entirely, but I'm willing to call a truce, because we have to work together on Karla the Killer.

"Good-*ish*," I say.

"I'll take that for now," Will says with a relieved smile. We start walking to Ms. McKissack's room. "So, are you up for seeing a movie this weekend?"

#Irony

"Funny, someone else just asked me the same question." I don't tell him that it was Sam and that I might have left Sam hanging.

"Really? Who?"

"Sorry, Will," I say, tossing my head airily. "I'm not going to tell you for . . . let me see . . . four months."

He laughs. "Fair enough. But I was planning to go anyway, so if you go on a date with mystery guy, I'll just sit in the back and spy on you."

"Okay, fine, it was Sam."

Will's grin gets even wider. "He finally asked you! About freaking time."

"Wait, you knew he was going to—"

"MJ, the dude's been crushing on you forever. I told you that, like, over a year ago!"

Now that he mentions it, I have a vague memory of him saying something to that effect when we were in the middle of an intense game of *Injustice 2*. I thought he was just trying to distract me so he could catch up, because I was beating him at the time.

"So what did you say?" Will asks.

"That I didn't know. Then I freaked out and ran."

Will makes a pained face at me. "Oh, MJ. You've probably crushed the guy's spirit. Poor Sam."

"Poor Sam?" I say archly. "What about poor *me*? He blindsided me!"

"But—"

"What if things don't work out and we still have to work on Karla the Killer together?" Then I have another horrible thought. "What if Sam is a bad kisser?" I've never thought of Sam this way before and I immediately worry he's a bad kisser? What's wrong with me?

Will laughs. "I'm sure Sam is an awesome kisser, MJ. Just think about it and if you're into it, go on the date. If not, no big deal."

I raise an eyebrow. "Okay, fine. But what if it gets awkward?"

Will gives me a look.

Oh.

"Exactly," he says, looking sheepish. "But look how that blew up in my face. So . . . do you forgive me?"

"Will, it's no good giving me that puppy dog look. I'm a cat person."

"How could I forget?" he says. "No living person could ever compare to Pascal."

"Most dead people can't, either," I say. "I mean, look at this fuzzy wuzzy little face." I pull up the latest picture I've snapped of his feline adorableness on my phone and shove it under Will's nose.

"If I say Pascal is the cutest cat in the world, will you forgive me?" Will says, pushing my hand farther away so he can actually see the pic.

"Possibly. If you actually *mean* it, that is."

"I mean it! I mean it!" Will says as we walk into Ms. McKissack's room for Robotics.

"Fine. You're mostly forgiven," I say. "On the condition you don't ever hide stuff from me again."

"Deal," Will says, and then he grabs me in a giant bear hug and squeezes until I'm laughing so hard I can't breathe.

"Will," I gasp between giggles before he finally releases me.

"Hey, MJ, we've got a problem with Karla only you can solve," Sam calls out.

"About time you guys finally made it," Ada shouts from across the room. "Come on, Karla the Killer needs your expertise if we're going to beat Boris the BotBeast."

"Dude, you guys don't have a chance," Tony Ortega says. "Boris is going to whip Karla's butt!"

"Dream on, Tony," Ada says. The two of them talk smack all the time, but the general consensus is that they have the hots for each other, even though Ada denied it when I asked her.

"Yeah, Tony, Karla is going to smash Boris into pieces so small you'll need an electron microscope to find them," I say.

We trash talk each other all the time in Robotics Club. But we're united in our unabashed geekitude.

I haven't one hundred percent forgiven Will, but as soon as we start working on Karla, it becomes all about solving the problem. We want to win. I might not have gotten into Carnegie Mellon, but building things is still what I like to do best.

RUMOR HAS IT

Good morning, Greenpoint Panthers! It's Tuesday, December 20, which means we only have three more days of school till winter break and FREEDOM! Well, unless you're one of those people planning to develop a parentally approved and very convenient illness a day or two before break starts so you can get a jump on vacation travel. *cough*cough* As they do every year, the administration has sent an email to parents threatening "dire consequences" for removing kids from school for vacation, but we all know it's going to happen anyway.

You know who can't wait for winter break? Taylor van C. He's been telling everyone who will listen that he's going to Telluride. Taylor, we know your granddaddy has a big freaking house there. Dude, give it a rest, okay?

I bet Ms. Johnson is counting down the days to break, too. She was spotted crying at her desk on Friday. Don't worry, Ms. J, it'll be better in the New Year.

I'll tell you two people who *won't* be having such a happy New Year. That would be Dara S and Will H . . .

Today's Rumor Has It bombshell is gonna cause some trouble in paradise for the formerly secret lovebirds. Watch and see for yourself:

Rumor-Has-It.com/willhbombshell

Here's a transcription, just in case you're in class and can't watch right now, because you do NOT want to be late to *this* party.

Dara S: Oh, come on. Everyone knows Will paid someone to take the August SAT for him. I mean, his scores went up by how much? Like, two hundred points? Who does that—especially when they've told you how they suck at standardized tests?

From 1250 to 1460? Will's a smart guy, but that's just ridiculous.

Maybe the pressure from his dad just got to be too much? Maybe Will didn't know about it and his dad arranged it, like in that celebrity college admissions scandal?

Whatever. Either way, it's not right, because he's taken the spot away from someone who really deserves it.

Like I said, it's a bombshell. Duck and take cover, Panthers!

DARA

Ada and I are both in AP Physics when she texts me saying Rumor Has It just posted something new about Will and me.

What now? I don't know why they are so obsessed with us.

Hiding my phone under the desk, I check out Rumor Has It and see a video's been posted. I can't watch it in class, but then I realize there's a transcript. And it's me. Saying stuff. In this video.

As I read, the hairs on my arms start to tingle with the feeling I get when something is about to go very badly wrong. The same feeling I've been getting ever since that Sunday in sixth grade when Dad went to the supermarket to get Mom and me ice cream and never came home because some idiot drunk driver T-boned his car at an intersection two minutes from our house. That same sick-to-my-stomach feeling I got when we started hearing sirens, and I knew, somehow, deep down, that they were for Dad.

I'm trying to read, but my phone is blowing up with text messages from Ada that I keep ignoring. When I finally understand what I'm supposedly saying in the video, I just stare at my phone. The words on the screen blur together as my mind spins in confusion.

Because I never said those things.

My phone vibrates again and I switch to my texts.

Why would you say that about Will? Ada's latest text reads.

I didn't! I text back. I don't know what's going on!

She turns and gives me a skeptical look, then looks back to the equation on the board Mr. Buckley is talking about in front of the room.

One by one, other kids in the class start looking in my direction.

Word of Rumor Has It's latest post is spreading.

Has Will seen it yet?

My fingers trembling with panic, I text him.

Will, I don't know what is going on. I never said what Rumor Has It says I did!

I keep checking under my desk to see if he's replied, but there's nothing.

Just texts from other people either asking me if it's true or why I'd tell everyone that my boyfriend cheated on the ultimate test.

I know I'll see Will at lunch next period. But it's fifteen minutes away and I can barely concentrate with this knot in my stomach.

When the block ends, I race out of the classroom, ignoring Carly Vickers, who calls out, "Hey, Dara, wait up!" I have to get to Will, but first I have to see this video. I head to the nearest bathroom so I can watch it without being watched myself. Locking myself into a stall, I press play. As I watch, it feels like I'm in a sci-fi movie. There's someone who looks exactly like me, wearing my clothes, with my voice, saying things that I know for a fact I never said.

How is it possible?

I play it again, and bile rises into my throat. I have to talk to Will. Somehow, I have to make him understand that I never said any of this.

But how? *I* know I didn't say it, but there's this video. I mean, I'm watching it. It doesn't make any sense.

I text Will again.

Will, can you meet me somewhere other than the student center? WE HAVE TO TALK.

I wait, willing the little speech bubble to appear so I know he's texting me back.

It doesn't.

I'm not at all hungry, but I force myself to head down to the student center because Will has lunch now, too. The last thing I want to do is to have this conversation in front of half the school, but I have to see him.

People I barely know are giving me strange looks as I walk down the hall. Denice Jones asks me if it's true. I just shake

my head and hurry past because I don't want to talk to anyone except Will.

Amir and Sam are sitting at our usual table. "Have you
seen Will?" I ask.

"No. But I'm not sure he wants to see you," Amir says. "Not
after that video."

"That's what I need to talk to him about," I retort.

"I'm shook, Dara, so you can imagine how Will feels. I
thought you were into him. Like, *really* into him," Amir continues. "I mean, even if Will *did* cheat, which I can't see him
doing, why would you accuse him like that?"

"I *am* really into him!" I exclaim. "And I didn't accuse him
of anything!"

"Then why is there a video of you doing just that?"
Sam says.

"I *don't know* how there's a video!" I explode with frustration. "All I know is that I never said that stuff!"

They stare at me, and it's clear from their faces that they
aren't convinced.

"*Please*, where's Will?" I beg them. "I really need to
see him."

"Looks like you're about to get your wish," Amir says. "He's
heading this way."

I turn and see Will storming over to the table. People notice
and are watching his progress across the student center, antic-
ipating drama, phones pointed at us. I can't help wondering if

Rumor Has It is here somewhere, reveling in the chaos they've caused.

"How could you, Dara?" Will shouts at me. "*Why* would you?"

I step back. I've never seen Will like this. "*I didn't!* I never said any of it!" I say, trying to keep my voice calm, even though my body is starting to shake.

"You're un-fricking-believable, Dara! How can you stand there and lie straight to my face? There's literally a video of you right here"—he jabs a finger at his cell phone—"saying I *paid someone to take the SAT for me!*"

It's impossible to get enough oxygen in my lungs.

"I know it looks like I did," I say, breathless desperation making my voice unnaturally high-pitched. "I don't understand how, because I swear that *I never said those things.*"

"Yeah? So what's your brilliant explanation for the video showing you doing exactly that?"

It feels like all eyes and phones in the student center are focused on us, probably because they are.

"I don't have one," I'm forced to admit. "I don't know where that video came from." I try to put my hand on his arm, my eyes pleading with him, but he flinches away from me. "Will, please . . . you *know* me. You've got to believe what I'm telling you. I would *never* do this to you."

"Except you did," he says. His gray eyes are glacial. "And now I don't know what to believe about you anymore. We're done. Finished. Over."

I feel a small flame of fury. Will's shutting me out, not even giving me a chance. If that's how he feels, fine. But I'm not going to stand here and take it. And if he can end us just like that, then whatever. I guess he isn't who I thought he was after all. Steeling my shoulders, I walk the gauntlet of staring eyes to leave the student center.

WILL

How could she do this to me?

Why would she do this to me?

I kissed those lying lips. I was looking forward to the next time we were alone so I could kiss them some more.

Now I don't even want to see her face.

I can't understand how Dara could be so deceitful.

Was everything she said to me a lie? Even when she told me she loved me?

But . . . *why*?

"I just don't get it," Amir says, shaking his head slowly. "Dara's always been cool. I can't believe she'd do something this messed up."

"Yeah, especially since it turns out you guys have been dating for months," Sam says.

"You think you can't believe it? This is a total gut punch," I say. "I mean, I told that girl I *loved* her."

"I'm sorry, Will," Sam says. "That really sucks."

Amir looks at me, and there's a flicker of doubt in his dark brown eyes. "Don't come at me, but . . . you didn't do it, did you? What Dara says in that video?"

Wow.

"Thanks for nothing, Amir," I say. "Do you even know me?"

"Sorry, dude. It's not like I thought you would," Amir says. "But . . . I didn't think Dara would do something like that, either."

"Well, she did," I say, slumping in my chair.

"Hey, Will," MJ says, arriving at the table with Ada. She's hovering a bit awkwardly, shifting from foot to foot. "Um, how are you doing?"

I get it. How do you talk to your best friend about the fact that the girl he's been dating just turned his life into a dumpster fire? "Great. Real freaking great," I say bitterly.

"We saw Dara rushing out on our way into the student center," Ada says. "She looked pretty upset. I asked her if she was okay and she blew me off."

"*Dara's* upset?" Sam says. "After what *she* did to *Will*?"

MJ grimaces. "The video?"

"Yeah." I turn to Ada. "You've been friends with Dara for a long time. Can you explain why she'd do something like this?"

"No," she says. "I couldn't believe it when I saw it."

"You mean saw the video of it?" Amir says.

"Yeah," Ada says. "But still . . ." She frowns, her brow furrowed. "There's something that's bugging me."

"Yeah? What's that?" I ask. "It seems pretty clear to me."

"I know, but . . . well, it's just that I've known Dara since I moved here in third grade," Ada says slowly. "She was my first friend. We've been best friends ever since and . . . even though

I've seen the video, I'm having a hard time accepting it. It just seems so . . . not her."

She puts her finger on the thing that keeps running around my brain every time I watch that video. The Dara in the video looks just like the girl I've been with since the summer. She's wearing that COLLEGE sweatshirt that her mom bought her as a joke when she was freaking out about whether she'd get into school somewhere, and she has her hair down, spilling around her shoulders. I can't tell exactly where it was taken, but it's definitely her. Even if what comes out of her mouth is so *not* her. It feels like it can't be true, but there's a video.

"I mean, even when her dad died in that car crash and her mom got really depressed, Dara was still always trying to make things better for other people," Ada continues. "Why else did she spend all those hours to get certified as an EMT?"

"Wasn't that like ninety hours of classes or something?" MJ asks.

"More like one hundred and twenty," Ada says. "And now she spends, like, all her time volunteering as an EMT. Someone who cares enough about people to put in that kind of time *and* still be top of our class . . . Even after watching that video a few times, I don't know. It's just kind of hard to believe that Dara would say that about her boyfriend. Even if it's true."

First Amir, now Ada?

I stare at her. "What do you mean, *even if it's true*?"

She doesn't flinch, her eyes steady as they meet mine. "I

mean, your scores *did* go up a lot between the May and August SAT, didn't they?"

"Will did not cheat," MJ jumps in, furious.

Even though I'm about to explode, MJ being on my side so immediately feels good. Like finally someone has my back, without question. I force myself to take a deep breath.

"My scores went up because I did practice tests every spare moment," I say, biting out the words. "Not because I paid someone else to take the freaking test."

"Seriously, Ada, how can you even think that?" Sam says. "You know Will!"

"Yes, I do," Ada tells him, but her eyes stay focused on me. "And *you* know Dara."

"So you're saying you believe Dara when she says I cheated?" I ask her.

"No," Ada says. "I'm just pointing out that you guys are really quick to believe the worst of her."

"Just like you seem to believe the worst of *me*," I say.

"No, I'm just—"

"If you believe Dara, then you must think I'm the kind of person who would cheat my way into Stanford."

"Will, dude, hold on," Amir says, trying to dial things back. "Ada's just—"

"You know what? Fine!" Ada says, picking up her lunch. "I'll go eat somewhere else since you're determined to make me take sides instead of trying to actually think this through."

I watch her as she goes to sit with some of her other friends, speaking to them angrily, probably telling them what a cheating jerk I am.

Fine. I'm angry, too.

I want everyone to pick a side, and I want it to be mine. I want my friends to prove they really *know* me; know me well enough to be sure that I'd never do what Dara accuses me of in that stupid video.

MJ slumps into the chair next to me with a heavy sigh. "Maybe Ada's right, too," she says in an uncharacteristically quiet voice.

I stare at her. Two seconds ago, she was on my side. She's one of my closest friends. She of all people should know the real me.

MJ continues, "I mean, not only would this be totally out of character for Dara, she also really *likes* you." She bites her lip and shakes her head slowly. "Or at least she *did*. From the look on her face when she was leaving before, I'd say that your relationship is roadkill."

"Good riddance," Sam says.

MJ is looking down at a blob of mayo on the table, like it's the most interesting thing she's seen today. "Yeah," she says, in that same quiet voice. "Yeah. I guess."

The whole school might think I'm a cheater, but at least my closest friends are on my side.

I just hope this whole thing blows over when Rumor Has It

posts about someone else. But even if it does, I'll never be able to see Dara the same way again.

I'm in Spanish when I'm called to the main office to see Principal Joyner. Guess this isn't blowing over anytime soon. I can tell from their reactions that everyone in my class has seen the video. It's hard to meet people's eyes as I gather my stuff and walk out of the room, but I force myself to do it, because *I* know I'm innocent, even if other people don't.

When I get to the office, Mrs. Martinez, Principal Joyner's administrative assistant, tells me to go right into his office because he's expecting me.

"Good afternoon, Will, have a seat," Principal Joyner says, gesturing to the chair facing his desk. "We have a lot to discuss."

My stomach, already growling because I was too mad to eat anything at lunch, starts churning as I sit down. Joyner tilts back his chair and crosses his arms over his chest.

"Will, I'm not one for gossip and I'd love to shut down the whole Rumor Has It tradition because it causes no end of problems," he says. "But a serious allegation about academic dishonesty showed up on the site this morning, one that I can't ignore . . . particularly given how much your scores did improve from the May to August SAT."

Not him, too.

"That's because I spent all summer studying," I point out. "I worked my butt off to bring those scores up."

"So then why would Dara say you cheated?" he asks.

"I don't know" is all I can say.

"Did you have a fight? Could this be her way of getting back at you?"

"What? No! Everything was fine between us." As soon as the words leave my mouth, the doubt takes over. I must have missed something; some important clue that might have warned me. "Well, at least I *thought* things were fine."

He looks like he doesn't believe me and taps his lips with his forefinger, thinking. "I've known you and Dara Simons for four years," he finally says. "I'm in a quandary because you are the last two students I'd ever thought would get tangled up in a mess like this. You've both been exemplary in every way. So now I have a she-said-he-said situation and it's impossible for me to know who or what to believe."

"I swear to you, I didn't do it," I say. "I've got a 4.9 GPA. Why would I blow that by doing something stupid and dishonest like paying someone to take the SAT for me?"

"I've been a high school principal for over twenty years, Will," he says, shaking his head. "You have no idea of how much stupid I've seen." He leans forward. "It has got nothing to do with grade-point averages or IQ. Sometimes it's the smartest kids who do the dumbest things."

"Maybe," I say, feeling unsure where this is going. "But I'm not one of them. I swear to you, I didn't cheat."

"I'll be speaking with Dara after this. And then I'll make a decision about next steps."

"What do you mean, next steps? You can't punish me for something I didn't do!" I say, starting to panic.

Joyner stands up, signaling our meeting is over.

"As far as what those next steps might be, I'm reserving judgment," he says. "I'll be in touch with you and your parents after I've had a chance to speak to Dara."

I can't believe this is happening.

How has my life turned from great to crap so quickly?

DARA

When I'm called down to Joyner's office, a few of the kids in my English class go "Ooooooooh" just like they did in elementary school. The rest turn and look at me as I gather my things and leave, some with curiosity and others like I'm the worst person in the world. Ada, at least, seems sympathetic because she whispers, "Hang in there." She means well, but the words off a kitten poster in the guidance counselor's office can't fix this mess. MJ, who is sitting in front of Ada, seems to be making it a point not to look at me.

But she's Will's best friend. She probably believes I would do something this awful to someone I really like. Someone I've been dating. Someone I risked saying I loved. Or at least I thought I did.

People in the hallways have been asking me why I'd do that to Will. At first I tried just telling the truth—that I didn't do it. But no one really wanted that answer. So my reply became: "I don't know, because I *didn't* do it. Why do *you* think I would?"

Most of the replies people gave me were nasty. I've been trying to pretend I'm encased in ice and I can't see or hear anyone. If everyone is so quick to jump to conclusions and think of me as a horrible person, ignoring them can't make it that much worse.

At least now the hallways are empty because people are in class, so I don't have to pretend. But that leaves me time to think, which is almost worse.

When I enter Joyner's office, he gestures to one of the chairs in front of his desk and I sit on the edge of it, my knee bouncing with nervous energy.

"Dara, I've asked you here because you made substantial allegations in the video posted on Rumor Has It," he says. "Allegations that I have to take very seriously." He leans forward, pinning me with his gaze. "How about you tell me what you know about Will paying someone to take the SAT for him?"

I put my hand on my knee to try to stop it bouncing so Mr. Joyner will take me seriously. "So . . . I know this is going to sound totally ridiculous but . . ."

"But?"

"Mr. Joyner, I never said the things in that video."

He raises an eyebrow. "Then how would you explain the fact that this video of you making the accusation exists?" he asks.

"I don't know!" Desperation claws at my belly. "Will is my friend . . . We've been dating—" I have to stop and swallow the lump rising in my throat. "At least we were, until this happened."

Joyner leans back in his chair and eyes me thoughtfully. In the silence, I feel my heart starting to beat even harder in my chest and hear blood rushing in my ears. He has to believe me. He has to. If he doesn't . . . I don't even want to think about it.

"Dara, you're the top student here at GHS, and I've always had the greatest respect for you," Mr. Joyner says. "But here's what I think happened. I think you and Will had a fight, and you decided to get back at him by revealing what he did. And now that you see how it's blown up, you're having second thoughts and denying that you had anything to do with it."

Seriously? He thinks I would do something like this because of a fight with my boyfriend?

Anger gives me the courage to push back. I force my voice to stay even, despite wanting to pound on his desk. "Mr. Joyner, you're not listening to what I'm saying. I don't know anything about Will paying anyone to take the SAT, and I never said he did."

He frowns. "To the contrary, Dara. There's a video of you saying exactly that. But your contention notwithstanding, I'm going to have to investigate. News of your accusation has spread very rapidly. Thanks to Rumor Has It's reach, I've already had members of the school board calling, wanting me to do damage control. It's not every day a school's prospective valedictorian accuses the prospective salutatorian of academic dishonesty."

"But I didn't say he did it!" I repeat. "I don't think there was any academic dishonesty."

"Thank you, Dara. You can return to class now."

My fists clench. Why won't he listen to me?

I get up, holding on to that tiny piece of anger.

Everyone thinks this video is the truth, because they can see me saying those things. I don't know how anyone could fake me doing that, but I have to find out a way to prove they did. Because I realize, this isn't just about Will. It's also about me.

WILL

After school, I head straight out to the car. Most days I've been going to the weight room because track season starts in a couple of months and I want to stay in shape. But the thought of more people staring at me made me text Sadie to tell her I'd give her a ride home. While I wait for Sadie, I watch the video over and over. Each replay hits me with the same cutting feeling of betrayal, even though I already know what's coming. Eventually, I can't take it anymore and lay my head on the steering wheel, trying to close myself off from the world and the dumpster fire that is my life.

Sadie startles me back to reality when she opens the passenger door and plops into the seat.

"From what frozen part of Hoth did Dara Simons pull that stupid video?" is the first thing out of her mouth.

"I wish I knew," I say, backing out of the spot and following the stream of cars and buses out of the parking lot. When we're on the main road, I tell Sadie what's really making me crazy. "The worst thing is that she won't even admit to what she did. She denies everything. She told me she never said any of it."

"Are you serious? It's right there. I had half the sophomore class asking me if you really *did* pay someone to take the SAT for you. The other half wanted to know if you and Dara have broken up yet."

She glances over at me, eyes narrowed. "You *have* broken up with her, right? You'd have to be an idiot not to, and even though we both know I inherited the brains in this family, I don't think you're an idiot."

I ignore her arguable claim to be the family brain. "I made it pretty clear that she is no longer my favorite person and that we're done," I say. "Then Ada Thompson was like, 'It's not something Dara would do' and she . . ."

It's hard to admit that one of my friends thinks I might be guilty, even to my sister.

"She what?"

"She pointed out that my scores went up. Like she was basically implying that it was suspicious and maybe *I* was the one who is lying."

"What? No way!" Sadie exclaims. "I think I can take her if you want me to beat her up."

I snort, because Sadie takes after Mom in the height department. I can't imagine her taking on anyone, much less Ada, who's, like, half a foot taller.

"Yeah, I don't think so," I say. "But . . ."

"But what?"

"I just don't get it. I saw Dara this morning, right before Rumor Has It posted, and everything was . . ." I shake my head, gripping the steering wheel as I remember how glad I was that we were finally out in the open about us dating. "There's like this piece of me that doesn't want to think that the Dara I know—at least I thought I knew—would do something like this."

"Oh brother," Sadie sighs. She raps my head with her knuckles. "*Wiiiiillll*, use your brain."

"I *am* using my brain," I say, shaking her off. I really don't *want* to believe that everything she and I had was fake. It felt real.

"Do Mom and Dad know about this?" Sadie asks.

"I don't know," I say. "Joyner said he was going to call them once he'd met with Dara and talked to the superintendent and the school board about 'next steps,' whatever they are."

A wave of nausea crashes over me as I think about my parents finding out. Ever since I got into Stanford, they've actually been getting along. Well, okay, that's probably overstating it. For them "getting along" means not being complete jerks to each other. They're too busy telling everyone who'll listen that I got in, because it's proof that their bitter two-year divorce didn't mess me up so badly I couldn't get into a top school. They're probably proud of me, too, but honestly, I think the proof thing is what makes them happiest, which makes me feel even worse about the fact I'm not sure if Dad's school is the right place for me.

My phone rings. Sadie looks at the screen because I'm driving.

"It's Mom," she says. "Good luck." She answers and puts it on speaker.

"Will, I just got a call from Mr. Joyner. He said there's a video going around accusing you of paying someone to take the SAT for you!" Mom says, her voice frantic with disbelief. "It's not true, is it?"

I glance over at my sister, and she's rolling her eyes.

"Mom, of course it isn't true!" I say. "Do you think I'm stupid? Why would I risk everything to do that?"

"Because your father has been putting so much pressure on you to go to Stanford?" she says. "I keep telling him you might be happier at a different school, but he won't hear about it. Oh god, if he convinced you to do something unethical—"

"Mom!" I interrupt to stop her from singing the familiar your-dad-is-such-a-jerk refrain. "Stop. It has nothing to do with Dad. I didn't bribe anyone. *Dad* didn't bribe anyone. I don't know why Dara said I cheated."

"An accusation that Mr. Joyner is taking very seriously," Mom says. "He's also calling your father, and he wants us to come in for a discussion tomorrow morning." She sighs. "I suppose this means we're going to have to have a family meeting tonight."

Like I'm not stressed out enough about this, now I've got to deal with my parents being together in the same room.

"Great, your father's on the other line," Mom says. "I'll call you back." She hangs up.

Sadie sighs. "You know they're going to make this about them instead of you, right?"

"Yep," I say with a sigh of my own.

"The whole thing is just . . . weird," Sadie says. "We need to figure out why Dara made the video and how Rumor Has It got it."

"I hate that stupid site," I say. "If I ever find out who is behind it . . . they're dead."

"Maybe that's what you should do," Sadie suggests. "Figure out who Rumor Has It is. Then you confront them and get them to tell you who made the video."

"Easier said than done," I say. "All we know is that Rumor Has It always picks a rising senior as their successor at the end of the year, but there are, like, two hundred and twenty-five people in the senior class. It could be any one of them."

"Well, we know it's not you, right?"

"Fine, it could be any one of two hundred and twenty-four people," I say. "Glad we're able to narrow things down."

Sadie gives me a death look. "Don't be a jerk."

"Sorry," I say. "But you know it's not going to be easy to figure out."

"As Dad and Mom are always so quick to point out the minute I get anything less than an A on a test, you have the second-highest GPA in your class," Sadie says. "All your geeky friends are super smart, too. But suddenly you're too dumb to solve a problem because . . . why?"

She has a point. I've got some of the smartest kids in school on my side.

Well, except for Ada.

And Dara.

Even Amir had a moment or two of doubt before he believed me.

"You *are* pretty smart," I admit to Sadie. "But I'm still the family brain."

She snorts. "Yeah, right. You don't see *me* being accused of cheating on anything."

I'm about to remind her that I didn't cheat when Mom calls back.

"Your father is swinging by after work," Mom says as soon as Sadie answers. "I'm going to stop on the way home from work and pick up a pizza from Saucy Sue's."

Saucy Sue's is my favorite pizza place, but that's not enough to make up for everything that's happened today, especially because I have a feeling the worst is yet to come.

Mom arrives home from work with a large pizza and a salad.

"Get some plates and silverware and let's eat," she says while she's taking off her coat. "Your father said he'll be here at seven thirty." She frowns. "Which, knowing him, probably means eight thirty."

"Can you just call him Dad?" Sadie asks. "We *know* he's our father."

"He's not *my* dad," Mom says.

"So call him Gary, then," I tell her. "That's his name."

Mom emits an exasperated sigh. "Will, I was married to the guy almost twenty years. I *know* his name."

Sadie and I exchange a glance.

It's already been a bad day, and it's clear tonight won't be a whole lot better.

I help myself to pizza, even though my stomach is churning like it always does when I know my parents are getting together—especially when it's to talk about me. Maybe if I throw up, they'll stop fighting. Actually, I don't even think puke would stop them. They'd just figure out a way to blame each other for my vomit.

"Mr. Joyner sent me a link to the video," Mom says when we sit down to eat. "Wasn't that girl Dara a counselor with you at Camp Terabyte over the summer?"

"Yeah," I grunt through a mouthful of pizza.

"Don't talk with your mouth full," Mom says.

I finish chewing and swallow. "If you don't want me to talk with my mouth full, don't ask me questions when I'm eating."

Mom gives me a don't-get-fresh-with-me look.

Sadie tries to cut the tension by telling Mom about the art project she's working on, but it doesn't help. We're all on edge as Mom keeps glancing at the clock and making increasingly loud sighs of annoyance as the minutes tick past seven thirty.

We pick at the rest of our dinner in silence.

The doorbell rings at seven forty-seven, which is probably the timeliest Dad has ever been. He's either really mad about his canceled date or really worried about me. Possibly both.

Mom says, "Can you get the door?"

Like I have a choice.

"Hey, Will," Dad says, pulling off his leather gloves and tossing his keys on the hall table like he still lives here, which drives my mom nuts. "So when do I get to take you out to dinner to celebrate you getting into Stanford? Katelyn is really excited to meet you."

"I don't know," I tell him. "There's a lot going on right now."

"It's probably going to have to wait till we get back from Aspen, then," Dad says. "We leave on Friday."

"I guess it'll have to wait. But . . . uh . . . I'm looking forward to meeting her, too," I say, lying through my teeth.

Dad takes off his coat and throws it over the banister. "So what's this mess you've gotten yourself into?"

"I didn't get myself into anything," I say.

"That's not what Mr. Joyner seems to think," Dad says. "Otherwise he wouldn't have insisted we all come in for a meeting tomorrow morning."

"I know but—"

"Come on, let's get this family discussion over with," Dad says. "I've had a long day, and dealing with your mother is just going to make it longer."

I hate when Dad asks me questions and then interrupts me before I can answer them, but he's already heading into the kitchen. Sadie calls it the Dad Deflection.

Mom's cleaned up the plates, but the remains of the pizza are still on the table.

"I'm starving," Dad says, taking one of the two slices remaining in the Saucy Sue's box.

"Gary, it's polite to ask if you can have it before taking," Mom says.

"Tell that to your divorce lawyer," Dad mutters through a mouthful of pizza.

"Really?" Mom says, her hands on her hips. "You're going to bring that up again? Now? In front of the kids?"

"I was supposed to have dinner with Katelyn tonight," Dad says. "The least you can do is spare me a slice of awful pizza."

Saucy Sue's used to be his favorite pizza joint, too.

"Oh my god, Mom! Dad! Will you stop?" Sadie says. She's twisting her paper napkin in her hands and looks like she wants to send it as a projectile but can't decide which parent to aim at first.

"Yeah," I say. "Can you guys try to not kill each other for, like, half an hour? Today has already been total crap."

Mom tosses a look in Dad's direction, then sits down, her hands folded on the table. Dad sits at the other end of the table, as far from Mom as he can get.

"So . . ." Dad says. "Did you pay someone to take the SAT for you, Will?"

"Why does everyone keep asking me that?" I say, frustrated.

"Because, Will, there is a video of some girl claiming you did," my dad replies.

"But you asking makes it seem like you think that's something I would do. I wouldn't. *Obviously*, I wouldn't. It's like no one knows me or something." I put my head down on the table in exasperation.

"Then why is this girl saying that you did?" Dad asks. "She sounded pretty convinced."

"I don't know!" I tell them. "I thought we were—"

I almost slip and tell them Dara was my girlfriend, emphasis on the *was*. But it's too late. Mom already picked up on it.

"You were what?" Mom says with narrowed eyes. "Did something happen between you and this Dara?"

I look down at my hands, not trusting myself to keep a poker face when it comes to this.

"Will, were you involved with her?" Dad asks.

I raise my head and nod, slowly.

"You've got to be kidding me! Your future could be ruined because of some girl?" Dad says. "Did she make it in retaliation because you broke up with her?"

"That might make sense if I *had* broken up with her," I say. "But I hadn't." Well, until after the video. "I thought things were good. This morning everything was great. Even if she is technically beating me for valedictorian at the moment." I don't know why I feel the need to brag about how smart Dara is. I guess because it's one of the best things about her?

"So why would she lie?" Dad says. "Tell us the truth, Will. We can't help you unless you're one hundred percent honest with us."

"Gary, Will said he didn't do it," Mom says.

My parents exchange a weighted glance.

"Will, I want to take you at your word," Dad says finally. "But Mr. Joyner sent me the link and I saw the video."

"I. Didn't. Do. It," I bite out through gritted teeth.

"I believe you, Will," Mom says, with a pointed look at Dad, which makes me wonder if she really does believe me, or if she's just saying it because Dad doesn't.

"The problem is that the school isn't convinced," Mom continues. "They're taking it very seriously. Mr. Joyner said he might bump it up to the College Board to investigate. And they could tell Stanford."

Wait, what? My stomach drops. If they tell Stanford, I'll be kicked out before I even start. No way would they let an accused cheater attend. Then I wonder if that would be so bad. I flush with guilt and glance at my dad. I'd never hear the end of it.

"They can't do that," Dad says. "We'll sue if they do."

Of course that's my dad's reaction. I swallow hard and try to stop the panic from rising.

"Sue who?" Mom asks. "The school district? Stanford?"

"Both, if necessary," Dad says. "They can't take away Will's place."

"They can if cheating is involved," I say. "Which, I will repeat again for those in the back, *I did not do.*" Frustration is coloring my words, but it's better than the other feelings.

"Are you going to pay the lawyer's fees if we sue?" Mom asks. "Because I can't afford to finance a big lawsuit."

"I gave you all that money in the divorce and you're complaining that you can't pay for a lawyer if Will needs one?"

"There he goes again," Mom says, rolling her eyes. "You just can't get over the fact that the judge awarded me alimony, can you?"

"STOP!" Sadie shouts. She gets up, her fists clenched. "I'm so sick of you two fighting!"

I shove my chair back. "No, Sadie, it seems about right they'd make this about them. That's what they always do."

"Hold on a minute, that's not fair," Dad says.

"Sure, just like it's not fair that you two got divorced and hate each other," Sadie says, her voice rough with anger. "Deal with it, Dad! We have to."

She stomps out of the kitchen, and I follow her, ignoring my father's stern admonition to "Get back in here right now, Will!"

As I storm upstairs to my room, I hear my parents start to argue about whether I did cheat and blaming each other for the mess I'm in.

Looks like Team Will has one player: me.

I am so screwed.

DARA

"What are you doing sitting here in the dark?" Mom asks when she gets home from work and finds me in the living room with no lights on.

I've been sitting on the sofa all afternoon, watching the video over and over, obsessively searching for clues to prove it's fake. No luck so far. All I've got are tired, gritty eyes.

"Dara, what's going on? Why haven't you put the casserole in the oven yet?" Mom flicks on the lights, making me blink. "Does this have to do with the phone call I got from Mr. Joyner today about some video? He sent me a link to watch, but I was totally slammed at work and didn't have time."

"Yes," I say, pointing to my phone screen.

Mom comes over and sits next to me.

"Before you watch this, you need to know something really important." I look straight into her eyes. "I never said this."

Mom's brow furrows. "How about you just play it for me?"

I exhale as I press play and watch my mom's reaction to the video. Her eyes widen when she hears me say that Will paid someone to take the SAT for him.

She shakes her head, confused, when the video ends. "So are you telling me this video is . . . fake? That you never actually said this, but somehow there's this video of you doing it?"

"You don't believe me," I say, unable to keep the hurt from my voice.

"I didn't say that," Mom says. "I'm just trying to be clear about what you're saying, because this is . . . extremely confusing."

"Tell me about it," I say. "No one is more confused than me. How do you think I felt when I watched this the first time, knowing I never said that?"

"I just don't understand how—" Mom bites her lip. "Wasn't Will one of your coworkers at camp this summer?"

I nod. "And we were dating."

"Dating?" Mom exclaims. "You never told me you were dating anyone!"

"We didn't tell anyone," I say. "But can you, like, forget that for a second? It's not the point."

Mom frowns. "So what *is* the point, besides the fact that my daughter is hiding things from me?"

"*The point* is that I never said this," I explain. "Yet somehow there's a video of me doing that. And now Will hates me, and my friends hate me, and Mr. Joyner called me into his office and implied that I made it because of some fight Will and I had and—"

"Hold up," Mom says, raising her hand. "The principal accused you of making this because of a fight with your boyfriend?"

I nod, and Mom mutters something impolite about Mr. Joyner under her breath. I think she believes me, which fills me with relief because it means I've got at least one person on my side.

"I know," I say. "But that's not the biggest problem. I need to figure out how to prove that this video is fake."

Mom taps her index finger against her lip. "Where did it come from?"

"Remember I told you about that anonymous gossip site at school called Rumor Has It?" I say.

"Yes, ridiculous," Mom says, shaking her head.

"Rumor Has It posted the video this morning."

"And you have no idea who this Rumor person is?"

"No. Or how this video exists."

"It's bizarre," Mom says.

"I know. It's freaking me out."

"I have to ask you this," Mom says. "*Did* Will pay someone to take the SAT for him?"

"Mom—no!" I say. "But it looks really bad for him, because his scores increased a lot from May to August."

"So . . . are you sure he didn't?" Mom asks.

I hesitate for a second before answering. Can I be totally sure? I mean, he said he loved me a bunch of times before this morning, but then he wouldn't even listen to me, much less believe me, when I told him I never said what was in the video.

As much talking the logic through with myself as answering Mom, I say: "I saw him practically every day over the

summer. He was always talking about taking another practice test. I don't think he was lying about that. So if he
cheated, he never told me."

"As long as you're as sure as you can be," Mom says. She
hesitates. "Do you want me to talk to Ted about this? He
might know about how the video could be manipulated, and
given his line of work, he might have the tools to help prove it."

Ted's my mother's boyfriend—excuse me, her fiancé—and
he does video editing for the local TV station. He proposed to
Mom right before school started, and now it's all wedding
this and wedding that constantly. I'm still getting used to the
idea of things going from just Mom and me to becoming part
of a family of five, with Ted as my stepdad and Carson and
Saffron as my stepsiblings.

"Aren't you two too busy planning the wedding?"

Mom inhales quickly and gives me a sharp look. She swallows visibly and then speaks in a slow, measured tone. "Do you
really think I'm incapable of doing anything except planning
a wedding?"

"No, but it's been pretty much the number-one topic of
conversation around here for months."

Mom frowns. "I get it, Dara. You're upset about what's happening to you, and you're unsettled by me getting remarried,"
she says. "But please don't forget that I love you, and you've
always been my priority."

I feel bad that I kind of want to roll my eyes, because I know
she's being sincere. She just doesn't get that this is weird for

me. That I'll leave for college and be replaced with two other kids. Instead of saying any of that, I just say, "I'm . . . sorry." And I mean it.

"We'll figure this out," Mom says.

I want to believe her. But right now I don't see how.

WILL

The meeting with Joyner is at nine this morning. When I get to the office, Mom's already there, looking at her watch because of course Dad is late. When Mrs. Martinez says Mr. Joyner is ready to see us, Mom stands up and says, "Come on, Will. If you father can't be bothered to show up on time, we'll begin the meeting without him."

This is off to a great start.

"Good morning, Mrs. Halpern, Will," Joyner says as we walk in, gesturing for us to sit. "Mr. Halpern isn't coming?"

"It's Ms. Rose, and he's allegedly on his way," Mom says.

Mom really hates being called Mrs. Halpern since the divorce, which feels weird since Sadie and I are Halpern, too.

"I'm so sorry, Ms. Rose," Joyner says. "It's always difficult to figure out how to address people in today's families. Our computer systems haven't caught up yet." He glances at the clock on the wall, which now reads ten past nine. "Would you prefer to wait for Will's father?"

Mom opens her mouth to say no just as Dad comes barreling into the office. "Sorry I'm late," he says. "Got stuck behind some grandpa driving below the speed limit."

I can only imagine the language in Dad's car while that was

going on. His road rage accelerates faster than the Maserati he bought himself after the divorce.

"That's fine, we were a little late getting started," Joyner says.

One thing Dad is really good at and I'm not is schmoozing. Watching him in action makes me even more aware of my limitations. He moves straight in to break the ice by commenting on Joyner's collection of signed baseballs. I'm forced to sit there listening to them bond over sports while the amorphous threat of "next steps" is hanging over my head. It's making me even more fidgety and stressed out. Mom's next to me with her hands clasped in her lap so tightly her knuckles are white. Finally, she snaps. "For goodness' sake, Gary, we're here to talk about Will, not baseball."

Dad looks annoyed, but Joyner apologizes and says, "Yes, I'm sorry," before taking a seat on the other side of his desk.

"So . . ." He clears his throat. "I'm afraid I've had to call you in today because of the video that surfaced on the Rumor Has It website, which contained a very serious allegation." Fixing his eyes on me, he continues. "We try to maintain high standards of academic integrity here at Greenpoint High."

"That's very important," Dad says. "But as you also know, my son has worked extremely hard to be a good student. He's currently second in the class and gained admission to one of the top schools in the country. Do you really want to jeopardize that for him?"

"Of course not," Joyner says. "But we can't condone academic dishonesty. It wouldn't be fair to the other students."

"Mr. Joyner, I swear to you, I didn't cheat," I say, since Dad neglected to mention this very important point.

The principal shakes his head as he glances over at me. "Will, I'd love to believe that. I can't tell you my shock when I watched the video. But I've got myself a situation here. There's a video of your girlfriend—"

"*Ex*-girlfriend," I point out.

"Your ex-girlfriend saying that you engaged in illegal and unethical behavior," he continues. "She claims that she never said the things in the video but has no explanation for how and why it exists. Meanwhile, it has circulated widely. I'm getting calls from angry parents, and I've got the school board breathing down my neck."

Joyner looks at me with narrowed eyes. "I don't know what went on between the two of you, but whatever it was, you would have done yourselves a big favor if you'd dealt with it privately."

"I don't know what happened, either," I say. "As far as I knew, everything was good."

Joyner looks skeptical. "There are too many open questions, so after consulting with the school board, the decision was made to bump this up to the College Board to investigate, given that the accusation involves the SAT. We'll wait on their decision before deciding what actions to take here. But in the meantime, Will, you're on disciplinary probation."

Disciplinary probation? I don't even know what that means.

"What are the chances that the College Board will inform Stanford?" Dad asks.

"They do reserve the right to tell higher education institutions of any investigations," Joyner says. "I realize that reporting might have serious consequences—but likewise, so would ignoring an allegation of academic dishonesty."

"Mr. Joyner, I hope you'll think very carefully about this," Dad says. "I wouldn't want to have to sue the school district because you rushed to unfounded conclusions about my son."

All the chumminess Dad schmoozed his way into at the beginning of the meeting disappears the minute he threatens legal action.

"Mr. Halpern, we can't overlook such serious accusations," Mr. Joyner says. "And threatening the school district with legal action isn't particularly helpful at this juncture. Our responsibility here is to take the allegation seriously and follow the proper protocol. At this stage, it's in the hands of the College Board to investigate further and determine guilt or innocence."

"Of course, Mr. Joyner, it's much too early to consider legal action," Mom says in her best smooth-things-over voice. "But I watched my son study every day before retaking the SAT in August. So I'm sure when this investigation is over, you'll know, as I do, that Will would never cheat."

"I sincerely hope so, Ms. Rose," Mr. Joyner says, standing to usher us out of his office.

It feels good to hear my mom is behind me, quietly and firmly. Dad makes threats, but I think it's more to do with him not wanting me to lose my place at his beloved Stanford than because he actually believes that I didn't cheat.

"Well, I'll see you after Aspen," Dad says. "Hang in there, buddy."

"I'll try," I say.

"And as soon as I get back, we're going to have that dinner with Katelyn," he says.

Mom rolls her eyes behind Dad's shoulder.

Once again, I'm caught in the middle between them, not wanting to upset Dad but not wanting to hurt Mom, either.

"Yeah, okay," I mumble, giving him an awkward hug. "Have a great trip."

"I'll see you at home later," Mom says, just as the end-of-period buzzer sounds.

"I better get to my next class," I say, hoping my parents don't fight all the way back to their respective cars.

When I'm halfway down the hallway in the science wing, I hear, "Will, wait up! Please!"

At first I speed up, wanting to run away from the sound of the voice that only two days ago made me smile and made my chest expand with a feeling I thought was love. But then I realize that there's something I need to say to her.

My jaw clenches as I turn to face her.

Dara, standing there in all her glory. Her ponytail perfectly centered, looking hot in a soft off-the-shoulder sweater and neon-blue high-top Vans.

The girl who landed me in this mess.

"What do *you* want?" I ask, not even trying to hide my anger and contempt.

"Will, I know you're mad at me but—"

"Mad? That doesn't even begin to describe how I feel about you right now. Haven't you heard? Our relationship is canceled."

The hurt expression flits across her face so quickly I might have missed it if I wasn't staring at her with fury in my eyes. She takes a deep breath and steps toward me.

I step back. I can't be near her. It's too confusing.

She nods once, like she gets it. "I'm going to figure out how this happened. I'm going to prove that you never cheated and that I never said you did."

She looks me dead in the eye. "I can understand why it's hard for you, but . . ." Her gaze hardens, then she says, "Just try to remember who I am. I would never, *ever* do this to you."

Memories of the last few months while we'd been dating start fighting with the anger about that video for space in my head, but I push them out and take another step back. "Remember who you are? Dara, if I had my way, I'd never have to see or speak to you again."

With that, I turn my back on her and stalk the rest of the way to physics, doing my best to delete the image of Dara's angry expression from my brain.

RUMOR HAS IT

Well, *helllooo*, Panthers! It's Thursday, December 22. Happy Hanukkah! Or is it Chanukah? However you spell it, hope you're enjoying the Festival of Lights. Have you been spinning those dreidels and eating latkes and doughnuts?

I'm gonna jump right into the news, because I haven't posted in a few days and things have been W-I-L-D here at GHS!

Y'all thought soccer team hunk Jermaine K getting dumped by Mykala J for basketball center Nate A was the biggest news this week, right? It's true, Jermaine's Instagram post-breakup was truly heartbreaking and gave Rumor Has It the sads, but this little love triangle has been overshadowed by the latest events.

Who needs to watch soap operas or reality TV? We've got all the drama you need right here at Greenpoint High!

So just what has toppled the sports love triangle from first place? The drama, drama, drama between Will H and Dara S in the student center on Tuesday at lunchtime, that's what! It looks like the relationship between recently revealed lovebirds and valedictorian competitors might not survive Dara's fifteen minutes of internet fame, at least judging by the harsh words Will threw at her in front of a gawking lunch crowd. It was savage.

Dara denied that she said what was in the video posted here Tuesday but couldn't seem to explain how a video of her saying it exists. Hmmmm . . .

Meanwhile, Will is denying that he paid someone to take the SAT.

Who is telling the truth?

The drama continued Tuesday afternoon with them being called down to Principal Joyner's office separately, and an investigation is underway.

Yesterday, Will and his parents had a meeting with Principal J. That looks ominous, doesn't it?

But the biggest news?

Will H and Dara S are coupled no more.

Will was overheard telling Dara that if he had his way, he'd never have to see or speak to her again.

You can hardly blame him for dumping her after what she did.

Especially since a little birdie told me that Principal J is referring the explosive video posted here yesterday to the College Board.

Will GHS's number-two brainiac lose his place at Stanford?

Will he still be here at graduation, or will he get the boot?

Should I be changing my bet to MJ M as salutatorian?

Stay tuned here for more . . .

DARA

I turned off all my social media notifications because the people who believe Will—in other words, like, everyone—have been going off on me. It's Friday afternoon of the worst week ever, and as much as I love being a volunteer EMT, I really want to go straight home after school. It's been another day of being alternately stared at and shunned. At least winter break starts right now, so I don't have to face everyone for two weeks.

But I still have the rest of my shift to get through first, and I can't let anyone down. It turns out to be a good thing, because it takes me out of my own problems for four hours. Helping other people does that.

One call was from Mrs. Odekembo, an elderly lady who lives on her own in an apartment on Jones Street. She fell, but luckily she always keeps her cell phone in her pocket, so she was able to call 911. She had the most amazing plants in her apartment and told me about them on the way to the ER.

Almost immediately after we got her to the hospital, we had another call to a house where a ten-year-old named Joey had been climbing on the top of a chair to reach the place where he'd figured out his mom was hiding the Christmas presents. He fell and broke his collarbone, and hit his head pretty hard in the fall, so we also had to check to see if he had a concussion.

"Isn't he still supposed to believe in Santa at that age?" Isaac, the paramedic on the shift, said. "Man, kids just grow up too fast these days."

I tried to remember when I realized that Santa was really my parents. It was definitely before my dad died, but I know I pretended to believe for a while longer than I actually did because it seemed to make them so happy. Especially Dad, who loved eating the cookies I left out for Santa. I think that's part of the reason I figured it out, because Dad was so insistent that I leave out the cookies, and Mom was all, "I don't know, I think Mrs. Claus's encouraging Santa to lay off the cookies because of dad bod," and I started wondering who Santa's kids were (the elves?) and thinking how awesome it would be to live in a toy shop at the North Pole. Well, except for the cold, that is.

My shift ends after we drop Joey at the ER. Even though he was in pain, he was really excited to be riding in the ambulance. He was kind of hilarious about it.

Despite being cheered up a bit, the absolutely last thing in the world I feel like doing is having Friday night dinner playing happy families with Ted, Carson, and Saffron. But the wedding show must go on, despite Dara's drama, or at least that's how I imagine the conversation between Mom and TV Ted went.

Also, I should probably stop thinking of him as TV Ted because pretty soon he'll be my stepdad.

The Taylors are coming about the same time my mom gets home from work, and she left me a list of instructions for dinner. She already made the Bolognese sauce and prepared the garlic bread. I just have to heat up the sauce, boil water, put in the spaghetti, and get the garlic bread in the oven.

Cooking is more Mom's thing than mine, but I've become ace at heating things up.

I put the sauce on to simmer, start a big pot of water for the pasta, and set the oven to heat up for the garlic bread.

While that's all going on, I take out my phone to watch the video again. It's become an obsession. I see it playing behind my eyelids when I'm trying to get to sleep.

Somehow I have to figure out a way to prove that it's fake.

But no matter how many times I watch it, I can't find any clues to help me do that.

After playing it a few more times, I give up because the water's boiling and it's time to put in the pasta.

That's when I hear a key open the front door. "Hello, we're here," Ted calls over the noise of his family's arrival—the shuffle of coats being tossed aside and the thuds of kicked-off sneakers.

Mom gave him a key to our house even before they got engaged, which freaked me out because it's *our* house—as in hers and mine, and the memories we have of Dad. Giving Ted a key felt like we were betraying my dad. It's just another of the things I've had to get used to and accept.

"Hey, Dara," Ted says, entering the kitchen with Saffron and Carson close behind. "It sure smells good around here."

"This is for dessert," Saffron says, handing me a box.

"What is it?" I ask.

"Don't open it! It's a surprise," Carson says.

After the week I've had, I'm not sure I want any more surprises. The timer starts beeping for the garlic bread.

"I better go get that," I say, setting the box aside and grabbing an oven mitt. I wonder how long it's going to take for someone to bring up the video.

"Need help?" Ted asks.

"Nope, I think I got it," I reply as I open the oven.

"Carson, how about you set the table? Saffron, help me get water for everyone," Ted says, stepping out of my way.

While we're getting everything on the table and organized, Ted tells us a funny news story he edited today about a local Italian restaurant, Morello's, which has been around forever. Someone apparently stole a set of salt and pepper shakers, and then returned them a few weeks later with a note saying that ever since walking off with the restaurant's seasonings, they had been stuck with bad karma. So they returned the stolen goods in the hope that things would change for the better.

"Meanwhile, the restaurant didn't even know they were missing," Ted says.

"Did your reporter interview the thief?" Carson asks.

"No, because it was returned anonymously by mail, with a note of explanation," Ted says.

"Why don't more bad things happen to really bad people?" Saffron asks. "Or more to the point, why do bad things happen to good ones?"

Ah, to be a freshman and so idealistic.

I've been asking that question ever since my dad died. He didn't deserve to be killed by that drunk driver. Mom didn't deserve to lose her husband, and I'm not saying I'm the perfect kid, but I didn't do anything so terrible that I deserved to lose my dad.

Mom gets home as I'm cutting up the garlic bread. Ted goes out to greet her as soon as he hears the garage door.

"Wow, Jana, you timed that perfectly," I hear him say from the hallway. "Do you and Dara always time dinner with such military precision?"

Mom laughs and I hear them kissing.

I glance at Carson and Saffron, and the looks on their faces reflect the awkwardness I feel. I guess we have that in common.

"If my life's taught me anything, it's that I can only *try* to plan for things to work out perfectly," Mom is saying as they come into the kitchen. "If they actually *do*, it's all random chance."

"Tell me about it," I say, in a tone that probably reveals a little too much, because Ted looks at me intently. I ignore his glance, focusing instead on draining the spaghetti.

"Let's eat," Mom says, and we all take seats around the table.

Ted and Mom talk about their respective days. Carson and Saffron and I just eat and listen. I like them both well enough, but it still weirds me out that we're going to be stepsiblings. It's not like we've got so much in common. Carson is really into theater. Saffron is on the girls' soccer team. We travel in different friend groups. We probably wouldn't have hung out much at all if our parents hadn't started dating.

"Dinner is delicious," Ted says finally, looking at me.

"Yeah, this is awesome," Carson says.

"Dara, you're a really good cook," Saffron adds. "Too bad you're going to school next year. My dad is the worst." She grins at him.

"I'm not *the worst*," Ted says in mock defense. "Back me up here, Carson."

"Uh," Carson says around a piece of bread. He swallows. "Well, we're not dead yet, so points for that, I guess."

"Ouch," Ted replies with a laugh. "You guys know how to hurt me."

"Actually, I just heated things up and made the pasta," I confess. "Mom's the one you should be complimenting."

"Great food, Jana," Saffron says.

Mom and Ted smile at each other, like this is all part of their strategy to win Mom's way into his kids' hearts through their stomachs and things are going according to plan. It's strange to think that Mom's still going to have a daughter living with her when I'm away at college. What if she ends up being closer to Saffron than she is to me? I'm not used to having to share her. I feel a pang in my chest at that thought.

"So, kids, we've got the venue for the wedding," Ted says. "It's going to be the Waterfront."

"If it's a nice day, the ceremony will be outside by the water," Mom says. "If not, we'll have both the ceremony and the reception in the ballroom overlooking the water."

"Sounds like something out of a magazine," I say, trying to push down my complicated feelings and just be happy for them.

"Is that a good thing or a bad thing?" Ted asks.

I shrug. "It's a wedding thing, I guess."

He exchanges a weighted glance with Mom, who quickly changes the subject. "So, kids, tell us about your day."

"Mine was terrible. My history teacher is just . . . ugh," Saffron says. "He assigned us a paper that's due *after break*. What part of *it's our vacation* doesn't he understand?"

"Is it Mr. Higgins?" I ask. It has to be—it's his favorite thing to do. He does it every break. He'd assign a paper over the summer if he could. He gives a ton of reading as it is.

Saffron nods.

"Advice from a Higgins survivor: Do it this weekend," I tell her. "Get it out of the way so you can enjoy the rest of break without it hanging over your head."

"But I've got Christmas shopping to do! And Jayda's having a party tomorrow night."

"Forget about all that," Carson says, waving a hand in Saffron's direction. "Did Will really pay someone to take the SAT for him? Like, how do you even *find* someone to do that for you?"

I knew the odds of us making it through dinner without someone bringing this up was, like, zero to nothing.

"For the record, you better not be thinking of doing something that unethical," Ted says, giving Carson a warning glance.

Carson shakes his head. "Duh."

"I don't know anything about Will cheating, and I never actually said he did. I don't know how someone managed to make a video of me doing that," I say. I've been saying the same thing on repeat the last few days. Too bad no one's listening.

"I do," Ted says. "It's getting scarily easy."

"What?" I say, looking up in surprise. "Really? How?" I narrow my eyes at Ted and hold my breath.

"Using deep learning," Ted says.

"What?" Great. I've been reduced to one-word questions. I stare at Ted. "You mean like artificial intelligence?"

"Deep learning is a subset of machine learning, which is a subset of artificial intelligence," Ted explains. "AI is a simulation of intelligent behavior in computers."

"Can you give us the For Dummies version?" Mom asks. "Without all the tech speak?"

Yeah, Ted, what my mom said.

"Okay. Do you know what a neural network is?" Ted asks patiently.

The rest of us look around the table at one another.

"I don't," Mom says.

"Neither do I," Carson says.

"Nope!" Saffron says.

"Right. Okay, an artificial neural network is a series of algorithms that tries to recognize relationships in big sets of data in a way that mimics the operation of the neurons in the human brain," Ted explains. "So deep learning teaches itself the way to categorize things rather than it being programmed by a long series of human instructions."

"I thought we were getting the dummy version," Saffron mutters.

Ted laughs. "It just means setting up computer hardware and software algorithms so the machines teach themselves by finding the relationships between things," he says. "But you'd need an amped-up computer with extra graphics cards, a heat sink, and some strong fans."

"Okay, but how does that have anything to do with

someone making a video of me saying something I never said?" I ask him.

"Because if someone had sufficient computing resources and enough pictures and videos of you, they could train the algorithm to create that video," Ted explains. "It's what's called a deepfake—a combination of *deep learning* and *fake video.*"

"Ted, this is completely terrifying," Mom says. "Why would anyone create such a thing?"

"Deep learning has legitimate applications," Ted explains. "Like the driverless car. Or interpreting medical imaging to detect cancer."

"But what about that video of Dara?" Carson says. "I mean, I think I've seen some where they put Nicolas Cage into all these different movies, and they're pretty hilarious, but this one of her . . . isn't."

"Is there any way I can prove it's a deepfake?" I ask.

"Millions of research dollars are being spent on just that," Ted says.

"Seriously?" Saffron asks. "Why?"

"National security. Deepfakes could be used to disrupt the political process. Or the financial markets," Ted says. "Look at how this one video impacted Dara and Will, two high school students. Can you imagine these being used in an election or a war—or to destabilize everyday life?"

My heart sinks.

"Great. So basically I'm screwed is what you're telling me," I say.

"Not necessarily." Ted gives Mom a meaningful glance. "How about we help clean up, serve up the surprise dessert we brought, and then watch that video on the big screen in the living room? I've got my work laptop, which has some tools that might help us."

"Sounds like a plan," Mom says.

Carson and Saffron clear the dishes while Ted puts the leftovers in containers. I rinse the dishes and load them in the dishwasher, and Mom gets out dessert plates and fiddles with the mystery dessert box.

"Dara, why don't you take the dessert plates and silverware into the living room and help Ted hook up his laptop to the TV or whatever it is he needs to do," Mom says. "The rest of us will bring in the dessert."

I open my mouth to say that TV Ted doesn't need me to figure out what to do, and he doesn't have to hook anything up because it's a smart TV. But everyone is looking at me like, *Do it, Dara!* So I pick up the plates and forks Mom put on the counter and follow Ted into the living room.

I don't know what's going on with everyone and this dessert—they're all acting so weird, like it's a big secret they're in on and I'm not. My birthday is in July, otherwise I'd be convinced they were about to put those trick candles that won't blow out onto my birthday cake.

I pull up the Rumor Has It site and find the video, and Ted

downloads it to his laptop so he can manipulate it with the TV station software he has.

After a few minutes Saffron comes in carrying a cake, a broad smile on her face, followed by Carson and Mom each carrying a present.

"Congratulations, Dara!" Saffron says, putting a cake in front of me on the coffee table. It's got *Congrats, Dara! Go, Blue Jays!* in icing on top, as well as what I think is supposed to be a blue jay but looks more like a Smurf with wings.

Ever since Rumor Has It posted that video, it's been all I've been able to think about. The fallout has made it easy to forget the good things that have happened in my life, like getting into Johns Hopkins. A thrill goes through me remembering that I'm excited for next year.

"We're so proud of you," Mom says, handing me her present.

It's a Hopkins Blue Jays hoodie.

"Thanks, Mom," I say, giving her a hug.

"Saffron said that all the other kids who got in early finally started wearing their college gear," she says with a smile. "So I figured you needed one with the actual name of the college you're going to—to replace that hoodie I gave you at Thanksgiving."

There's a twinge in my chest as I remember Will's smile as we joked about my lack of a Hopkins hoodie. It seems like a million years ago.

I also try not to let it bother me that Mom and Saffron

already seem to be kind of chummy. Yes, we're going to be stepsisters, but I don't want Saffron to take my place when I'm away at college. Still, I smile and thank her for giving Mom the idea.

"And here's a present from us," Carson says, handing me a bigger wrapped gift.

Inside is a duffel bag with my initials, *D.E.S.*, embroidered on it.

"I know how much your mom's going to miss you next year, so this is to encourage you to come home and visit," Ted tells me.

Home is going to be really different next year, once he and Mom get married and things get reorganized to make room for Carson and Saffron, I think with a pang. But at least Ted seems convinced that Mom will miss me, even though she'll have him and his kids to keep her company. I'm oddly touched.

"Thanks, Ted," I say, getting up to give him an awkward hug, then exchanging even more awkward ones with my soon-to-be stepsiblings.

"Can we cut the cake already?" Carson asks. "I've been waiting for this since we stopped to pick it up on the way here."

Mom laughs. "Sure," she says, reaching for the knife.

Once we all have cake, I push play on the video.

Everyone watches in silence as we chow down. When the video is finished, I play it again.

"There's definitely something weird about it," Mom says,

putting down her half-eaten piece of cake. "I've only realized it now I've seen it on the big screen."

I sit up, suddenly alert. Has she spotted something I missed in the many times I've watched it?

"What's weird?" I ask, feeling a tiny sliver of hope.

"That's the problem," Mom says. "I don't know exactly. It certainly looks and sounds like you, but there's something not quite . . . right."

"Let me play it again," I say. I've watched the video more times than I can count since it was posted, but now that Mom's mentioned it, there *is* something off about video me.

I press play again and feel the familiar prickling of horror at the back of my neck as I see myself saying words that I know never came out of my mouth.

"I think it's your eyes," Carson says. "They don't look right."

"How?" I ask.

"I don't know," he says. "They're not as . . . like . . . *animated* as when you normally speak."

Huh.

"I've loaded the video into the editing software we use at the TV station," Ted says. "Let me play it on the big screen slowed down as much as I can. Maybe that will help us."

Played super slow, my voice sounds really freaky, like the serial killer guy from *Scream*.

"I know what it is!" Saffron exclaims suddenly. "You don't blink!"

"You're right!" Mom says.

Carson is already looking it up on his phone. "Get this," he says, reading off his screen. "The average person blinks every four seconds, or fifteen to twenty times a minute."

Google for the win.

Ted pushes play again. Saffron nailed it. I don't blink at all. But my gut is telling me there's something else, which my brain hasn't figured out yet.

At second twenty-six, there's a series of sounds apart from my serial killer voice. "What's that?" I ask. "Can you stop and play it again from the beginning? I just heard something."

"What's what?" Ted asks. "I'm not sure what we're listening for."

"Neither am I," I admit. "But there's another sound in the background, besides my voice. Maybe if we can figure out what it is, it'll give us another clue."

"Can we try playing it a little faster?" Saffron suggests. "It's hard to tell what the sounds are when they're so slowed down. Dara sounds like a total psycho at that speed."

"I know, right?" I say.

"I'll speed it up a little bit at a time," Ted says.

When it gets to second twenty-nine, I close my eyes, so I can focus better. It sounds more familiar but . . .

"Doesn't sound like anything I recognize," Mom says.

"There's something about it," Carson says. "It makes me annoyed, and I'm not sure why."

"Okay, I'll try speeding it up a little more," Ted says.

When the video starts again, we're all listening intently. "Wait a minute!" Saffron exclaims. "Play it again!"

Ted plays it again at the same speed, then speeds it up a little more and plays it a second time. That's when Saffron says, "Okay, you'll probably think I'm nuts, but that sounds like a few notes from the *Gutter Girlz* theme song."

Gutter Girlz was this awesome show that was really popular when I was in middle school. It was about a high school bowling team, and I loved it because there was a character, Rosie, whose dad had died, too. The fact that she could be sad and miss her father but still be able to laugh and do fun things with her friends made me feel like maybe it was okay for me to feel happy sometimes, even though I missed my own dad. It made me feel less alone. I was so into it that I used to have the theme song as my ringtone.

"How can you tell it's that from a few notes?" Mom asks.

"Trust me, she listened to that song enough times she could probably tell it from one note," Ted says. He plays it again.

"Saffron, I think you're right. You're a genius!" I exclaim.

"No wonder hearing it annoys me!" Carson says. "Saffron was obsessed with that show and I hated it!"

"Because you have no taste," Saffron says.

"Clearly," I agree.

We start singing the *Gutter Girlz* song together, and Carson makes a big deal of covering his ears, which just makes us laugh and sing louder.

Maybe having stepsiblings won't be so bad after all.

Still, there's something poking at the back of my brain, and I ask Ted to play the video one more time.

"Haven't we watched this enough?" Mom asks. "Can we just enjoy the cake?"

I flap a hand to shush her, and this time I keep my eyes open as I listen. I hear the faint *Gutter Girlz* theme ringtone in the background and hear the words come out of my mouth as I stand there wearing the hilarious sweatshirt with generic COLLEGE on it.

The sweatshirt . . .

"That's it!" I say, jumping off the sofa and standing in front of the TV. "The ringtone! And the sweatshirt!"

Four very confused faces stare back at me.

"What's it?" Ted asks.

I grab my phone off the coffee table and play my current ringtone, which is the *Wonder Woman* theme song. "Will changed my ringtone last summer, when we'd just starting being a thing," I explain. "It's been 'Wonder Woman's Wrath' since the beginning of August."

"But . . . I didn't give you that sweatshirt . . ." Mom's nose crinkles as she thinks. "Not until . . . Thanksgiving weekend!"

"If this isn't enough proof for Joyner, I don't know what is," Carson says.

My heart is racing like I've had too much coffee. Finally! Proof that this video isn't me.

"Oh my god, you are all the best!" I exclaim, grabbing my

cell. "Thanks for the cake and the presents and, well . . . everything."

With hurried fingers, I text Will.

Hey, I know you don't want to talk to me.

I found something in the video.

It's fake.

I can prove it.

PART TWO

AUGUST
BEFORE

RUMOR HAS IT

Hey, Panthers! Hope you're enjoying the dog days of summer. Could it be any hotter?

Oh yes it could! Here's the latest steamy gossip from my sources around town:

A little bird tells me that Mykala J and Jermaine K are an item, and have been since a party at Kwame D's last weekend.

I'm also hearing rumors that rising sophomores Paola Q and Phil D are now a thing. They were spotted looking cozy at the movie theater last Friday night.

But longtime senior couple Mason P and Logan W took the express train to Splitsville after Mason found out that Logan was hooking up with Josh J on the side while he was away on vacation. Logan . . . you are a bad, bad boy.

But fear not, Panther cubs! From what I hear, Mason hasn't sat around bemoaning the breakup. He's been seen out and around Greenpoint with Cody T.

The Panther football team has already started practice and they're looking fierce.

Make sure you start working on those summer assignments you

put off doing because you thought summer vacation would last forever. Especially if you have Mrs. Dougall or Mr. Higgins. They never give extensions. Only eight days until school starts. Unless you're fresh meat—then it's just seven.

Party on while you can, people. September will be here before you know it!

WILL

How did I end up here? I think as I try to make sure ten hyped-up eight-year-olds don't do anything stupid on the Slip 'N Slide, one of the many activities for Carnival Day here at Camp Terabyte.

It's a computer camp, so I thought it would be about teaching kids to code. Then they told me I was going to be a "bunk leader"—even though it's a day camp and there aren't any actual bunks. What that means is that I'm in charge of ten eight-year-old boys. I have to make sure they don't maim themselves or each other, while ensuring they have fun, too. I should have known when the camp director, Mrs. Hermann, got so excited when she saw I ran track; she probably thought I'd be able to catch any little monsters who try to run away.

To top it off, Carnival Day is the hottest and most humid day we've had so far this summer—and that's saying something.

"When do the counselors get to go on the Slip 'N Slide?" I say to Dara Simons, who is also a counselor here, as well as being one of the required medical staff, since she's some sort of super-overachiever EMT.

"Sorry to tell you, Will, but never," she says, pulling her

Camp Terabyte shirt away from her tanned skin. "It's dangerous for teenagers and adults because the slide isn't long enough. A bunch of people got paralyzed from the sudden stop at the end."

"Wow, Dara, I can always count on you for not-so-fun facts," I say.

Her face is already pink from the sun and the heat, but the color deepens.

"I can't help it. I'm in EMT mode," she says. "In every situation I'm looking at how someone could get hurt and thinking through what I'd do if it happens."

"So I take it I'm never going to persuade you to go skydiving with me, huh?" I say.

"No way," she says with a shudder.

Then I catch sight of Jimmy McCormick pushing Lyssa Black. "Jimmy, get to the back of the line. You just forfeited that turn."

"Aw, Wiiiill," Jimmy complains, but Dara backs me up.

"We said no pushing," she says. "If you keep complaining, we'll ban you from the Slip 'N Slide altogether. Safety first!"

Yeah, she just "safety firsted" Jimmy. I want to laugh, but I swallow it.

Grumbling under his breath, Jimmy moves to the end of the line. Lyssa smiles and takes a running leap, screaming, "OOOOHHHHH YEAAAAAAAH!" as she slides. She gives Dara and me a high five as she skips by us back to the end of the line.

"Remind me never to have kids," I say.

Dara gives me a sidewise glance. "Remind me why you decided to spend your summer as a camp counselor for, uh, *kids*?"

"I didn't realize how much work they are," I say. "I'm sure I wasn't nearly as impossible as Jimmy McCormick."

"Right. I bet your mom might have a different opinion on that," she says with a grin. "I'll have to ask her sometime."

"File that under reasons I'm gonna make sure you and my mom aren't ever in the same place at the same time," I tell her. "At least until graduation. Then I'm stuck."

"I'll just have to ask Sadie, then," Dara says. She makes brief eye contact with me before looking away to scan around. "We bump into each other at school all the time."

"Note to self: Swear younger sister to secrecy about any and all things to do with me."

Dara lets out a snort of laughter.

"Nice," I say.

"I'm sorry, it's just the thought of you asking Sadie *not* to dish dirt on you. I bet she *loves* discussing your many flaws."

"True. Times like this, I envy you being an only child," I say with a sigh.

"It's got its pros and—"

There's a loud scream from the Slip 'N Slide. Caleb Johnson is lying on the ground holding his arm as Jimmy slides to the end and jumps up looking guilty. Dara immediately picks up the first aid bag that looks like it's as heavy as she is and sprints over to Caleb like it weighs nothing.

"Hold off, everyone!" I shout to the kids waiting to go. "Camper down!"

"It hurts! It hurts so bad!" Caleb moans over and over. He's clutching his arm at an awkward angle.

We took our eyes off the little monsters for literally, like, seconds, and this happens.

"I'm going to touch your arm," Dara says. "Tell me where it hurts the most."

She gently moves her hands over Caleb's arm, until there's one spot where he shouts, "Owww! Stop!"

Dara removes her hands and opens up the first aid bag. "Okay, so it looks like you might have managed to break your arm," she tells Caleb in a steady, soothing voice. "I'm going to splint it to avoid any further injury, and then we'll get you to the ER."

"It's Jimmy's fault!" Caleb says. "You said we had to go one at a time, but he cut the line and pushed me out of the way!"

"No, I didn't!" Jimmy shouts.

"Yes, he did!" Lyssa says. A bunch of the other campers voice their agreement.

Jimmy, my little friend, you are so busted.

"Yo! People! Not important at the moment!" I call out, shutting down the chorus of voices.

"Mrs. Hermann can deal with that," Dara says. "Right now, I want to get this splinted, because that should relieve some of Caleb's pain."

She takes a few foam-lined cardboard splints from the first aid bag. "Let's see which of these is the best fit."

"Don't move my arm!" Caleb pleads.

"I'm not going to," she says. "I'm just lining it up to figure out what size to use."

Caleb looks up at her with damp brown eyes. "You promise?"

"I promise," she says. "I'll let you know everything I'm doing."

Dara picks one of the splints and puts the others away. "Now I'm going to put the splint under your arm and move it into place." She smiles at Caleb. "Yell if it hurts, but I'm going to do my best to make sure it doesn't."

She gets it in place and says, "Okay, now I'm going to tape it above and below the break so it stays where it's supposed to."

As Dara is doing that, Mrs. Hermann comes over, and she doesn't look happy.

"What happened?" she asks.

"Jimmy pushed me!" Caleb says.

"I think his arm's broken," Dara says. "He'll need an X-ray to be sure."

Mrs. Hermann nods and says, "On it. I'll get in touch with his parents and the ER." She turns to Jimmy, who is shuffling his wet feet in the grass, avoiding eye contact with her. "Jimmy, come with me to the office."

Reluctantly, he follows her off the field.

"Caleb, I'm going to slide this roll of gauze into your hand.

I want you to hold on to it like this"—Dara holds up her hand to show him, her fingers slightly curled—"got it?"

"Okay," he says.

She slides it into his hand. "Now let's get you some ice for that arm." She takes an instant ice pack out of the first aid bag. "Feel it," she tells Caleb, holding it near his good arm.

"That's not cold," he says.

"Aha, but wait, there's more!" Dara says, smiling. She breaks it and then shakes it. After about a minute she has Caleb feel it again.

"Cool!" Caleb exclaims.

"It's going to get even cooler," Dara explains with an even wider grin. "It's science."

"Caleb has a broken arm and you're giving give him a science lesson?" I say. "Just when I thought you couldn't get any geekier . . ."

"What do you mean?" Caleb asks. "Wait . . . it *is* getting colder! The cold feels good."

That's when I realize that she's trying to get him to think about something other than how much his arm hurts.

Dara gives me a triumphant glance and then turns back to Caleb. "It's what's called an endothermic reaction. Inside the pack are two chambers—one with water and one with ammonium nitrate. When I broke the pack, they started mixing, and that caused the breakdown of chemical bonds. To break down those bonds, energy has to be absorbed, which lowers the temperature."

"Way cool!" Caleb says.

"That's right. Way, *way* cool," Dara says. "Science is like that."

She smiles at him, and I'm hit by the sudden realization that Dara Simons is . . . hot. I don't know if it's the smile, or her total chill when dealing with a kid in pain, but I wonder why I didn't notice before.

"Come on, let's get you out of here so we can get you to the ER," Dara tells Caleb.

Slowly and very, very carefully, she helps him stand up. Mrs. Hermann radios to Terry, the head counselor, that she's already got Mr. Tyler lined up to drive Caleb to the hospital, and she's on the phone with Caleb's mom.

"Come on, let's get you to the hospital," Terry tells Caleb. Slowly, they walk off the field. Dara picks up the first aid stuff and zips the bag.

"Okay, campers, you can go back to sliding," I tell them. "But safety first, okay? We don't want any more broken bones!"

Now Dara's got me safety firsting.

"You were amazing," I tell her. "I knew you qualified as an EMT, but I've never, like, seen you in action."

She flushes. "Oh, uh, thanks. It's practice and experience. The first few times, I wasn't nearly as calm." She looks up at me. "If you want to know the truth, I was kind of freaked out. But Caleb was in pain, and he was scared enough. It wouldn't have done him any good if I was losing it, too."

As the kids hit the slide again, I steal quick glances at Dara and start noticing little things about her, like the beads of sweat on the small of her back where she's tied up her camp T-shirt and the way her ponytail swings when she moves.

"Hey . . . do you want to go to the Dairy Barn after work today?" I say. "My treat."

She turns to look at me and smiles. "Have you ever known me to turn down free ice cream?"

"Cool," I say, hoping that maybe the reason she wants to go is more than just free ice cream.

I tell myself to stop getting carried away. Just because I've had this sudden epiphany that I want her to be more than a friend, it doesn't mean she feels the same way.

I'm strangely nervous when Dara slides into the passenger seat after work.

"I've been dreaming about ice cream all afternoon," she says. "I think it's the only thing that kept me going. The carnival was exhausting!"

"Yeah, I'd rather teach a LEGO robotics workshop any day. But it's finally Friday," I say. "True confessions: I'm glad we only have one more week of camp left. Senior year is going to be easy after this."

Dara laughs and something inside me expands. "I know! Just this week I've had to deal with a broken arm and Bobby Tremel barfing on a drone right before the kids were going to fly it."

"No way! He barfed on a drone?"

"Way," she says. "The day before yesterday. And it was after lunch and he'd had a blue freeze pop, so it was very . . . colorful."

"Gross!"

"At least I only had to clean up Bobby, not the drone. I felt bad for Beth when I saw her taking it apart later. But I was gagging enough as it was."

"What, you mean EMT training doesn't include being able to withstand barf smell without wanting to puke yourself?"

"Ha!" she says. "Actually, I learned a trick from some of the more experienced EMTs."

"Yeah? What's that?"

"Sniff an alcohol wipe."

"I'm going to have to remember that fun fact," I say. "What else ya got?"

"Oh, the human body has lots of disgusting fun facts," she says, flashing me a wicked and kind of adorable grin. "Here's one: A university in Sydney, Australia, found that belly buttons contain all kinds of gross stuff in there, like dead skin, dust, sweat, and fat."

"Barf. So, wash belly button more—got it," I say. "Does it matter if it's an outie or an innie?"

"Innies are more prone to collecting stuff, obviously," she says. "Here's another gross fun fact: Earwax isn't actually wax."

"For real?" I ask, glancing over at her. "It sure looks like wax to me. Not that I spend that much time examining the junk that comes out of my ears on a Q-tip but . . ."

"It's actually a delightful combination of hair, dead skin,

and the secretions from oil and sweat glands in your ears," she says. "And you can tell if you've got an infection from its color, just like you can with nose snot."

"Okay, I think I've had enough gross fun facts for one day," I say. "I still want to enjoy my ice cream."

"So . . . you mean whenever I want your ice cream as well as mine, I just have to tell you more gross human body fun facts?"

"Yeah. I mean, no! I don't want to let you know all my weak spots," I say. "Not that I have weak spots. I'm a man of freaking steel. No, titanium."

Dara throws back her head and laughs. I like the way it causes her eyes light up, and it makes me want to keep saying funny things.

There are only a few open parking spaces at the Dairy Barn, which is hopping on this hot, humid afternoon, but I manage to snag one and we head to the line.

"Aaah! I don't know what flavor to choose!" Dara exclaims. "Do I want chocolate? Or do I want salted caramel? Or do I want cookie dough? Or . . ."

"How about you get salted caramel and cookie dough, and I'll get chocolate. Then we can share?"

"Sounds like a plan," she says.

The Dairy Barn makes the best ice cream, which is probably why there are so many parents with kids here. Dara manages to find us a small empty table in the corner.

"Oh my god, this is what I didn't know I needed today until you offered to take me here," Dara says. She leans across the table to snag a spoonful of chocolate, then grins when she tastes it. "Wow, the chocolate is amazing, too."

I whip out my phone and start recording her.

"What are you doing?" she asks.

"You being this happy over that ice cream is seriously excellent content."

She smiles and licks the ice cream off her lips, and suddenly I want to lean across the table and kiss her. Badly.

That's when her phone rings. It's the theme song from that really awful show Sadie was obsessed with a few years ago called *Gutter Girlz*.

"Hi, Mom!" she says. "Yeah, I'll be home soon. Will Halpern and I stopped for ice cream. It's been a day . . . Love you!"

"You can't be serious about that ringtone," I say when she's off the phone. "Are you, like, *twelve*?"

"What do you mean? *Gutter Girlz* was the best show ever!"

"I'm going to have to rethink our friendship," I tell her. "My sister has made me hate that song for life."

"You don't know what you're talking about, Will Halpern," she says, taking another bite of ice cream.

"You should hand over the phone."

She sticks her tongue out at me.

I stop the recording and place my phone on the table, then put my hand out for hers.

"Why, what are you going to do with it?" she asks.

"Give you the ringtone I think you deserve."

She tilts her head and eyes me, her mouth quirked into a half smile. "Oh? And what would that be, Will?"

Hope spreads through my chest. I think Dara Simons is flirting with me.

"You'll just have to give me your phone and find out, won't you?"

She swipes some more chocolate ice cream before saying, "Fine," and handing me her phone. "But only because I'm curious to see what you think of me."

"Don't worry," I tell her.

"Easy for you to say."

I search for the ringtone I have in mind and set it as hers. Then I hand it back to her and call her number.

"Wait . . . is that the *Wonder Woman* theme song?" she says, a slow flush rising up from her chest to her face.

I nod.

"That's what you think I deserve?"

"Definitely."

"Wow . . . I don't know what to say."

"How about that you'll go to the movies with me sometime?"

She looks up at me from under her lashes, her brown eyes lit up with amusement. "You think you're up for being Steve Trevor?"

She is so definitely flirting with me.

I smile slowly. "So, does that mean you'll go?"

She helps herself to another spoonful of my ice cream. "Sure."

Yes!

Guess I've got to thank Jimmy McCormick for being a monster after all.

DARA

When I walk into work on the last day of camp, Mrs. Hermann stops me. "Mrs. Johnson wanted to thank you for what you did for Caleb," she says, holding out an envelope. "She left this when she dropped him off this morning."

"She didn't have to do that!" I exclaim, taking it. "I was just doing my job."

"And a good one at that," Mrs. H says. "Mr. Tyler said the ER doctors told him that they wouldn't have done the first aid any differently."

I feel a glow of pride in my chest. I've worked really hard to get certified as an EMT, and it feels good to know the ER staff thinks I'm good at it.

On the way to meet my campers, I open the envelope. Caleb made me an adorable thank-you card. He's drawn the two of us, him with a very broken-looking arm and a speech bubble saying, "OWWWWW!" and me looking like some kind of superhero.

"Hey, Dara, whatcha got there?" Will says, bounding over.

"Caleb made this for me," I say, showing him the card.

"Caleb's got your number," he says. "Like I said, you are Wonder Woman. And now you've got the ringtone to match."

I feel the heat rising in my face and wonder if Will's noticed the way I've been checking him out for the last month, because I realized that he's actually kind of hot, even if we are mortal academic enemies.

"So, can I give you a ride to the party later?" Will asks. "I can't stay too late because I have to retake the SAT tomorrow but . . ."

One of the other counselors, Marina, is having an end-of-camp pool party for the counselors after work. She lives in the part of town where big houses have stupid-long driveways and a billion bedrooms, and everyone has a pool. It's basically the perfect place to have a party.

"Sure," I say, my heart beating a little faster in anticipation. "I'm fine with not staying too late."

"Great! Well, good luck surviving the last day," he says. "I hope it's free of any grossness."

I laugh. "Me too. Oh my god, me too!"

The camp day ends without me encountering any broken bones, barf, or other medical issues besides Zoey Carter needing a Band-Aid for a skinned knee. I count that as a win. After saying goodbye to all my campers and waving them off at pickup for the last time, I head to the bathroom to change before the party. I swap the simple tank bathing suit and Camp Terabyte T-shirt I've been wearing for work with a bikini, high-waisted white denim shorts, and a short-sleeve floral shirt that I knot at the waist. I don't wear makeup to camp because I'd just sweat it off, but I apply a bit of tinted lip gloss and brush out my hair before putting it back up in a messy bun.

"You clean up well," Will says with a grin when I meet him by his car.

He's changed out of his camp T-shirt into a GHS Track shirt and a different pair of swim trunks. The color accentuates his tan and makes his eyes pop.

"You clean up pretty well yourself," I tell him. We smile at each other, and I feel a tingle of anticipation creeping up my spine.

"Let's hit the party," he says, unlocking the car. "I'm looking forward to being by a pool where I'm not in charge of making sure kids don't drown each other."

"You and me both," I say.

The party is already hopping by the time we get there. Marina's parents have put out a great spread: barbecue and veggie burgers, plus lots of sides and salads. I'm suddenly starved and immediately start piling food onto my plate. I carefully balance it and drop down next to Will at one of the tables.

"How do you pack so much food into such a small you?" Will asks as he watches me devour what's on my plate.

"All my brainwork burns it off," I say, before taking another bite of my veggie burger.

"Okay, I know your brain is active, but I'm not sure that's how this works."

"Trust me, I'm an EMT," I say.

Will laughs. It's loud and deep, like he means it.

I grin. "It's true! Your brain is about two percent of your body weight, but accounts for about twenty percent of your body's energy use."

He gives me a skeptical look. "Riiiight. So I can give up track and still maintain this hot bod by just sitting at a desk and studying? I don't think so."

"Not exactly," I say. "Especially if you're eating chips and drinking Mountain Dew."

"Well, I guess that means I better swim," he says, shoving his plate away and pulling his T-shirt over his head. I try to concentrate on my burger, but his six-pack distracts me. I choke, and he gives me a series of increasingly less gentle thumps between my shoulder blades until I can breathe again.

"You okay?" he asks, looking at me with concern.

"Yeah . . . something just went down the wrong way."

"See you in the pool, then."

He dives in, and as I finish my food, I watch him swim a few laps, admiring the ripple of his muscles as he cuts through the water.

Time to cool off, Dara.

I cannonball into the pool when he's in the deep end, far enough to be safe but close enough that he gets splashed, big-time.

"Nice, Simons," he says. "You make a big splash for a small person."

"'Though she be but little, she is fierce,'" I say. "It's like Shakespeare knew me or something."

Will swims close to me and treads water, his long legs moving in a circular motion and bumping into mine. "You probably won't believe this," he says, drops of water clinging to his eyelashes and cheekbones. "But when we read *A Midsummer Night's Dream* sophomore year, I thought of you when I read that line."

"Yeah, right," I say, throwing a small splash at him.

"No, really! I did!" He grins. "Because you kept kicking my butt on every test. Made me realize I'm not always the smartest guy in the room."

"Or even the smartest person," I say.

"I stand corrected," Will says. "Or more accurately, tread water corrected."

He swims over to where a double pool float is drifting, empty. "Wanna share this?" he asks me, hauling himself aboard.

"Sure!"

He extends a hand and helps me get on it, and we lie down next to each other, looking up at the clear blue sky, decorated with puffs of clouds. The late afternoon sun warms my skin, and the water droplets beading on it slowly evaporate.

"So have you got anything fun planned for the last week of summer?" Will asks.

"Relaxing?" I say. "Oh, and I'm scheduled for a bunch of long EMT shifts."

"Do you ever get freaked out by the stuff that happens?" he asks. "I don't think I could handle blood."

"Fortunately, I've never been on a call with lots of blood," I say. "Hopefully I'll be cool, but I guess we won't find out until it happens."

"What made you want to be an EMT?" he asks. "It's, like, a huge time commitment, isn't it?"

"Probably no more than track during the season," I say. I falter for a moment. I still find it hard to explain the why. "But . . . my reason for doing it? It's really personal—and maybe not one hundred percent rational."

"You don't have to tell me," he says, turning his head to me so that our noses practically touch, and I feel his breath on my skin when he exhales and smell the chlorine on his.

I take a deep breath and look back at the clouds, because I feel too vulnerable looking into his eyes while I talk about it.

"It's just that . . . well, my dad died in a drunk driving accident. I mean, everyone knows that part, I guess. But the paramedics tried to keep him alive to make it to the hospital, but . . . they couldn't." I swallow, hard. "I was really messed up after. I probably still am." I try to toss that line off, but it gets stuck in my throat. "I know nothing will bring my dad back, but maybe, someday, if I'm a trauma surgeon, I might be able to save another kid's parent, so they don't have to go through what I did."

Will moves his hand slightly, so that his pinkie touches

mine. I glance over at him from the corner of my eye. He looks at me, his eyes darkening.

"I don't think you're messed up, Dara. I think you're pretty amazing."

"You two look way too serious," Marina shouts from the side of the pool. "Someone flip them!"

She doesn't have to ask twice. Tommy Walter and Bella Espinoza swim up under us and tip the float over. Will slides off over me, and he grasps my hand to pull me to the surface. A splash war ensues, until I have to swim to the side because I'm laughing so hard.

It's dark by the time we leave the party.

"I think every mosquito in the county bit me," I grumble as we head to the car.

"It's because you're so sweet," he says, flashing me a grin. "They didn't touch me."

"So unfair." I playfully bump him with my hip and am rewarded with his laugh.

We get to the car and I lean against it, waiting for him to unlock the passenger side door. He pauses next to me, key in hand. I suddenly realize we're in each other's space. I can feel the heat radiating from his bare skin. I move over a few inches, until I'm blocking the door he was about to unlock.

"So we're not leaving?" Will asks, his voice soft and languid.

I shake my head. "I mean, not unless you want to. Do you?"

"No. I mean, yes I want to." He looks confused for a minute.

I let out a low laugh.

"What's the question, Dara?" Will asks. Then his eyes flick to my lips, and he leans forward but stops to look me in the eye. Checking to make sure.

I nod and slide my fingers across his collarbone and around the back of his neck. I give a small pull and Will's mouth crushes against mine. He tastes like coconut and barbecue and sunshine, and a rush takes over my whole body. I can feel the thrum of my heart as Will tugs me closer and my fingers tangle in the ends of his still-damp hair. His thumbs graze my hips as he steadies me before he changes the angle and deepens things. The feeling of Will, summer, this kiss expands around us, and I'm lost in it.

Voices echo in the haze of our kissing, breaking the moment. I pull back, dazed, and scoot away from Will so he can unlock the door. He gives a slow laugh. "Time to go?"

I just grin at him, feeling too flustered for more. Will fumbles and pulls out his phone before swiping the flashlight on and aiming it at the ground. "Gotcha!" he says, standing up and pocketing his phone. He's holding his keys up triumphantly.

I just stare at him.

"I dropped them when you kissed me," he says with a sheepish smile.

A loud laugh explodes from deep in my belly. I don't know

why this is funny, but I can't stop laughing, even after Will's unlocked the door and I'm in the car. But it's okay because Will's grinning at me.

Finally, my laughter drifts off and he starts the engine. I keep glancing over at his profile as we drive to my house, exchanging funny stories about our campers.

I catch him doing the same, and he flashes a small smile.

"So . . . I've got the SAT tomorrow," he says. "That's part of the pressure my dad's putting on me. He said I need better scores to get into Stanford, so I've been doing practice tests every night. But . . . maybe I could see you tomorrow night after the test?"

"How about that movie?" I say.

"Awesome," he says, pulling into my driveway.

I jump out and smile back into the car at him.

"Thanks for the ride home," I say.

"Thanks for the kiss," he says with a grin. I blow him another one and shut the door. I watch him back out of the driveway, then I walk to the house, filled with an even greater sense of anticipation about the coming school year.

MJ

Zack picks me up from work on Tuesday, the day before he goes back to college in Maryland.

"Wanna go to the arcade?" he says. "We haven't been there in a while and I feel like kicking your butt at *Marvel vs. Capcom 2*."

"Like that's even possible anymore," I say. "I might be your little sister, but I can still destroy you."

"I'll believe it when I see it," he says. "I'm willing to bet you're going down."

"What are the stakes?" I say.

"Hmmm," he says. "Five bucks?"

"Five bucks? I think we need some real stakes."

"Okay, if I win, you have to let me take your *Legend of Zelda: Breath of the Wild* poster to school," Zack says.

"What? That's one of my favorite posters!"

"You said you wanted real stakes, didn't you?"

"Okay, fine. Then if I win, I get to use your cryptocurrency rig while you're gone."

My brother built his own rig to mine Bitcoin when he was in high school. Basically it's a tricked-out PC with extra features, which he used to do complex math calculations to earn coins.

He gives me serious side eye. "That's a big ask, MJ."

"If you're so convinced that you're going to be able to kick my butt, it shouldn't be a problem."

"Fine. If you win, you can use my rig."

Yes! I've wanted to play around with some stuff for a while, but my laptop doesn't have the resources. I've been thinking about building a PC of my own, but since Zack's got one sitting on his desk doing nothing while he's at school, I figure I can save the money for college instead.

Now I just have to beat him.

What Zack doesn't know is that Will and I practically lived at this arcade while he was away at school and my *Marvel vs. Capcom* game is a lot better than he remembers it.

We warm up by playing a few games separately. I play a few rounds of pinball, and then Zack and I play *Space Invaders*. He wins that, but I don't mind because it makes him over-confident.

"Okay, MJ, you ready to cry?"

"Cry tears of victory because I beat you worse than you used to beat me in *Mario Kart*."

"Ha! Dream on, MJ. You will never beat the Zackanator."

Famous last words.

I destroy him. I know I should be a good sport, but I can't resist throwing Zack a few Nelson Muntz HA-HAs.

"That's right, go ahead and gloat, MJ," he says. "Because you will never beat me again."

I give him a look of mock confusion.

"Is that never as in 'you'll never beat the Zackanator'? That kind of never?"

Zack shakes his head. "What has happened to that sweet, gullible little kid who believed it when I said she was playing with me, even though I handed her a controller that wasn't even hooked up?"

"Come on, that was when I was, like, three!" I say. "I've learned a thing or two since then. Also, that was really mean."

"It wasn't mean, it was problem solving! I didn't want you messing up my game, and if I said you couldn't play, you'd run crying to Mom."

Part of me has to admire his cunning tactic. I really did believe that controller worked.

"So when did you get so good?" he asks as we head back to the car.

"I think the real question is when did you get so bad," I say with a grin.

"A hazard of making dean's list," Zack says, unlocking the car doors. "I didn't spend nearly enough time keeping my arcade skills from getting rusty."

"I question your priorities," I tell him as I slide into the passenger seat.

"Says the girl who is currently number three in her class," he says.

"Aaaaaannnd the girl who is really looking forward to using your rig."

The pained look on his face makes my victory even better.

"I should have known you'd been here practicing," Zack mutters. "You suckered me into that bet."

"That'll teach you to underestimate me," I say.

"We're having a rematch when I'm home for Thanksgiving," he says. "I will have my revenge."

"Sure, Zack," I say, patting his shoulder with mock condescension. Then I break into a painfully out-of-tune rendition of the *Rocky* theme just to rub it in.

"Is that everything?" Dad asks Zack early the following morning. "It better be, because there's no more room in the car."

"Yeah, that's it," Zack says.

Mom and Dad are driving Zack back to school. I'm staying home because I couldn't get off work. At the end of junior year, I asked my computer science teacher if she knew of somewhere I could get a job for the summer and then after school during senior year. A paid job, not an unpaid internship, like some of the other kids can afford to do. She recommended me to a local insurance company. I started off doing data entry, but now I'm helping them make sure their databases and systems are more secure, after I showed them how easy they were to hack.

It's better than the job I had checking out at the supermarket last summer. At least I can work in my own little cubby with headphones on, instead of having to deal with annoying people constantly. It's still hard when my friends ask me to do stuff now that their summer jobs have ended and I can't because I'm working.

"If you're done packing, can I show Zack my surprise?" I ask.

"Yeah, do it now, because we need to get going," Dad says.

"Come check it out, Zack," I say. "You have to see this before you leave."

"MJ's got a surprise for me? Is, like, the front door rigged so I walk into the house and get a bucket of water dumped on me?"

"So suspicious," I say.

"Yeah, with good reason," Zack says. "I still remember the time you set up that crazy prank in my bedroom where I walked into the room and got sprayed with shaving cream."

"It was a hint that you needed to shave!" I say. "Anyway, if you're going to be such a wimp, I'll go in first."

"After you," he says, sweeping his arm and bowing like a courtier in a Shakespeare play.

I lead the way into the house. "Hand me your phone," I say to Zack when we get to the living room.

He looks at me doubtfully. "Why? What are you going to do?"

My brother has spent so much time trying to hack into other people's devices that he's super cagey with his own. Once he hacked the robot vacuum cleaner so that he could make it say things to freak people out. The best was when Dad fell asleep in front of the TV and Zack had the vacuum play "The Imperial March." I almost peed my pants laughing. Even Mom thought that was very amusing. But for some strange reason, she didn't find it nearly as funny as the time Zack changed it to make a variety of ever more disgusting fart sounds while we were watching a movie together. Neither did Pascal, who ran under the sofa. Dad, Zack, and I all laughed so hard we cried.

"Come on, give it to her," Dad says. "Trust me, it'll be worth it."

Reluctantly, Zack hands me his phone.

"Duh, you've got to unlock it," I say.

"Fine," Zack says, thumbing in his passcode.

I download the app, connect it to the surprise, and then enter the password.

Handing the phone back to Zack, I say, "Now go into the kitchen with Dad."

My dad is in on the surprise. It was my idea, but he paid for it, and we planned in advance how we would show my brother.

They go into the kitchen while I take a seat on the sofa with Mom and Pascal.

Even though the camera is pretty well hidden on the shelf, I hear it moving.

"Hey, Mom! Hey, favorite sibling!" I hear Zack say through the newly installed CatCam. "Oh, look, and MJ's there, too."

I stick my tongue out in the direction of the camera and hear Zack laughing. I watch the camera pan from right to left as Dad shows my brother how he can move it remotely using the app.

They come back into the family room. "You complained so much about missing Pascal, MJ figured it would make it easier for you to see him from college," Dad says.

Zack comes over and leans down to give me a hug. "Thanks, MJ, it's awesome." Then he reaches out his arms. "Hand me my kitty."

"What do you say?" I ask, keeping a firm grip on Pascal.

"Hand me my kitty or I'll give you a noogie," he says.

"Manners, Zachary!" Mom says.

Zack rolls his eyes at her and turns back to me. "Fine, MJ, *please* hand me my kitty."

"Now that you've said please, here's *my* cat," I say, handing him Pascal, who is clearly reaching the end of his affection limit and wants to escape.

Zack cuddles Pascal to his chest and tells him how much he's going to miss him. Then he flashes me a wicked grin. "Hey, I can spy on MJ and report back to you when she's up to no good!" he says to Mom and Dad.

"Yeah, like I ever get the chance," I say. "I'm too busy kicking academic butt, running track, and building robots."

"True," Zack agrees. "It'll be like watching C-SPAN. No, wait, that's more exciting. MJ-SPAN would bore me to tears!"

"You're soooooooo funny," I say. "But if I ever *do* get up to no good, I'm putting something in front of the camera."

"I've got a better idea," Mom says. "How about not getting up to anything?"

"Booooring," I say, rolling my eyes.

Dad looks at his watch. "We better hit the road. We've got a long drive ahead of us."

Zack puts Pascal down and fist-bumps me. "Later, MJ. Don't do anything I wouldn't do."

I follow my parents and brother out of the house and stand waving in the driveway until the car disappears from sight. Zack might tease me and use up all the hot water in the morning, but the house always seems much too quiet when he's gone.

I only have to work till two the next day, so I text Will and see if he wants to hang out. We've hardly done anything together the last few weeks. I know he was busy studying to retake the SAT, but that's over now so I'm hoping I get my friend back.

Today he says yes. He comes over to my house around three when I'm back from work. Better yet, he brings some of those ridiculously fancy macarons, the kind that his mom gets but my parents will never buy because "they're too expensive and we have to save for your tuition." I've made us each a glass of chocolate milk, which is what we always drink when gaming. That plus Will and macarons makes me so happy.

"Good to see you *finally*," I say. "Where have you been? I thought the SAT might have killed you."

"I know," he says. "I'd been spending pretty much every waking moment doing practice SAT tests. You know I suuuuuuuck at testing and my dad . . . ugh. You know him. Gotta get those scores up for Stanford." Will rolls his eyes.

The thing is, the SAT was last Saturday, and I asked him to hang out on Monday, but he was busy again.

"So what's really going on with you?" I ask as we settle into the couch to figure out what game to play. "You've been acting kind of weird. And the SAT is done."

"Nothing," he says, sounding defensive. "I've just been really stressed out. You know my dad's been pressuring me about Stanford since, like, forever. And I don't know. I'm just . . . like, what if I don't get in? Then what?" Will looks a little helpless.

I feel for Will, I do. But there's a twist in my gut, too. I get the pressure he's feeling, but his parents support him. Which is more than I can say about my parents.

"I *wish* my parents would be pressuring me to go to Carnegie Mellon," I say. "I'm planning to apply early decision. That's how sure I am about it—if I get in, I have to go there. But all I get is how expensive the tuition is and how maybe I should apply to some cheaper schools because they don't want me to graduate with hundreds of thousands of dollars of student loans. They want me to go to a state school like Zack."

"You're number three in the class," Will says. "You should get some pretty decent scholarship money."

"I'm number three in the class *as of now*," I say. "Watch your back."

He grins. "I will. And Dara better watch hers."

"Too right." I help myself to another macaron. Yum.

"So do you actually *want* to go to Stanford?" I ask. I've never asked Will that before. I assumed he did. I knew his dad was being extra about it and that he's been worried that he wouldn't get in. But this seems like something else.

Will doesn't answer right away, and I wonder if I'm wrong that there's more than the usual stress around his choice of college.

"I . . . think so? I mean, if I'm going to be the next Steve Jobs or Bill Gates or Mark Zuckerberg, I need to go to a top-tier college," he says.

"You do realize that each of those tech titans you just named dropped out of their top-tier college, right?"

"Exactly what I told my dad."

"Great minds," I say, trying to get Will to smile.

"Yeah, but then he responded that they'd already proved they could get into those colleges," Will says with a sigh.

"Ouch," I say. "Well, at least Stanford is early action, not early decision, right? So you don't have to go there, but at least you know you've gotten in somewhere before the regular decisions come out. Carnegie Mellon is early decision, which is why my parents are all over me to apply elsewhere. They just can't get beyond the cost." I savor the last bite of my macaron. "These are so good. Good enough I might just forgive you for blowing me off the last few weeks."

"You're so easily bought," he says, nudging me with his shoulder.

"So other than the fact that your dad is pressuring you so

much, are there other reasons you're not sure about Stanford?"

Will sighs. "It's just that . . . my mom thinks maybe I'd be happier at somewhere a little less . . . intense. She might be right, but . . . you know my parents hate each other so much, and I don't know if my mom really thinks I'd be better off at a more laid-back school or if she's just saying it because Dad wants me to go there so badly."

"That sucks," I say.

"He's been on me to go to Stanford for as long as I remember. I mean, there are pictures of me as a baby wearing a freaking Future Stanford Graduate onesie."

I laugh. "No pressure or anything."

"But you know what I have been thinking about a lot?"

"Will, I've barely seen you for the last few weeks. I'm not a mind reader."

Something I can't read flashes across Will's face. "Okay . . . so I finished that biography of Steve Jobs over the summer."

"Finally! I've only been telling you to read it for, like, three years."

Will gives me a sideways glance. "I know! So anyway, you know how Jobs was this total visionary, but he was also, like, such a jerk?" he says. "Same with Zuckerberg, especially in the early days. And Bill Gates. And then there are the frauds, like Elizabeth Holmes and Ramesh Balwani. I mean, I want to be a billionaire as much as the next guy—" He pauses, then says, "As much as the next *person*, I mean."

I laugh but nod in encouragement at him.

He continues, "So I got to thinking—is it possible to build a start-up into a billion-dollar-plus company without being a complete jerk or a total liar? Because I want to be super rich, but I don't want to treat people badly while I go about it."

"I don't know. Does wanting your product to be the best it can possibly be automatically make you a bad person?"

"Not necessarily," Will says. "I guess . . . maybe it's not the perfectionist part that's the problem, but how you deal with it when the people around you aren't living up to that perfectionism? These guys were the worst to the people who worked for them. I know how that feels." He glances over at me. "But sometimes it also seems like that's the only way to make it. I don't know. I don't want to be that guy."

"Is this where I'm supposed to say #notallbillionaires?"

Will laughs. "I guess so." But then he sighs. "I think what scares me most is that even though my dad's not a billionaire, he's done really well financially, and honestly? He can be a total jerk, too. It's like he majored in making me feel less than."

"So here's the plan: I promise that no matter how rich you get, I'll be that friend who still tells you when you're being an idiot. Okay?"

"And I promise to do the same thing for you," he says, sticking out his hand. "Let's shake on it."

I shake his hand briefly and then pick up my controller. "Come on, it's time for me to whip your butt."

"You mean it's time for me to slay you?"

We look at each other and crack up.

"Not being a jerk didn't last long," I say.

"Nah, this is just friendly banter," he says, grinning.

For the next few hours, all we do is play games and trash talk each other.

Because we're the kind of friends who can do that.

WILL

Dad texts me while I'm at MJ's and asks me to have dinner with him. He offers to take me to my favorite dive restaurant, Buddy's.

The fact he's willing to go to a place he considers both unhealthy and tacky makes me uneasy. Is it a prelude to him asking me to do something I don't want to do?

But I say I'll meet him there anyway and text Mom to let her know I won't be home for dinner.

It's crowded at Buddy's when I get there, but Dad's already got us a table.

"So what have you been up to since your camp job ended?" Dad asks as soon as I sit down.

I think about making out with Dara.

What I actually say, though, is: "Did like a million practice tests for the SAT, retook the SAT, and researched colleges. Slept. Oh, and I hung out with MJ this afternoon."

"Yeah? How's your girlfriend doing?"

"How many times do I have to tell you? She's not my girlfriend."

"She will be someday," Dad says.

"No, she won't. I—"

I almost slip up and tell him I *am* seeing someone (kind of? I think?) and it's not MJ, but luckily I bite my tongue in time.

"MJ, my friend-who-just-so-happens-to-be-a-girl, is fine, Dad."

"You spend so much time with your friend-who-just-so-happens-to-be-a-girl, I worry that you're never going to have an actual girlfriend," Dad says.

"I'm hungry. Can we just order?" I say, trying to change the subject.

He nods and picks up the menu.

I order the usual, a loaded steak sandwich and onion rings. Dad shakes his head, but before he can launch into his usual that's-a-heart-attack-on-a-plate lecture, I remind him that I've been running every day all summer.

"I invited you out to dinner because I want to talk to you about your college strategy," Dad says after the waiter walks away.

There it is. The price of dinner at Buddy's.

"What do you mean?" I ask, barely holding in a sigh.

"You should apply to Stanford early," Dad says. "The acceptance rate for early action is nine percent, versus less than four percent regular admissions. Between that, track, Robotics Club, and being a legacy, you'll have better odds, because the pool you're competing against is smaller, and they know you really want to go there."

What if I don't know if I really want to go there?

That's what I would say to my dad if I wasn't so much of a coward.

Instead, I ask, "What if my SAT scores didn't improve enough?"

"All the more reason to apply early. The smart move is to use every advantage you've got." He leans forward. "And forget about all the it's-not-fair-to-everyone-else garbage. Do you think if other people had the edge you do they'd refuse to use it?"

"Okay, I'll think about it."

"Don't think too hard. Just do it," Dad says. "Listen to your old man."

"You said old, not me," I say, trying to lead the conversation away from college.

"Yeah, and the reason I'm still in such good shape for a not-so-old man is because I don't usually eat at places like this."

I sigh. Guess it's two-for-one lecture night here at Buddy's.

The next day when Mom's at work and Sadie's over at a friend's house, I text Dara. We're going to the movies tonight, and maybe I'm not playing it cool enough by doing this, but I want to see her.

Me: Hey. I'm sitting in an empty house.

Me: Wanna come over and pick up where we left off on Friday? 😃

Dara: 😊 Okay.

Dara: As long as you have AC, because I'm going to ride my bike over and it's disgustingly hot and humid.

Dara: I hope you're not squeamish about sweat.

Me: Like I never saw you sweaty at camp?

Dara: Ha-ha, true.

Me: See you in half an hour! 😃

I spend the next thirty minutes in a state of nervous anticipation. I've been thinking about Dara constantly since Friday night. Figures this happened right as camp ended. I kind of miss seeing her every day.

When the doorbell rings, I walk to the door, my heart beating fast and my mouth dry.

Dara's on the front step, in cutoffs and a slightly cropped tank top, leaving a line of tanned stomach showing. Her skin glistens with perspiration.

"Hi!" she says.

"Hi. Welcome to my air-conditioned abode," I say. "Can I get you a cold drink?"

"Yes, please!" she says, following me into the kitchen and dropping her helmet on the counter.

When we get there, I turn and put my arms around her.

"I'm so gross and sweaty," she says, pulling back.

"Don't care. I've been thinking about you nonstop," I reply.

I kiss her and she winds her arms around my neck. She smells of sunscreen, vanilla, and sweat.

She finally breaks away and says, "I need a drink, please."

I feel like a selfish jerk.

"Sorry," I say. "What can I get you? Water, soda, iced tea?"

"Iced tea sounds perfect," she says.

I get her a glass and then we head into the family room. She sits next to me on the sofa, and I pull her close.

"So what have you been up to?" I ask.

"Went to the office supply store to get school supplies, Ada and I went to the mall to shop, and other than that, a whole lot of nothing. Watching TV and reading and taking it easy, because once school starts . . . well, it's going to be all go, all the time." She looks up at me. "Oh, and on Saturday I have a six-hour EMT shift. What about you?"

"Hung out with MJ," I tell her. "And Amir and Sam." Then I tell her about last night's dinner with Dad and how he's pressuring me to apply early to Stanford.

"Why wouldn't you want to apply early if it gives you a better chance of getting into your first-choice school?" she asks. "That's why I'm applying early decision to Johns Hopkins. I'm sure it's where I want to go."

"Can I tell you something?" I ask. "Something I've only told MJ?"

"Of course you can."

The scent of her makes my heart thud in my chest. At least I want to think it's that, and not that I'm afraid to confess this to someone as motivated and driven as Dara.

"I'm not sure I want to go to Stanford."

She tips her head and looks at me. "Why not? Their computer science department is one of the best in the country and you'd be right there in Silicon Valley."

"I know, I know. But . . . it's also really high pressure."

"You'd give up the chance to be at one of the top schools in the country, where you're going to make really great connections, because you want to be more chill?"

She makes it sound like I've lost my mind, and I start to wonder if maybe I have.

"It's not just that. There are really good programs for game development at other schools," I say defensively. "Besides, not everyone who is super successful goes to a top-tier school, and lots of smart people can't afford to go even if they *do* get in."

"I'd be one of them if it weren't for my dad's life insurance. There's no way I could afford to go to Johns Hopkins if my mom hadn't put most of that away to pay for my college," Dara says. She looks down. "It makes me feel guilty . . . like, assuming I can get in, I can afford to attend a top-tier school and still be able to graduate with little to no debt."

Now it's my turn to look at *her* like she's crazy. "Yeah, but you've had to *grow up without your dad*. Being able to graduate debt free is great, but it doesn't sound like nearly enough to compensate for that."

"I know," she says. "But lots of people grow up without one or both of their parents, for a lot of different reasons, and they don't all get a pile of money to pay for college."

"True. Still, there's no reason why you should feel guilty about it." I reach for her hand and her fingers twine with mine.

She stares at our hands, where my thumb has started to run circles on her knuckles. "Can we talk about when we go back to school?" she asks.

"What, you mean like next week?"

"Excellent calendar skills, Will," she says with a wry smile. "I'm proud of you."

"I'm not second in the class for nothing," I tell her. "Well, at least second *for now*. I'm planning to take you down, Dara Simons."

"In your dreams," she says. "But . . . can we be serious for a second?"

"What makes you think I'm *not* serious about beating you for valedictorian?" I say.

"Ha-ha. Okay, well, serious about . . . whatever this is." She gestures between us with her free hand. "And going back to school."

"What do you mean?"

"I've been thinking . . . maybe we should keep our relationship on the down low."

My hand stills. "Why?"

She looks up at me. "Funnily enough, because of what you just said."

"What did I just say?"

"About taking me down as valedictorian," she says.

"That was *a joke*!"

Dara raises her eyebrow. "Was it, though?"

She has me there.

"I guess I'm . . . half-serious," I say slowly. "I do want to be valedictorian, and you're the person I have to beat to do it. But MJ told me yesterday that she wants to beat both of us, so it's not like the competition is just between us two."

"I know. But this thing, us, whatever it is, it's been less than a week. We made out. And it was awesome," she says before I can object. "This is not a relationship, though. Maybe it will be, but who knows. And it's weird enough that we've got overlapping friend groups and we're in competition to be valedictorian. You and MJ being best friends is just another aspect of it. Adding the layer of us dating is just going to make people focus on it and talk about us even more."

"Who cares what people think?" I say.

One of the things I like most about Dara is also one of the things about her that drives me crazy: namely that she isn't afraid to call me on my crap. She did it. All. Summer. Long. Now she sits up, untwining our fingers, and turns sideways on the sofa to face me. "Really, Will? So . . . have you told MJ about us?"

I push myself to sitting, too, and run my hand through my hair because I know I'm busted and it gives me a few extra seconds to come up with an answer.

"No," I admit.

"Look, I'm glad you haven't, but why not?"

"I don't know. I guess because we haven't been more than friends for very long and I wasn't sure where this was going. And because there's enough stress in my life right now, what with Dad pressuring me about Stanford and—"

A broad smile cracks her face, and I realize I just walked right into the trap.

"Bingo!" she says. "Because I have enough stress in my life, too."

"Fine. Maybe you do have a point," I admit.

"So you're okay with it?" she says. "Staying in stealth mode?"

"Stealth mode . . . I like it," I say, leaning forward so our lips are almost touching. "Now that I think about it, it's kind of . . . hot."

"Will, you think that everything is hot," she says, smiling as she closes the distance between us.

Stealth mode it is.

When I pick Dara up for the movies later that evening, she looks like a different person. She's changed from her shorts and tank into this floaty sundress, and her hair, which is usually up in a high ponytail, falls around her shoulders.

"Wow," I say when she gets into the car. "You look different!"

She tilts her head to one side. "Um . . . thanks?"

"Oh! I mean, not that you don't look good. You look amazing. Wait, I don't mean you normally don't look amazing. I mean . . ." I hit my head on the steering wheel. "Ugh, that was supposed to be a compliment, but . . . I think I'll just stop talking now."

Dara laughs. "You need to work on your game."

"Obviously," I say. "I'll spend the entire movie trying to think of a better compliment. Hopefully by the time I drop you home I'll have thought of something."

We head to the multiplex at the mall. While we're in the line for the box office, one of the other movies lets out, and people stream into the lobby.

"Oh my god, Dara! What are you doing here?" Ada comes over with her older sister, Grace, and some of Grace's friends.

"Um, seeing a movie?" Dara says. "That's kind of what you do at a movie theater."

"You didn't tell me you were going to the movies!" Ada says. Then she looks from Dara to me, and back to Dara. "Uh . . . what movie are you seeing?"

"*The Mind Paradox*," Dara says.

"That's what we just saw," Grace tells us.

"It was really good," Ada says.

"What's not to love about a movie starring Morgan Riley?" Dara says. "She's amazing."

"And Martin Cain is a snack," Ada says.

"I know, right?" Dara says. "Can't wait."

"Come on, Ada, the chili fries at the diner are calling my name," Grace says. "I'm heading back to Tulane on Monday, so see you at homecoming, Dara."

Dara hugs her and wishes her a good semester.

As their group walks away, I see Ada texting and then hear Dara's phone buzz. She looks down at it and then stuffs it in her pocket. It buzzes again. And again. And again while I get the tickets.

Finally, she pulls it out and types furiously.

"Everything okay?" I ask her.

"Yeah. Just . . . well, Ada is asking what's going on. Like, you know, are we dating."

"Huh. And what did you tell her?"

Dara shrugs. "She knows we worked together at camp. I said we were friends." She looks up at me. "I feel bad about— well, if not exactly lying, not telling her the truth. But the truth is, we don't know what we are exactly, right?"

"Right," I say. "And anyway, we agreed to keep whatever we are top secret for now."

The smile of relief lights up Dara's face. "Yeah."

"So . . . you think Martin Cain is hot?"

Dara gives me a sidelong glance. "He's not bad to look at," she says. "But I *really* stan him because he's funny."

As the trailers start, and the lights go down, I reach over and take Dara's hand. I also resolve to google some jokes. I can be funny, too.

RUMOR HAS IT

Can you believe this heat? It's fine if you can chill at the pool all day, but if you can't, then . . . not so much. To top it off, near a hundred percent humidity has turned this week into one long bad hair day. For all of us.

But the weather isn't the only thing that's hot around here—that's why I'm here to share all the steamiest scandals. Rumor Has It isn't deterred by muggy weather or bad hair!

First up, the latest with Logan W and Mason P. I'm told that Logan got hot under the collar when he ran into Mason and Cody T at the movies. Let's hope Logan manages to cool off by the time school starts.

Panther girls' soccer has a new teammate, Graciela D, who just moved here from Michigan. I'm told she has feet of FIRE. Welcome to GHS, Graciela!

Head cheerleader Vicky H got back from cheer camp and has been showing the squad some new moves. Trust me, you do *not* want to miss the halftime show this fall.

Not long till we'll all be back in the halls of dear old Greenpoint, so enjoy yourself while you can!

If you know of excessive enjoyment, entertain us by emailing rumorhasitghs@gmail.com.

DARA

It's hour four of my last six-hour EMT shift before school starts, and so far it's been relatively quiet for a sticky summer's day, so we stop at the Daily Grind coffee shop to get iced coffee.

I started with the Exploring program when I was a freshman and did the EMT course last year, so now I get to ride as the third person on the ambulance when we go out on calls. Mom was worried that it was too much on top of taking AP classes and SAT prep and all the rest of it, but I begged her to let me do it because it's the kind of thing I need to get used to if I want to be a trauma surgeon. Being on the ambulance showed me what I already knew: I love it.

"So, Dara, how about that Yankee game last night?" Alex asks, rubbing his hand over his short, tight curls. He teases me trying to talk about baseball, because he knows I think it's like watching paint dry. He's been an EMT for five years, and despite the teasing, I've learned so much from him.

"There was a baseball game?" I say. "How many hours of boredom did it take before something exciting happened?"

He shakes his head in mock disgust. "And you call yourself an American . . ."

"But I love our troops and apple pie!" I say. "Two out of three, buddy. I still qualify."

"That's up for debate," he says.

"Forget baseball, did you guys see the latest episode of *Medics*?" Natalie asks. She's been a paramedic for ten years, and I love working with her, because she's really good at what she does and because we share a love of *Medics*, this show about a busy urban emergency room.

"Oh no, not this again," Alex groans.

Ignoring him, I say, "Can you believe that Dr. Jasmine hooked up with Hot Nurse Nick? My mom was so jealous!"

Mom has a major crush on Hot Nurse Nick, this super-buff guy who looks really good in scrubs. I love spotting things the show's EMTs do wrong. Besides having a fervent appreciation of Hot Nurse Nick's finer points, Mom gets all worked up about the bad life choices people on the show make. Stuff like "You do *not* want to date Dr. Hopkins! Yes, he's good-looking, but he's a class-A jerk!"

I think it's her way of giving me dating advice without me asking for it. Just another reason I don't want her to know that Will and I are hanging out.

The radio squawks and the dispatcher reads the call: "Medic Two: Motor vehicle accident on Jonas Ridge Road. Two vehicles, one on its side."

We throw out our half-finished iced coffees and run back to the ambulance. Natalie radios in that we're responding, then flips on the lights and siren.

"It couldn't come in five minutes later, when we'd finished our drinks, right?" Alex grumbles as we're bracing ourselves in the back.

I'm always kind of nervous with anticipation on the way to respond to a call, because even for the most boring-sounding thing, you don't know what you'll find until you get there. But now my heart feels like it's beating so hard it's going to break through my rib cage. I've never had a car accident call, and it doesn't take Freud to figure out why I'm amped up and twitchy. I put my hands under my thighs to hide the tremors and take some deep breaths.

"You okay?" Alex asks.

"Yeah," I say. "It's just . . ."

"First hot motor vehicle accident?" Alex guesses.

I nod. By *hot*, he means that we're traveling with lights and sirens.

"When we go in, focus on the task," he says. "It's all about the task. Remember your ABCs, Airways, Breathing, Circulation, and if we've got trauma, which is a given in an Echo response, remember your DCAP-BTLS."

I run through DCAP-BTLS in my head. *Deformities, Contusions, Abrasions, Punctures and Penetrations, and Burns, Tenderness, Lacerations, Swelling.*

"Okay," I say. I chant through them in my head. Over and over.

"Follow the procedure," Alex says. I can hear the unsaid words—he knows about my dad. He's reminding me that I know what to do.

I nod, because my mouth feels too dry to speak.

"If you're anything like me, this stuff hits you afterward," Alex warns me. "When it's all over, and everything starts replaying in your head. Remember, you can talk it through with us, okay?"

"Okay," I say.

Natalie slows down, and we get ready to jump out.

Police and fire are already on the scene.

"What have we got?" Alex asks the nearest police officer.

"Two-car accident—vehicle one crossed over double yellow line. Vehicle two had to swerve to avoid, lost control, flipped, and hit a pole. Driver of vehicle two, the SUV, is trapped and unconscious. Passenger in vehicle two is conscious but has visible cuts and bruises and possible broken leg. She is extremely agitated about her husband. Fire department is assessing extraction. Driver of vehicle one is being interviewed and tested for DUI."

I hear *DUI*, and my stomach turns over, but I take a deep breath and push thoughts of my dad to the back of my mind. I have to focus on the now. I have to do my job.

"Let's get another unit here," Natalie says, calling for backup.

We grab what we think we might need and run over to the car. Alex tries to assess the driver, while the Greenpoint firefighters are figuring out the best way to extract him.

Luckily, the passenger door is still functional, even though the window is broken.

"What's your name?" Natalie asks her.

"Caroline," she says, grimacing. She's clearly in pain.

"Hi, Caroline, I'm Natalie, and I'm going to check out a few things, then Dara and I will get you out of here and on the way to the ER."

"What about my husband?" she says. "Is he going to be okay?"

"My partner is trying to assess him now," Natalie tells her. "It's going to take a while to get him out because of the damage to your car. But he's in good hands. Can you tell me what hurts?"

"My arm. My chest. My neck," she says. "I tried to brace when we started swerving, and I think my wrist is broken."

I jump in. "I'm just going to take your vitals—"

"Dara!" Alex shouts. "I need an IV, stat. His blood pressure's dropping!"

I run around to the other side of the car and hand him a bag of saline. The firefighters have removed the driver door, and Alex crawls into the small space to start an IV line.

Caroline cries out, "Jerry! Jerry! Is he going to be okay?"

"We're going to do everything we can to make sure he is," I hear Natalie tell her.

I can see Jerry has facial lacerations.

"Dara, I need a cervical collar," Natalie shouts. I grab one and take it around to the other side of the car. Once she's got that on, she asks me for an arm splint. "We're going to splint your arm to prevent further injury," she tells Caroline. "Then we're going to get you out of here."

"What about Jerry? I'm not going anywhere without him!" Caroline cries.

We hear the siren of the second ambulance in the distance. "Let's get this splint on so we can get you out of the car," Natalie says in a calm but firm voice.

Our backup arrives as the firefighters are carefully lifting Caroline out of the car. I'm assisting Alex to administer whatever first aid he can in the cramped space where Jerry is trapped. We have to move so the firefighters can use the Jaws of Life tool to cut the damaged car away and extract him.

I go to help Natalie get Caroline into the ambulance so we can rush her to the hospital. When Caroline hears the horrible grinding noise, she starts struggling on the stretcher and she screams her husband's name. "No, no, I can't leave him!"

"He'll be right behind us as soon as they can get him out of the car safely," Natalie says.

Alex hops into the back. "Caroline, Dara and I are going to take good care of you, and Jerry is in great hands. He'll be at the ER with you before you know it."

"Is he going to be okay?" Caroline asks Alex once we're on our way.

He catches my eye briefly, then takes Caroline's good hand. "Everyone's working hard to get him out of that car and to the ER," he says, giving her a true but vague answer, because we don't want to give her false assurances.

"We were going out to buy a present for our grandchild," Caroline says. "Our daughter is due next week."

"That's so exciting," I say. "Do you have other grandchildren?" I've found people who have grandchildren love to talk about them. Anything to keep her mind off worrying about her husband.

"This is our first," she says. "Jerry said we should wait and go Monday, but I was worried in case the baby came early." Her lower lip trembles. "If I'd just waited, we wouldn't have been—"

Her heart rate increases as she becomes agitated. "It's not your fault, Caroline," Alex says.

She won't be consoled. She starts screaming and struggling. "I need to be with Jerry!"

"Caroline, we have to get you to the ER so you can be in shape to help him," I say.

It doesn't work. She keeps calling for her husband, her cries filling the tight space in the back of the ambulance and piercing my brain, making it hard to think.

Alex keeps assuring her that her husband is on his way, even though we can't know that yet. His blood pressure was dropping. Hopefully the IV fluids will help with that, but what if . . .

Then, as quickly as she started screaming, Caroline falls silent. It's like she's withdrawn into herself. For some reason, this makes me nervous; it's even more disturbing than her screaming. Alex checks her vitals again, and I try to estimate how much longer it'll be before we get to the ER. Soon. I can hold it together, even though Caroline's unfocused eyes and sudden silence are opening a door I try to keep nailed shut.

The ambulance halts to a stop.

I put my hand on Caroline's shoulder. "We're here," I tell her, but she doesn't respond.

Natalie opens the doors and we wheel her into the ER, where the team there will take over.

I'm walking alongside her, and she grabs my hand suddenly, making me jump.

"Don't call Anna," she says. "Stress might hurt the baby."

I want to tell her that Anna would want to know if her parents had been in a car accident, baby or no baby, but I don't want her to get agitated again. So I put my hand over hers and say, "Let's get you taken care of first."

It seems like . . . not enough. Not nearly enough. But I don't know how to make it better for her.

The locked door inside me starts rattling, and I'm afraid of what will happen if it opens.

One of my favorite nurses, Jeanne, is on duty. "Caroline, I'm Jeanne. I know Alex and Dara have done a great job of taking care of you, but we're going to take it from here."

Caroline doesn't say a word, but a slight movement of her eyes acknowledges that she heard. She's wheeled off to triage, and just like that it's over.

Alex makes sure the paperwork handing the patient over to the ER staff is signed, and then Natalie radios in that we're done.

Suddenly, my legs feel like Jell-O and I grip Alex's arm to steady myself.

"You okay?" he says.

"I don't know," I admit. "I feel . . . shaky."

"That was a tough one," Natalie says. "And I bet it was especially hard for you."

"Yeah," I say. A wave of sadness rolls through me. I miss my dad. I miss who my mom and I were before he died. I wonder who we'd be now if he were still here.

"You did great," Alex says.

His words pull me back into the moment. I blink.

"And it's perfectly normal to feel shaken up after a call like that," Natalie says. She looks at her watch. "Not long till the shift ends. Let's just hope it's quiet till then."

We're luckier for the rest of the shift. It's just a call to a house where someone fell and hurt their leg, and another to a store downtown where someone fainted.

I'm usually pretty tired after a long ambulance shift, but the emotional roller coaster of today has left me more drained than usual. I keep wondering how Jerry is doing, and if he'll live. I wonder how Caroline is doing; if she's by his bedside or in shock and having to make funeral arrangements. I think about how awful it would be for her daughter to have to face her dad's funeral when she's about to give birth.

I don't know the answers, so the questions just keep running around and around in my head, mingled with the image of silent Caroline staring with unfocused eyes.

When Mom picks me up, she takes one look at me and says, "What happened?"

"I'll tell you when we get home. I just need to . . . not talk or think for a little while."

Her brows knit with concern. "I worry this is too much for you," she says.

"Mom, please. Not now." I can't tell her I'm fine, because I know I'm not right now. But I will be. Later.

At least I think so.

Mom tells me about her day, and I stare out the window, half listening, replaying everything we did in my head and wondering if it was enough to save Jerry. I mean, I know it's not just what we did—it's up to the surgeons now.

One day, that'll be me. It'll be up to me.

At least when I'm a trauma surgeon, I'll be a step removed from having to go on the scene of car accidents. Like, I'll still be trying to save lives, but without being confronted by all the twisted metal and blood, which starts making me think about how Dad died and worrying if he was in terrible pain all over again.

"Did you hear a word I just said?" Mom asks, interrupting my spiral of thoughts.

"Uh . . . no, sorry," I admit. "I've got a lot on my mind."

We get home, and I collapse into one of the kitchen chairs because I don't think I can walk another step.

"Okay, kiddo. Spill," she says as she takes leftovers out of the fridge and heats them in the microwave.

So I do. I worry that maybe I shouldn't, but the words just come out. "When it was happening, I just felt so . . . overwhelmed. I mean, I functioned enough to do my job, but it was different from other stressful calls I've been on. And now I feel like a squeezed-out orange," I say. "No juice left."

Mom puts the heated casserole on the table and sits. "Does it . . ." She bites her lip as if hesitant to continue. "Does it . . . bring back feelings about when Dad died? Did Caroline's behavior remind you of how I got so depressed afterward?"

I stare at the fork next to my food. Suddenly, even the act of lifting it feels too much. "Why do you think this is about you?" I say defensively. "It isn't." But even as I deny it, I recognize there's a familiarity about that overwhelmed feeling I experienced in the ambulance today. Caroline alternated between crying, screaming, and being totally out of it.

My mom perfected the art of all three for a very long time.

"I'm not saying it's about me, per se. Just that you had to grow up fast because I fell apart. Because I wasn't able to be the mom I wanted to be back then, because I felt like I was drowning in grief."

She reaches over and takes my hand. I want to pull away. I

don't want to talk about that time. How it felt like I lost both my parents.

"I'm sorry, Dara. I let you down. I know that time is gone, and there's nothing I can do to fix it, but I can be here for you now."

I let her hold my hand for a moment, then tug it free. "You are," I say. "Like you say, it's the past. There's nothing we can do about it." My mom's apologized so many times since then, but I never know what to say. I mean, it's not okay what happened, but *I'm* okay. And, like, she can't change it, and her talking about it just reminds me how mad I used to be at her. And I just can't go there—when she was so depressed that she could barely get out of bed in the morning, when I had to start making my own lunches and most nights had to try to figure out dinner for us. I did the only thing I could: I shoved the feelings deep inside and did my homework and studied all the time. Which got me to the valedictorian spot.

Responding to the motor vehicle accident today threatens to call up those feelings. But I don't want to open that box. Not now. Not ever.

"I know you're tired and upset, so this probably isn't the best time . . . but I need to talk to you about the future," Mom says. "I want you to hear it from me."

"You mean college?"

"Not college," she says. She clears her throat and starts fiddling with a ring on her left hand.

I notice a flash as it catches the light.

"Wait . . . is that an engagement ring you're wearing?"

I've been so wrapped up in my own thoughts that I didn't even notice it till now.

Mom looks down at the ring, then back at me.

"That's . . . why I wanted to talk to you," she says. "Ted and I have been dating for a few years now, and . . . well, he's asked me to marry him."

Something shifts and a wave of anger burns through me. Mom watches me, nervous and expectant, waiting for my reaction to the news.

"But *why*?" I exclaim. "Everything's fine the way it is!"

From the expression on her face, I can tell this isn't the reaction she was hoping for.

"It is, for now. But you'll be going off to college next year, and . . . well, Ted and I, we love each other. Your dad will always be in my heart—he was my first true love, and he gave me you." Her lips tremble. "But he's gone. He's been gone for six years. And I need to seize happiness while I can. It's time."

"But you're happy already!" I say. "Why can't things just stay the way they are?"

"Because you're leaving and I don't want to be in this house all by myself, just me and the memories," Mom says.

"You're going to sell the house?" I say, my heart starting to pound in my chest.

"We haven't one hundred percent decided yet," Mom says. "Most likely, Ted will move in here."

Into our house.

"What about Saffron and Carson?" I ask. "What about my

room? Are you going to give it to Saffron?" The questions are just tumbling out now. I knew things would probably change when I left for college, but this is a lot more than I was prepared for.

Mom, in contrast, replies slowly and calmly. "There's a lot we haven't decided yet," she says.

There's already so much uncertainty in my life what with college and wondering if Caroline is going to be okay and whatever is going on with Will and senior year starting—I can't handle this right now.

"I'm going upstairs," I say, getting up and leaving my untouched dinner on the table.

"But you haven't finished your—"

"I'm not hungry!" I shout from the stairs, taking them two at a time until I get to my room and slam the door. I throw myself on the bed, emotions speeding around me like race cars at Le Mans. I feel blindsided, but as I lie staring up at the ceiling, I wonder why. It's not like Mom's kept her relationship with Ted a secret. He comes over for dinner several times a week and brings Carson and Saffron when they're staying with him instead of their mom.

I should have realized that it was all leading here.

I text Ada.

Me: Mom just told me she's getting married.

Ada: !!!!!!!!! To TV Ted?

Me: No, to some rando she met on Old People Tinder.

Ada: Oh cool. So happy for your mom. 😄

Me: 😕

Me: Of course it's to TV Ted!

Ada: So do I say congratulations?

Ada: Or offer my condolences?

Me: I don't know. I'm not sure how to feel about this.

Ada: Wait—so Carson and Saffron are going to be your family?

Me: My stepfamily.

Ada: Are stepdads as evil as the fairy tales always make out stepmoms to be?

Me: I'll have to let you know.

Me: At least I'm going off to college next year, so they can't make me into their unpaid servant and force me sleep by the fireplace ashes.

Me: That's good, I guess.

Ada: And I guess your mom must be happy—at least she won't be as lonely when you leave for college. Congrats, Mrs. S!

I stop and stare at the last text.

It pricks a sliver of guilt into the storm of self-pity and anxiety that swept over me when Mom told me her news. I've worried about her being alone when I'm gone next year, but in all the questions and emotions I had about her and Ted getting engaged, I haven't once thought about her happiness, the happiness that the rational side of me knows she deserves.

I pick up the picture that's never left my bedside table since my dad died. It's one of the three of us on the beach at Cape

Hatteras, North Carolina, where we went on vacation a few weeks before the accident. It was, and still is, the best time of my life, maybe because of what followed.

We biked and caught waves with our boogie boards and sat on the balcony of the rental condo at night watching the lights of boats out on the ocean.

That vacation is gilded in my memory by sunshine and laughter and my not knowing what was coming.

Mom has the same picture next to her bed. All this time dating Ted and she's never moved it. I wonder if it'll end up in a drawer when they get married.

I don't want that to happen. But I don't want Mom to be sad, either.

So I get off my bed, change into my pajamas, and head back downstairs. Mom's sitting in the living room, which is completely dark except for the light from the TV.

I sit close to her on the sofa and lean my head on her shoulder. She puts her arm around me, and I exhale into her embrace.

"I'm sorry," we both say at the same time.

And then we start laughing and we can't stop. We carry on until my sides hurt and Mom has to wipe away tears, which I think are from laughing, but I can't be sure.

"So, what are you sorry for?" Mom asks. "Or should I go first?"

"You first," I say.

"Okay. I'm sorry for breaking the news to you when you

were so obviously tired and stressed out. It was insensitive of me."

"Honestly, I'm not sure if any other time would have been better," I say.

"Maybe not," Mom says. "But I've been so anxious about how you were going to react since Ted asked me, and I didn't want you to find out from Saffron or Carson."

"When did it happen?"

"Ted's working the night shift tonight, so he invited me to lunch today," Mom explains. "We've talked about getting married at some point in the future, but I never expected . . . this."

She holds out her hand and admires the sparkle. I take her hand and bring it up to my face, so I can check the thing out more closely.

"It's a beautiful ring," I say. "Not too flashy. Just right for you." I glance at her and then look back at the diamond. "I guess the guy really knows you."

Mom smiles and gets this goofy faraway look. "Yes, the *guy* does really know me." She takes my hand in hers and gives it a squeeze. The stone is unfamiliar and uncomfortable against my finger, and I slide it to a more comfortable position. Mom focuses back on me. "I want you to remember that you're my baby. It's important to me that you're okay with this."

I swallow, hard. "That's what *I'm* sorry about. I know I didn't react well. And I will be okay with it because I want you to be happy. I just . . . need some time to adjust to the idea."

"I know," Mom says. "I understand. It's a lot to take in."

"So much is changing," I say. "Like, I don't even know where I'm going to be this time next year, and now I don't even know if I'm going to have my room to come home to."

"You'll always have *a* room to come home to," Mom says. "As long as you want and need one."

"But will it be *my* room?" I ask. "Or will it be Saffron's? She's only going to be a freshman this year. She's got four more years at home."

"I know, but she lives with her mom most of the time," Mom says. "We'll figure it out. I know there are going to be some bumps along the way, but we'll get through them together, just like we always have."

Exhausted, I put my head back on Mom's shoulder. I know she's right. We will get through the changes. If we got through losing Dad so suddenly and unexpectedly, we can get through anything.

"I miss Dad."

I feel the hitch in Mom's breath. "Oh, Dara, honey, I do, too. Sometimes when you smile, I see his features in your face, and I'm just so grateful to have you, our amazing daughter, who has the best qualities of both of us."

My heart feels like it's suddenly too big for my chest. I swallow a few times and, desperate to change the mood before I start to cry, I pick up the remote.

"It's been kind of a heavy day," I say. "Since you're getting married, what do you say we watch *Bridesmaids* again?"

"Sounds like a great plan," Mom says.

We share a blanket on the sofa, and I lean my head back on her shoulder. It's like so many other nights when it's just been the two of us, but suddenly more precious because of the knowledge that we don't have that many more left to us.

RUMOR HAS IT

Welcome back! It's August 28 and the start of a brand-new year here at Greenpoint High. For all you new Panther cubs (aka fresh meat): Welcome to GHS! You've gone from being the big bad eighth graders to the bottom of the food chain. Time to pay your dues and work your way up again.

Just remember: Rumor Has It is where it's at if you want to know what's *really* happening at GHS.

Who am I?

That's the best kept secret here at Greenpoint High. There's only one person who knows who I am—the previous holder of this exalted position.

Who knows, one day Rumor Has It could be you.

But let's get down to the back-to-school news:

Austin W is going to be returning to GHS on crutches. He broke his ankle playing hoops last week. Good luck getting to class on time!

Don't look for your favorite chips and candy in the vending machines. The school board voted to remove unhealthy products (aka the stuff we actually like).

I heard through the grapevine that Candace M is dating Jason P's older sister.

But that's not the only GHS keeping-it-in-the-family news. This one's hot off the press: Senior Dara S's mom got engaged to junior Carson and freshman Saffron T's dad. Congrats on becoming one big happy GHS family!

Speaking of Dara S, she's starting the year as number one in the senior class, but Will H and MJ M are hot on her heels, closely followed by Ada I and Amir H. According to Principal Joyner, it's the tightest race ever for valedictorian. Who do *you* think will win?

Send your best guesses and any scintillating start-of-school scandals to rumorhasitghs@gmail.com.

MJ

"I don't understand how Rumor Has It found out about my mom and Ted Taylor getting engaged," Dara says before AP English on the first day of school. "I've barely told anyone. Honestly, why would anyone even care?"

"*You* might not have told anyone, but Saffron told my little sister," Carly says. "I don't know who else she told, or who Carson might have blabbed to."

"I can't believe it. You all probably knew before me," Dara mutters. "And Mom picked when I was exhausted after a really stressful shift on the ambulance to tell me."

"But . . . are you okay with it?" I ask her. "Them getting married?"

Dara pushes her hair back from her face. "I guess. I mean, I want my mom to be happy, and she's definitely been happier since Ted's been on the scene. It's just . . . a lot."

"So is he going to move into your house?" Carly asks. "Or is your mom going to move in with him?"

"They haven't decided yet," Dara says. "Um . . . can we not talk about this?"

Ada gives her a worried glance, but Dara's looking down at her desk. With a shrug, Ada turns to me.

"MJ, are you doing Robotics Club again?" she asks. "Ms. McKissack said there's a new county-wide bot battle competition in January, and GHS Robotics is going to enter."

"Wow, awesome!" I exclaim. "That'll be so cool."

Mr. Block starts handing out the syllabus, but I spend most of his first day of class sketching an idea for a bot that will destroy in the competition. I can't wait till the first meeting so I can make sure the smartest people are on my team to build her.

Over dinner, I tell my dad about the bot battle competition and the rough design I came up with.

"Make sure you put it in the family calendar," Mom says. "We want to be there to cheer you on."

I raise my brows in surprise. "*You* want to come to the bot battle competition? Who are you and what have you done with my mom, who reads a book every time the *BattleBots* show is on?"

"The difference is *you*, MJ," Mom says. "I'm willing to sit through pretty much anything to show that I love and support you."

"Yeah, even those interminable elementary school concerts in the auditorium with no air-conditioning," Dad says.

"That must have been Zack," I say. "As we all know, I don't have any musical talent." I grin at Dad. "Just like you."

"Okay, okay, I get it: I'm not going to win any karaoke contests," Dad says.

"Except maybe the prize for worst voice," I say.

"I'm going to call Zack and tell him you've turned against me."

"Do it! Zack will agree," I tell him.

"Speaking of your brother, we wanted to talk to you about college," Mom says. "It's important to moderate your expectations early."

"What do you mean?" I ask. Although I think I know. I've been avoiding this conversation all summer.

"We know you want to apply to Carnegie Mellon early, MJ, but we want you to start considering other options," Dad says. "Carnegie Mellon is an extremely expensive school. We're not made of money. We've been saving to pay for your college, but you'd have to get a really substantial financial aid package for it to be enough to get you through that school."

"But it's the best," I say. "Especially for what I want to study. Why should only the rich kids get to go to the best schools?"

"It's not that you can't go there," Mom says. "The thing that worries us is that they only offer early decision, which means you *have* to go there if you get in. Maybe it would be better to apply regular decision and apply to an early action school instead. That way, you know what the aid package is before you have to make a decision."

"But I really want to go to Carnegie Mellon," I say. I realize I probably sound like a brat, but going to Carnegie Mellon is about going to the best of the best. It's about making the right choice for my future—shouldn't my parents want that for me?

"We understand that, but what if you get in and don't get a good enough aid package?" Dad says. "You're committed to going, but you'll end up with a huge mountain of debt."

"But the field I'm going into is where the jobs of the future are," I say. "I'll be able to get a good job and pay off the debt."

"Yeah, until they outsource your job to another country where they can get someone to do the same work for less money," Dad says. "Do you realize how many IT jobs were outsourced overseas in the last decade?"

"But the thing I want to study is where the action is at in tech," I argue. "Not only that, I'm a girl, and they keep saying how they want more women in STEM fields."

"Until you apply for a job and they tell you that you don't 'fit in with the corporate culture,'" Mom says, using air quotes.

I don't know what that means, but it's clear what they are trying to do. "Look, I get it!" I say, my fists clenching under the table. "You don't want me to go to the school of my dreams."

My parents exchange a loaded glance.

"That's not fair, MJ," Mom says finally. "We're just trying to explain the financial realities. We'd love to be able to afford to send you to any school you want to go to, but we can't. We had the exact same conversation with Zack, and he's at a state school, which is less expensive, but which still has a great department in his major."

"It sure feels like you don't want me to go to Carnegie

MJ

Mellon," I mutter. "I haven't even applied yet and you're already discouraging me."

"MJ, you're a very smart girl. Why can't you understand what we're trying to tell you?" Dad says, starting to sound irritated with me. "We just don't want you to be committed to going if the aid package isn't sufficient. We're not saying you shouldn't apply at all."

"Think about it, sweetheart," Mom says. "I spent twenty years paying off my student loans, and college wasn't nearly as expensive then as it is now."

"Yeah, we're counting on you to look after us in our retirement," Dad says. "Since you're going to have some fancy-schmancy high-tech job."

The scary thing is, I think he's only half joking.

"Fine, I'll think about it," I say, just to shut them up. Anything to stop this conversation.

But in my heart I know that Carnegie Mellon is where I want to be. I'm going to apply early no matter what.

Since it's still light for an hour or so, I decide to go for a run. I text Will to see if he wants to come with me. We've been running together since we started doing track in middle school, and we're pretty well suited when it comes to pace.

No can do, he texts back. Too busy.

What is with him? He seems to always be too busy lately.

Whatever. I head out, losing myself in the beats of the music

162

in my headphones and the tread of my sneakers against the pavement until the purple and blue hues of dusk tell me it's time to head home.

At the first meeting of Robotics Club, Ms. McKissack hands out a flyer for the county-wide Bot Battle Extravaganza.

"I'm really excited for this, and I hope you all are, too," she says.

"Do we all get to enter?" Ada asks.

Ms. McKissack shakes her head. "Each school gets to submit one entry. We're going to create two contenders and see which one holds up best. So I need you to divide yourselves into two teams of about equal size."

Will, Amir, Sam, and I immediately team up.

"Is it okay if I join you?" Ada asks.

"Sure," Will says, before even asking the rest of us. Not that I mind. Ada's cool.

"We've got two-thirds of the Robotics Club female population in our group," Amir says.

"That's not saying much," I say. "There are only three of us."

Ms. McKissack, Ada, and I have been trying to get more girls into the club. We recruited Tracy Washington, a sophomore, who's in the other group. But there's still a long way to go.

"Yeah, us STEMinists have our work cut out," Ada says with a sigh.

"The first thing you need to do in your groups is decide what kind of bot you want to build," Ms. McKissack says. "Do you want a wedge bot, a spinning bot, or a hammer bot?"

Amir and Sam look at each other. "Hammer!" they say in unison. I grin, because the rough design I made was for a hammer bot.

"Are we even going to vote on it?" I say. "Or do we all love the concept of smashing things to pieces?"

"I vote for smash and destroy," Ada says.

"Me too," Will says. He grins at Ada. "Does Dara know that her best friend has such violent tendencies?"

Ada looks at Amir, Sam, and me, and then smiles sweetly at Will. "You mean like all of your friends?"

Will laughs ruefully. "Yeah. Just like."

I show them the design I made, and everyone starts making suggestions for how to tweak it to make it better. Then we make a list of the parts we think we need.

"Forget the parts," Amir says. "We need to talk about the really important thing."

"Which is?" Ada asks.

"Duh. A name! Our beautiful hammer-wielding bot needs a name."

"Can I just point out we haven't even started building our beautiful hammer-wielding bot?" Sam says.

"So?" Amir asks. "She still needs a name?"

"Oh, we already know she's a she?" I say.

"You said you wanted more girls in Robotics," Amir says.

"We meant *human* girls," Ada says. "But okay, fine. What about Grace, for Grace Hopper?"

"Grace?" Will says. "You want to name a hammer-wielding battle bot *Grace*?"

Ada shrugs. "You might have a point."

"What about Stone Cold Crusher?" Sam suggests.

"Not bad," Amir says. "You're on the right track."

"Okay, how about BludgeonBot?" Will says.

"Getting warmer," Amir says. "MJ, got any ideas?"

I frown. It's got to be something that will strike fear in the hearts of the other team.

"I've got it!" I exclaim. "Karla the Killer."

Amir strokes his chin, and then a wide smile cracks his face. "Yes! Karla the Killer. I'm into it."

So is everyone else.

Now that we've named her, we just have to build her.

But that's the best part.

PART THREE

NOVEMBER
BEFORE

RUMOR HAS IT

Happy Thanksgiving, Panthers! PSA: While you're busy enjoying your turkey and pumpkin pie, give a thought to the Indigenous peoples, because I don't think their side of the story has made it into history books. Not in the way it should, anyway.

And here are some other things to think about this weekend as we head into Black Friday . . .

Happy out-of-control consumerism month!

Happy switch-from-pumpkin-spice-to-gingerbread-lattes time!

Are you going over the river and through the woods to grandmother's house for Thanksgiving?

Nikki T is flying all the way to LA to share turkey with her grandparents.

Jessie L is heading to Norfolk, VA, to share pumpkin pie with his relatives. Wondering if he's grounded after failing his last three AP Calc tests?

Angie B is heading to Utica, NY. Fun fact: Utica got its name by having it drawn out of a hat.

For those of you who are staying close to home over Thanksgiving break, I expect to see your faces at the homecoming football game to cheer on the Greenpoint Panthers against the Dariton Generals. Rumor Has It will be there taking names.

I'll leave you with a special Rumor Has It poll . . .

Sweet potatoes should only be served:

a) with marshmallows

b) with no marshmallows

c) as fries

d) I would rather die than eat sweet potatoes!

Much like the city that brings us the most ridiculous Thanksgiving tradition—a parade of giant balloons—Rumor Has It never sleeps. Which is more than I can say for some of your parents and Vice Principal Cagle during the freshman band concert last week. So stay tuned for more festive updates over the long weekend.

DARA

"Where did you get that sweatshirt?" Amir asks when he, Will, MJ, and Sam come to pick me up for the homecoming game. "I want one!"

I'm wearing the hoodie Mom gave me yesterday as a joke gift. It just says COLLEGE across the front.

"My mom got it for me," I say. "Because I've been driving her up the wall freaking out about college ever since I sent in my application."

"You and me both," MJ says with a sigh.

"My mom said she wants me to remember that I'm going to get into college *somewhere*, even if Johns Hopkins isn't smart enough to admit me," I continue. "Subtle hint taken, *Mom*."

"They'd be crazy not to," Sam says. "You're probably going to be valedictorian."

"Not if I have anything to do with it," Will says, flashing me a wicked grin in the rearview mirror.

"Or me," MJ says, socking Will on the shoulder.

"Hey!" Will cries out, laughing. "You know you have tiny fists of fury."

"Poor you," she says, laughing right back at him.

"It doesn't matter if I'm valedictorian, despite these two

goofballs," I tell Sam. "I bet at least half the people who are applying early are their school's valedictorian, too."

"You have a point," Amir says.

"Ugh. Okay, can we declare this a college-talk-free zone?" MJ begs us. "I'm desperate to forget about the whole thing for a while."

"Going to be kind of hard to have a college-talk-free zone at homecoming," Will points out. "Given that there will be a lot of people there back from, you know, *college*, talking about school."

"But can we at least avoid the subject in this car?" MJ says. "How about we talk about this brilliant tweak I thought of for Karla the Killer?"

She proceeds to explain some intricate detail of their battle bot, which means nothing to me, so I kind of stop paying attention to the words and just watch Will. He's so adorably animated when he talks about Karla. We haven't had any time alone over Thanksgiving, and I miss him. Sometimes I think that once we all find out where we're going and get our grades this quarter, maybe I'll be ready to stop keeping this a secret. Hopefully by then I'll have pulled enough ahead of Will and MJ that they won't be able to catch up, and nobody will care that Will and I are dating. I thought maybe this thing with Will wouldn't last past September, but now I'm going to a homecoming game with him? Not only that, we're in a pretty intense, if secret, relationship. We've even exchanged the L-word. That kind of intense.

I have to keep reminding myself that next September we could be on opposite sides of the country, and I'm not down for long distance. This isn't forever, this is for now. My heart tightens at the thought, and I shove it away and try to focus on what MJ is saying about Karla.

The parking lot at school is already crowded when we pull in. I spot Ada with her older sister, Grace, and run to catch up with them. I give them both giant hugs.

"You'll never guess what happened at Phil Dugan's party last night," Ada says.

"Um . . . you finally got with Tony Ortega?"

"I wish," Ada says. "But no, it's about Carly."

"Carly made out with Tony Ortega?"

Ada smacks my arm. "Hush your mouth!" she exclaims as I rub it. "No, Carly hooked up with Jayson Trantor."

"Shut up! What?"

"Yeah, I know," Ada says. "That'll teach you to bail on me to go to an Oversized Aviators concert with Saffron."

"It was a last-minute thing!" I say. "Saffron texted and said she had an extra ticket because her friend got sick and she knew I love the band. You totally would have bailed on me, too, and you know it. You stan Oversized Aviators even more than I do!"

"True," Ada admits. "I'm jealous, that's all."

"Understandable," I say. "But back to Carly and Jayson. I guess he's kinda hot, even if he's not my type."

"Yeah, I know. And so does he," Ada says.

I laugh. I don't know much about Jayson other than he's hot and he's on the wrestling team and aced our sophomore Spanish class. "One-time thing?" I ask.

"Nope. Carly and I were supposed to come to the game together, and she blew me off to go with Jayson instead."

"God, I'm so glad I don't have to deal with high school drama anymore," Grace chimes in, zipping up her jacket.

Ada gives her an are-you-kidding-me look. "Like you didn't spend most of Thanksgiving dinner catching us up on the latest sorority house drama?"

"Greek life, not geek life," Grace says, and Ada rolls her eyes at the ridiculousness.

"Hey, Dara and Ada, are you gonna sit with us?" Will shouts from behind us as we go into the bleachers.

"Yeah!" I call back. We wait for them to catch up and then we all go into the football field and search till we find an empty spot high up in the bleachers that's big enough to fit all of us.

"Oh, look, there's Carly!" MJ says, pointing to a spot lower down in the bleachers. She starts to wave to call her up.

"Wait, is she with *Jayson Trantor*?" Will says.

"Yup," Ada says.

"How did we miss that?" MJ says.

"Because we skipped Phil's party to play *Iron Harvest*," Will says.

"And I totally killed you both," Amir says gleefully.

The game starts, and I try to follow along, but I'm just not that into football. Mostly I'm here to hang with my friends. So I cheer at the right times but without really knowing what's going on.

Will is sitting between MJ and me, but he's focusing his attention on MJ. We always play it cool when we hang with everyone, but his leg drifts toward mine and then stays there, so I feel the heat of him and we're somehow connected.

"You know, that tweak you came up with for Karla might just be genius," Will tells MJ. "Karla's gonna whip Boris's butt."

"Remember, it's not just Boris we have to beat," MJ says. "It's all the other robotics clubs in the county."

"I'm not worried," Will says. "My girl Karla can take them all."

"*Your* girl Karla?" MJ says with a raised eyebrow. "Don't you mean *our* girl Karla? She's the monster of many Dr. Frankensteins."

"Karla's not a monster!" Will says. "She's neutral, like all technology." He grins at MJ. "Now, the people controlling her . . . that's another story."

"Speak for yourself, William," MJ says.

Will snorts. "Yeah, right. Weren't you the one who convinced me to eat a mud pie by telling me it was a brownie?"

"Oh my god, Will!" I exclaim. "You didn't."

"Oh yeah he did," MJ says with a grin. "He was such a gullible little kid."

"But I got back at you by coating a sponge with chocolate

icing and offering you a piece of cake," Will says, grinning back at her. "Your face when you tried to take a bite was meme-worthy."

"I still haven't forgiven you for that, by the way," MJ says. "Or for saying that cats are evil."

"They are!" Will says. "Remember how Newton scratched me and I got sick?"

"That wasn't Newton's fault! You invaded his space!"

"The little fleabag thought your entire house was his space," Will says.

"You can't speak that way about my dead pet—"

"Okay, kids," I say, interrupting MJ. "I'm going to go get a snack. Want anything?"

"I'll come with you," Will says. "Before MJ kills me."

My heart gives a flutter. Until Ada says, "Me too."

So no moment alone with Will. Sometimes I wonder if all the secrets we keep are really worth it. But then I think about the regular updates Rumor Has It has been posting on the valedictorian race.

"Can you get me some popcorn?" Sam asks.

We head to the snack truck, and just as we go behind the bleachers, the crowd on our side goes wild.

"Don't tell me I missed a touchdown," Will says. "Because that will make me very sad."

"TOUCHDOWN for the Greenpoint Panthers!" the announcer says.

"Okay, we won't tell you," I say, with a half smile.

"Not cool, Simons!" Will says with a look of fake menace on his face.

"I'm soooooo scared," I say, and start running, and Ada explodes into laughter.

"She thinks she can outrun a track star, does she?" Will says, and I hear the sound of his sneakers hitting the blacktop coming up behind me.

He manages to grab my hoodie and pulls me into his arms, and then lifts me over his shoulder like a sack of vegetables.

"Ada, I think Dara is an elf," he says, turning. I get a glimpse of Ada catching this on her phone. "She weighs, like, nothing."

"I'm not an elf, you're just a giant, you behemoth!" I say. "Put me down!"

"Say please," he says.

"Fine, *please* put me down."

He loosens his grip on me and I slide down his body. Our eyes meet and I feel the electricity between us. "Wish we were alone," I whisper.

"Me too," he whispers back.

I pull away from him then, because Ada is catching up.

It's getting harder and harder to keep us a secret. I wonder how much longer we'll be able to do it.

RUMOR HAS IT

Good morning, Panthers! It's Monday, November 28! Shake off your turkey comas, we have plenty of catching up to do.

Congrats, Greenpoint Panthers, for crushing the Dariton Generals! It was great to see so many of last year's seniors at the game.

Edgar P and Jeremy Y are official! After seeing them holding hands at the homecoming game, Rumor Has It can confirm they are dating. I predict they'll be voted Most Perfect Couple in the yearbook. They've definitely got my vote!

A little bird told me that Penny K dumped Orlando M on Saturday after the game. Is that why he's walking around looking miserable? Rumor Has It suggests a trip to the Dairy Barn.

Meanwhile, new couple Carly V and Jayson T don't seem to be feeling the chill. They were seen at the game keeping each other toasty and warm.

Have you bought tickets to the Greenpoint Players production of *The Addams Family* yet? I'm hearing that Carson T makes a very dashing Lucas Beineke.

The next few weeks are going to be nerve-racking for some of our seniors. You may notice them walking around looking either ecstatic (YAY!) or miserable (BOO!) because schools are starting to release their early decision and action notifications. Each college drops their decisions on different days—some this week, some next, and some the week after. It's going to be an intense month! And that's *before* we get to all the festive activities in the lead-up to winter break.

I'll be covering it all, so stay tuned.

RUMOR HAS IT

Hellooooo, Panthers! It's Friday, December 9. Are you feeling merry and bright?

I'll tell you who is—these seniors who got into their first choice schools early:

Amir H is heading to the Big Apple, New York, NY, to attend NYU. Purple looks good on you!

Jermaine K is going to be stampeding his way to Washington, DC, as a Howard U Bison. He's been stylin' in that red, white, and blue hoodie!

Destiny M is going to Boston to be a Harvard woman. Can you say Hahvahd Yahd? Does this mean she's going to start rooting for the Patriots and the Red Sox?

Christina M won't be looking for any knights in shining armor— she's going to be a Scarlet Knight herself. Go, Rutgers!

Stay tuned for more good news as it comes in. And be kind to seniors who look like they've got the sads.

Meanwhile, Alyssa S and Jay T are our latest Panther couple. Sources tell me they were seen not watching the movie at the Greenpoint multiplex last Saturday night.

Not such good news for Ray J and Samantha P, who had a loud and very public breakup at the basketball game on Tuesday. Oh, the drama! Despite that, the Panther b-ballers managed to beat Seymour Valley High 68–52.

That's all for now. Check back here for more college news and GHS scandals—and as always don't forget to send any news to rumorhasitghs@gmail.com.

WILL

All the seniors who applied early and haven't heard yet are on edge because a bunch more schools have early decision and early action notifications coming up this week. Stanford's isn't until the day after tomorrow, but I keep checking my email obsessively just in case they decide to release them earlier. Dumb, I know.

"Are you watching this show or not? You literally checked your phone, like, two seconds ago," Sadie says, poking at me on Tuesday night while we're watching TV with Mom.

"Incorrect use of the word *literally*," I say. "It was at least thirty seconds ago, and probably more like two minutes."

"Fine, I was using *hyperbole*," Sadie says. "But I'm warning you, if you keep checking every two minutes, I'm going to steal your phone."

"Sadie, wait till you're the one anxious to see if you got into the college of your dreams," Mom says. "Be a little more understanding of your brother."

My dreams? Ugh. I feel sick. Half of me hopes I get rejected so I don't have to go. The other half hopes I get in because I cannot deal with my dad. But then I might actually have to go to Stanford.

"We all know Will's going to get into college *somewhere*," Sadie says. "He's just freaking out because he wants to get into Stanford to be Dad's golden kid."

"That's what you think," I mutter.

Mom pauses the TV. Sadie narrows her eyes at me.

Crap. I didn't mean to say that out loud.

"What do you mean, Will?" Mom asks.

"Are you saying that you applied early to Stanford and you don't even want to go there?" Sadie adds.

"No," I say. "Not exactly. I'm just stressed. It's fine. Let's watch the show."

"No, let's not," Mom says. "Come on, Will, out with it."

The last thing I want to do is talk to my mom about the pressure I'm feeling from my dad to follow this path of his. My parents don't need me to add any more fuel to the fire of them hating each other. But both Mom and Sadie are looking at me expectantly.

"I don't know," I say finally. "It's just . . . well, for as long as I can remember, Dad's been all about me following in his footsteps and going to Stanford."

"Tell me about it," Mom says, rolling her eyes.

"It's gotten to the point where it's hard for me to even imagine going anywhere else, because I would be such a huge disappointment to him." I look at the frozen TV screen, where some actor's mouth is open in the middle of a sentence. It looks like the silent scream I feel welling inside me whenever I think about college.

"Don't freak, but . . ." I take a deep breath and risk honesty. "There's a part of me that hopes I don't get in, because then I'll have the option of going other places."

Mom's eyes widen. "Will, why would you think you only have that option if you don't get into Stanford? Even if you *do* get in, you can still go somewhere else," she says. "It's early action, not early decision."

"Mom, you know what Dad's like," Sadie says. "He's been pushing Stanford on us since the day we were born. And it's even harder to get into now than when he went!"

"We all know what your father is like," Mom says, her voice grim. "But it's *your* life, Will, not his."

I give a hollow laugh. "At least in theory."

"Even if Dad ends up being a jerk about it, I still think you should tell him how you feel," Sadie says.

"Life's stressful enough right now without me doing that," I say.

"I hear you," Mom says. "Do you want me to talk to him?"

"No!" I exclaim at the same time as Sadie says, "Oh god, Mom, no!"

We exchange a glance as Mom says, "Well. Okay, then," in a quiet voice.

I feel bad because I know she was trying to help. It's just . . .

"Mom, you know that if you say black, Dad says white," Sadie says. "Will's got to be the one to do it."

"He's not going to listen," I say. "He never does."

"Will, I've learned that even if the other person isn't capable of hearing you, it's important for you to speak your truth," Mom says. "Otherwise you just bottle it up inside and it ends up coming out in unhealthy ways."

It's hard to stand up to the combined force of Mom and Sadie. "Fine, I'll tell him. Just not right now."

"Whenever you feel the time is right," Mom says. "But I wouldn't leave it too long. Otherwise, he's going to think . . ." She bites her lower lip and sighs. "Never mind." She leans forward and puts her hand on my arm. "At the very least, you should apply to some other colleges. Explore some other options, so you have choices, even if you do get into Stanford."

The idea of having options, to not having my life mapped out according to Dad's plan, spreads out in front of me.

Now I just have to find the courage to tell him.

"I've decided to have a party on Saturday night," MJ says the next day in school. "To either celebrate or commiserate, depending on the decision. And you guys are all invited."

"Cool! I can drown my sorrows if I don't get in, which is what I've totally convinced myself is going to happen," Sam says. "If I sulk at home, alone in my room playing video games, my parents will be all over me about how I should be working on college applications, not gaming. Which will make me want to drown them out by playing *more* video games, which will only get them all over me again. Rinse and repeat until my entire family is dying for me to get in somewhere just so we don't have to live in the same house anymore."

"It's the total opposite in my house," Ada says. "*I'm* the one stressing about my college applications. My parents keep telling me to chill out and relax because I'll get in the school that's right for me, and if I don't, I can always transfer later."

"My parents seem convinced I'm *not* going to get into my first choice," MJ says, exhaling heavily. "My dad just keeps quoting the five percent acceptance rate in computer studies and tells me I should be thinking about plan B, preferably a state school because it costs less."

"Your dad has a point," Amir says. "It's a numbers game. It's all about probabilities."

"I know. It's just . . . why can't I be in that five percent? I mean, someone has to be," she says. "It makes me feel like they don't think I'm smart enough. And they tried to persuade me not to have the party 'just in case I'm not in the mood' by Saturday."

"It's what parents do," Sam says.

"Not my dad," I say. "He's so convinced that I'm going to get into Stanford that if I don't, he's probably going to insist on a DNA test to prove I'm not actually his kid."

MJ laughs out loud. "He doesn't need a DNA test. Anyone with two eyes can see you're a carbon copy of your dad."

My lunch sits heavily in my stomach. I love my dad, but I definitely don't want to *be* him.

The more I think about it, the more I half hope I don't get in.

• • •

Sadie is staying after for a Gay-Straight Alliance meeting, so I give Dara and Ada a ride home from school. I purposely drop off Ada first so Dara and I can hang out.

"Okay, we're officially alone for the first time in what feels like a century," I say. "Where are we going?"

"Let's go to the sculpture garden," she suggests. "The garden will be dead this time of year, but the sculptures are cool. I need to be outside."

"You know, we could always go for a run," I say as I back out of Ada's driveway.

Dara snorts. "Me? Run with Will Halpern, track star? No thanks, I've only got so much tolerance for humiliation." She glances over at me. "Maybe if you ran with your feet tied together?"

I chuckle. "Yeah, okay. I'll go for a run later. Walk around the sculpture garden it is." I glance at her. "Well, walk and hopefully some other form of distraction."

She bats her eyelashes at me, exaggeratedly flirting. "Why, what could you possibly mean, Will Halpern?"

"Having intense intellectual discussions about the sculptures, of course," I say. "Get your mind out of the gutter, Simons!"

She laughs. I love the way it sounds like it's coming from deep within her.

I slip one hand off the wheel and grasp hers. "So, what did

you think about the last episode of *Medics*?" I ask. "I can't handle that Dr. Jasmine and Hot Nurse Nick broke up!"

"I still can't believe you watch *Medics*," she says. "It doesn't seem like it would be your kind of show."

"Okay, confession. Before we got together, I only watched it when it couldn't be avoided. Like when Mom and Sadie were watching and I happened to be in the room." I flash her a grin. "But thanks to you, I'm hooked."

"Next I'm going to get you to binge-watch *Gutter Girlz* with me," she says.

I make a barfing sound. "No way. Been there, done that with Sadie. I love you, but not *that* much."

"Isn't love supposed to be limitless? I'm pretty sure I read that on some sappy Hallmark card a while back," she says.

"And if it's on a Hallmark card, it must be true," I say.

Her ponytail bobs as she nods with fake solemnity. "Which means you have a binge-watching date in your future."

"As long as we stop for frequent make out breaks, I might be persuaded."

Dara does a fist pump. "Yes!"

I'm relieved to see there are only two other cars in the sculpture garden lot, because it makes it more likely we'll be able to find a private spot.

It turns out the sculptures are a lot more interesting than I thought they'd be. There are two huge eggs nestled into the landscape like an enormous chicken laid them there. Then I spot it.

"Wow, is that a Möbius strip over there?"

"I was wondering when you'd notice that," Dara says, pulling me by the hand and walking toward it. "It's called *Eternity 2*."

We stand in the shadow cast by the Möbius strip against the late afternoon sun, which hangs low on the horizon. "New life goal: have one of these in my garden someday," I say.

"You're going to need a pretty big garden," she says.

I reach out and feel the cold copper of the statue underneath my fingers, its color oxidized to a cool greenish-gray shade that Dara tells me is called verdigris.

There's something about it that draws me; maybe it's the fact that it's infinite, with no boundaries, at a time where I feel boxed in by Dad's expectations.

We stand there in silence for a few minutes, just lost in the moment.

"I've missed you," she says.

"Same," I say, stepping closer to her. "But if we decided to tell, it would be a lot easier."

Dara doesn't answer and instead takes my hand and starts pulling me toward the next sculpture, which is the torso of a guy with, like, twelve-pack abs.

"What do you think?" I ask Dara.

"The model for this must have done a *lot* of crunches."

"No, about *us*!" I say. I know she's trying to avoid answering.

"It's not . . . forever," she says finally. "Just until it's obvious which of us is going to be valedictorian."

"A little less confident now, are we?" I observe. "Usually you're *sure* you're going to beat me."

"Oh, I'm still sure," she says with a smile. "It's everyone *else* who needs to be."

"The sooner the better," I say, taking her hand, and this time I lead her toward the sculpture of a horse that looks like it's made out of driftwood. "I want us to be out in the open. I'm tired of having to sneak around all the time and hide the fact that I'm into you."

"I know," she says. "Just a little longer, okay? As soon as second-quarter grades are released, it should be pretty obvious."

"Huh. Now I get it," I say. "This is your cunning plan to get me to slack off a little so you can clinch valedictorian. My reward is getting to go public."

She laughs. "Yup. Busted!"

"Too bad I'm not going to fall for it," I say. "I'm going to suffer through keeping us on the down low to keep you on your toes."

"Guess you're just too smart for me, Will Halpern," she says, a smile curving across her face.

New goals: get a Möbius strip sculpture *and* be too smart for Dara Simons.

We make our way around the lake, exploring the sculptures. At one point Dara climbs one of the interactive ones and gets stuck. I'm laughing too hard to be of much help, but eventually she gets down and chases me to the next one. By the time we get back to the car, I feel better than I have all week.

On the way home, Dara asks me how Karla the Killer is going.

"Great!" I say. "We already beat Boris the BotBeast. I think we've got a good chance of winning the counties. You'll come to the competition in January to cheer us on, right?"

She pauses, then says, "Yeah. I'll try to make sure I'm not scheduled for EMT duty that day."

"Cool!" I say as I pull into her driveway.

"Ugh, back to the books," Dara groans, leaning down to grab her stuff.

When she rights herself and swings her ponytail over her shoulder, she says, "I'll talk to you later?"

She looks so pretty in the fading light that I scoot closer.

"Oh, hey, Will," she says with a smile.

I smile back and lean in to kiss her. Her hands are tangled up with all her stuff, but mine aren't, and I pull her even closer. When we finally break apart, my heart is pounding everywhere.

She smiles again and kisses my cheek. "You need to go if you want to get that run in."

"There's this thing called reflective gear that means you can run in the dark," I say, my heart still racing. "I happen to own some for exactly that reason."

"But you'll be safer in daylight," she says. "Trust me, I'm an EMT. Now go. Love you."

"Love you back," I say as she gets out of the car, juggling her stuff and kicking the door closed with her heel.

I watch her walk away, arms full of books and ponytail bouncing.

Despite having gone out for a run after hanging with Dara, trying to clear my head and tire out my body, I still barely sleep the night before the big day—when Stanford releases its early action decisions.

I'm not the only one.

When MJ gets in the car with Sadie and me to drive to school, she leans her head against the passenger window and groans.

"I don't know how I'm going to keep my eyes open today," she says. "I barely slept last night."

"Will's got coffee," Sadie says from the back seat.

"Yeah, help yourself," I say, gesturing to my travel mug.

"You have yours with disgusting amounts of sugar," MJ says. "I'm desperate, but not that desperate."

"Do you want to stop at the Daily Grind?" I ask.

"Nah, then we'll be late," she says. "Just promise you'll wake me up if I start snoring in computer science."

"Only if you promise to do the same for me," I say. "Not that I snore. Ever."

Sadie snorts. "No, you just fart."

MJ laughs. I roll my eyes.

MJ and I manage to make it through our first-period computer science class without snoring or farting, but I know I'm going to have to reread everything Ms. McKissack talked about at home, because I found myself zoning out, wondering if the decision email had landed in my inbox yet.

It didn't. Between every class, I check again. Nothing. I go to the website and check what day they say they'll notify applicants. It's today. Is it a bad sign that I haven't heard anything? Do they notify people who are accepted first, then send out the rejections?

I'm especially anxious after I get a text from Dara the period before lunch that says, It's official! I'm a Blue Jay! Johns Hopkins, here I come!

Me: AWESOME! Congratulations!
Dara: Any news?
Me: Not yet. I'll keep you posted.
Dara: Got all my digits crossed for you. ☺

My stomach is churning from stress and coffee, and my head is just as messed up from lack of sleep and conflicting emotions. And at this point, I just want to know, because what-ifs are taking up too much space in my head.

As I get to lunch, I get the email saying I can go to the admissions portal for the decision.

My tongue feels stuck to the roof of my mouth as I log in, and my heart is pounding like I'm in the middle of the 400-meter sprint.

Dear Will,
Congratulations! It is with great pleasure that I offer you admission to Stanford University.

"I . . . I got in." I can't stop staring at the email.

"Stanford? Dude, that's awesome!" Amir says. He found out he got into NYU last week.

"Congrats," Sam says.

"I have to text my parents," I say. "Dad is going to be stoked."

I send Mom, Dad, and Sadie a quick text with a screenshot of the acceptance letter.

Then I send one to Dara: Stanford, here I come!

Dara: Yay!!!
Dara: If it's what you decide you really want, that is.

Yeah. If. That's the question. But for now, I push that question aside. I also post in the senior group chat, where people have been announcing their acceptances.

"Hey, where's MJ?" I ask, peering at our table. "She's normally here by now."

Amir shrugs. "No idea."

Sam looks around, his brow furrowed. "Yeah, I hope she's

okay." He picks up his phone to text her. The guy has been into MJ since sophomore year and hasn't had the courage to ask her out yet, no matter how much Amir and I tell him to just do it already because we're almost halfway through senior year and time is running out.

I get a text back from Dad: That's my boy!

Suddenly, the weight of the decision presses down on me, crushing the air out of my lungs.

Anyone with two eyes can see you're a carbon copy of your dad. MJ's voice bounces around in my head.

I should be ecstatic, but I'm just relieved that I won't be a disappointment to my dad. I try to think about telling him I don't want to go, but I just feel a different kind of stress.

I should have the courage to tell Dad that I want to explore other options.

But I know how that conversation will go. Talking to him about things that are really important to *me* is impossible. He either doesn't hear me, or he just, like, steamrolls over whatever I say.

As I listen to Amir talking excitedly about NYU, I can't help feeling envious. I should be feeling the same, and the fact that I don't, combined with the heavy feeling in the pit of my stomach, tells me something.

I decide I'm going to follow Mom's suggestion and apply to other schools. Just in case.

Maybe if I know I have options, that feeling will go away.

MJ

This feels like the longest day *ever*. It's only second period and I've already checked my email, like, fifty times, and that's an underestimate. I try to limit my checking to once every five minutes, but I only last two minutes and fifty-four seconds—which felt like an hour.

The period before lunch, Dara posts in the senior group chat that she's been accepted to Johns Hopkins. Meanwhile, I still haven't got an email. I'm the only one at our school who has applied early decision to Carnegie Mellon, so I don't even know if not having heard yet is a good or bad sign.

When I tell that to Carly as we pack up our stuff before lunch, she shakes her head. "I'm pretty sure they send out the notices all at once."

"I just want to *know*," I say.

"Hey, you're not the only one," she says. "I'm still waiting, too."

"Yeah. How can you be so calm?"

"I just look calm. Inside I'm anything but," Carly says. She shrugs. "I mean, it's not like we can do anything about it. Whatever is going to happen is going to happen."

I wish I could be that chill about it. Or even pretend to be.

On the way to the cafeteria, I check my phone again. Will just posted that he got into Stanford, and as happy as I am for him, it just makes the acid in my stomach churn more. I should send him a congratulatory text, but I just can't. Not until I know.

Then my phone buzzes with incoming emails, and I see there's one from Carnegie Mellon.

"Um . . . I'm just going to stop in the restroom," I tell Carly. "You go on ahead."

"Okay, see you there," she says.

I head to the nearest bathroom and lock myself into a stall. With trembling fingers, I log in to the admissions portal.

We're sorry, but your admission to Carnegie Mellon has been declined. We had many excellent applications for admittance, and this year was even more competitive than last. We wish you the best of luck with your college search.

I'm so stunned I can't move. I was convinced I was going to get in. Third in the class by only a few fractions of a percent, lots of challenging AP classes, good grades, Robotics Club, after-school job, track team. I'm a dream candidate—at least I thought I was.

They could have at least deferred me, so I had another chance.

Instead, they flat-out rejected me.

I feel like everything I've worked for is crumbling. Going to Carnegie Mellon was the first step. But if I can't even get that right, then it's like it's over before I even started. Like my future is a disappointment already.

Looks like my parents get their way after all. Now I'm going to have to spend winter break figuring out which other schools to apply to and finishing applications, instead of celebrating.

What makes it even worse is seeing all the posts in the senior class group chat. The other day Amir posted that he got into NYU. Will got into Stanford. Dara got into Johns Hopkins.

Ada got into Michigan! Carly texts me. Have you heard yet?

It feels like everyone in the world got into their first choice except for me.

I will not cry. I will not cry. I will not cry. I will not cry.

I get another text. I'm almost afraid to read it, in case it's another happy friend telling me they got in somewhere.

Sam: Everything okay? How come you're not at lunch?

It's sweet of him to ask, I guess. Will is probably too busy celebrating that he got into a school he's not even sure he wants to attend.

It's so unfair. I wanted to go to Carnegie Mellon so badly. Maybe if my parents were big donors like Will's dad, I would have gotten in.

As soon as I have the thought, I feel like the world's worst friend.

Ugh.

I can't face going into the cafeteria. I can't be around my friends whose lives are all going according to plan when mine isn't.

So I ignore Sam's and Carly's texts and stay in the bathroom for the rest of lunch. It's not like I'm hungry, anyway. Misery has taken away my appetite.

RUMOR HAS IT

Good morning, Panthers! It's Friday, December 16, and I hope you're all being nice because the holidays are just around the corner . . . like NEXT WEEK. Hope you've done all your ChrisHanuKwanzakahmas shopping!

But let's be real. You don't come to Rumor Has It to be nice, do you? You're here for the latest news, the dirt that only I can bring you.

Things like the school board looking into misuse of funds by the chairs of the Athletics Booster Club. Apparently over half the money we raised at the Athletics Booster bake sales was spent on giving Mr. and Mrs. Levandowski pedicures.

I guess they wanted to put their best foot forward at games.

Speaking of bad news on the sports front: Tyler J is in danger of being kicked off the wrestling team because he started his senior slide a semester early. Better hit the books over the winter break, Tyler, otherwise you're not going to be able to wrestle for the Panthers at state.

Have you noticed the sudden fashion trend of college

sweatshirts? Those are the lucky seniors who got into their first-choice schools.

We won't comment about the seniors who are walking around without the name of their fave college emblazoned across their chest. They are sad enough. Although . . . I hear that one of them is throwing a party this weekend. Got to hand it to her—not sure I'd be up for that.

That's it for now. Email your seasonal scandals and scribbles for Santa to rumorhasitghs@gmail.com.

MJ

I know it's me that Rumor Has It is talking about, and it makes me wonder how they know about my party. It's not like I put up a notice about it anywhere—I just told people at Robotics Club and let some of my track team friends know. It's kind of creepy.

But I keep reading it . . .

"Hey, MJ," Dara says when I get to English. "How are you doing?" Her brown eyes are warm with sympathy. "I saw that Rumor Has It wrote about your party."

I don't know why her friendly concern rubs me the wrong way. I know she's just trying to be nice, but she got into her first choice, so it just feels like she's being smug.

"Yeah," I say, my hands clenched under the desk. "At least they didn't mention me by name."

"I know," she says. "Then you'd have had to worry that lots of people would crash."

"Ugh," I say. "My parents would freak. They were not really into me doing this."

"Do you want me to come help set up?" Dara offers.

"I can, too!" Ada says.

I want to keep being annoyed with them, but it's hard when

they are being so nice. Guess I'll have to redirect my anger somewhere else.

"That would be great," I say, actually meaning it.

"Don't worry," Ada says. "It's going to be okay."

I don't know if she's talking about college or the party, but either way, it's easy for her to say.

"I don't even want to have this party anymore," I tell my parents the following morning. "It was supposed to be a celebration, and I got straight-up rejected."

"Oh, sweetie," Mom says. "I know you had your heart set on Carnegie Mellon, and this has been a huge disappointment for you. But there are lots of other great colleges out there." She cuts the crusts off another round of egg salad sandwiches. A small piece of me feels a little better seeing that. She knows how much I love egg salad and hate crusts. "I know you're going to get into one, and I bet you're going to be just as happy as you would have been at Carnegie Mellon."

"Maybe even happier," Dad says. "Things happen for a reason, even though we don't always know what it is at the time."

I get that my dad's trying to make me feel better, but I know the reason. The admissions people didn't think I was good enough. Now I'm starting to wonder that about myself, too.

"I know. But can I cancel the party? I'm really not in a party mood right now."

"I understand that," Mom says. "But I've already made three pans of lasagna and all these sandwiches. We can't afford to let all this food go to waste because you suddenly decided you're not in the mood."

"We did warn you that maybe you should wait until after you got the decision to invite people over," Dad says. "Sometimes, it pays to listen to your parents. We actually know a thing or two."

"Look at it this way," Mom says. "You can celebrate your friends who did get into their first-choice schools. Show them some support. That's what friends do, right?"

I hate it when my parents are right. Deep down, as miserable as I feel, and as much as I'd like to spend tonight binge-watching TV or working on my latest computer projects, I know Mom is right. I have to be happy for my friends. Or at least try.

"Okay, but you're still going to dinner and the movies, right? Otherwise you're just going to ask everyone where they're going and all anyone will do is talk about who got into their first choice and it'll be torture."

"I'm still not sure I feel comfortable with having kids over for a party when we're not home," Mom says, glancing over at Dad.

"I'm going to be away at college *somewhere* next year, so shouldn't you start trusting my judgment *now*?"

"MJ does have a point," Dad says.

Mom's jaw tightens. She hates when Dad is the weak link in the united parenting front. I can tell he's going to hear from her the minute I leave the room.

"Okay, here's the compromise. We'll see a movie, have a quick dinner, and then come home," Mom says. "That way we're building trust in baby steps."

"Fine," I say. I might be miserable about not getting into Carnegie Mellon, but it'll be easier to pretend I'm happy if I don't have to worry about my parents saying something that reminds me of it.

Ada and Dara are coming in about an hour to help with setup. They said Carly's also coming to help, so it shouldn't take us too long. Before they arrive, I go up to my room to get changed and try to psych myself up for this party I don't want to have. But instead of figuring out what to wear, I flop onto my bed and FaceTime Zack.

He's in his room with a bunch of friends. "Hey, MJ!" they all shout.

"Can I speak to you alone?" I beg Zack. "No offense, guys, I just—"

"We get it," his roommate, Pete, says. "You hate us."

"No, I don't! I love you all," I say, and then add quickly, "In a totally sisterly way."

"Hang on, MJ," Zack says over Pete's laughter. "I'll try to find a quiet spot somewhere in this place where I can deliver my brotherly wisdom."

The quiet spot turns out to be the bathroom. "I can't guarantee total privacy because someone's going to come in, but we're good for now," he says. "What's shaking?"

"It's this party," I say. "I thought I'd be celebrating getting in, but now . . . I'm going to have to listen to everyone else being happy. I wish I could cancel, but Mom and Dad won't let me."

"Look, I know you're really devastated you didn't get into Carnegie Mellon, but remember, I didn't get into my first-choice school, either," he says.

I'd forgotten that. Zack was really set on going to Purdue, but he didn't get in.

"The thing is, now I'm glad I didn't get in there, because I love UMD so much," he continues.

"Really? You're not just saying that?"

"For real," he says. "I mean, I'm sure if I'd got into Purdue I'd probably like it there, too, but I'm really happy right where I am *and* the program here is awesome."

"Maybe there's hope for me yet."

"Of course there's hope for you! Come on, MJ! You've had a couple of days to feel sorry for yourself, but you're gonna have to get past it."

I expected that from Mom and Dad, but Zack?

"Wow. Thanks for the empathy, bro."

"It's a downer you didn't get in, but you're going to get in somewhere great," he says. "So be happy for your friends and try to enjoy the party tonight."

"I don't know if enjoying the party is humanly possible," I say with a sigh.

"At the very least, pretend," he says. "You can do it, MJ. It's only for a few hours."

"It's only a few hours that will feel like an eternity."

"So? You sat through my performance as Dogberry in *Much Ado About Nothing* and survived."

"Oh god. You're right. That was excruciating," I say. "And I mean that with love."

Zack laughs. "Spoken like my sister."

I hear the bathroom door open, and someone says. "Hey, McKay, why are you talking on the phone in the bathroom? Is this some new girl?"

"None of your business," Zack tells the guy. "Hey, MJ, I gotta bounce. Hang in there."

"I'll try," I promise before ending the call.

Throwing my phone down on the bed, I open my closet, trying to figure out what to wear. My original outfit of jeans and the Carnegie Mellon sweatshirt Dad bought me when we toured the campus is clearly out. I bury the sweatshirt in the back of my closet. I'm going to give it to Goodwill, because seeing it will remind me that I didn't measure up.

A LOSER sweatshirt would reflect how I feel right now, but it's too late to get one. Besides, I have to try to follow Zack's advice to suck it up. There's got to be something else in my closet, something that will make me feel better. If only I could go to the party in my pj's, but I can just imagine the Rumor Has It post: "MJ M proved she has zero fashion sense by turning up to her own party in sleepwear. It set the mood for what turned out to be a total snoozefest . . ."

Ugh.

After trying on six different outfits, I settle on my black jeans and a sky-blue sweater that Carly said "brings out the color of your eyes."

Sighing, I gaze at my reflection. My makeup collection consists of blush, an eyeliner, mascara, and tinted lip balm. A lot of the time I don't even bother, but tonight's a party, so I do the best I can with what I've got. I wish my hair were a little longer, so I could do something different with it. I don't know what, exactly, but being me doesn't seem to feel like enough right now.

What if Zack's wrong and I'm not good enough for any school?

My stomach starts churning. I can't bear to look at myself anymore.

Turning away from the mirror, I see Pascal, who has been lazing on my bed and watching me with his big green eyes. "Okay, Pascal, it's time to party and pretend I'm enjoying it."

Pascal flips the bottom of his tail lazily. His green eyes regard me with the kind of scorn only a cat can convey, as if to tell me, *Yeah, you go, I'm gonna stay right here and avoid the ruckus.*

"Fine, be that way, you jerk," I tell him. Then I feel bad for calling him that. Picking him up, I cuddle him to my chest and carry him downstairs with me. "You know I love you, right?"

As soon as I reach the bottom step, he squirms and jumps down from my arms, dashing away to hide.

Like cat, like owner, I guess. I wish I could hide, too, but I can't because it's my fricking party.

DARA

"I love that sweatshirt so much," Ada says when I slide into the passenger seat.

"Thanks," I say. "I wasn't sure if we were still doing the whole sweatshirt thing or if it would make MJ feel worse."

Ada looks down at the MICHIGAN emblazoned across her chest in big yellow letters. "You're so much nicer than me," she says. "I didn't even think about that. Now I feel like a total jerk."

She puts the car in reverse and backs out of the driveway.

"You're not a total jerk," I assure her. "I'm probably just over-thinking things. Like I usually do. Besides, this is all I got."

"I love that you're a science geek, but you're superstitious about hoodies," Ada says with a smile.

"Yeah, I know. Shh. It's my dark secret."

"My lips are sealed," Ada says, taking one hand off the wheel and making a zipping motion across her mouth.

"So . . . can you believe Carly and Jayson are still together a month later?" I ask.

Ada makes a face. "I honestly don't know what she sees in him."

"I'm glad I'm not the only one who thinks that," I say.

"But don't tell that to Carly, though," Ada says. "After the party, I told her to just know what she's getting into. Jayson's never had a serious girlfriend and is always dating someone new. But Carly said she knows that and she's cool with it, because she's not looking to date anyone seriously, either."

"I wonder why Rumor Has It didn't repeat that warning when they posted about the two of them dating?" I say. "Because you're right, they've posted about Jayson *a lot*, and it's usually when he's onto a new girlfriend."

Ada shrugs. "I don't know," she says. "So how are the plans for your mom's wedding coming? Or is that a sore topic?"

"This probably makes me the worst, but I'm trying to avoid the wedding stuff as much as possible," I confess. "Like, I'm happy for Mom and everything, but I don't feel the need to be involved in every little detail."

"I can totally see how it might be weird," she says as she pulls the car into Carly's driveway and honks to let her know we're here. "It doesn't make you the worst."

I know Ada's right, but it's hard not to feel that way, especially when I remember how my mom was after my dad died and seeing how much happier she's been since Ted. It's not like she met him and suddenly she was magically better—she went to a grief support group, saw a therapist, and took medication for a while, so she'd already climbed most of the way out of the pit by the time she met him. But since she and Ted got together, she smiles a lot more and seems genuinely content.

"Hey," Carly says when she slides into the back seat of Ada's car. "Are you guys psyched to party?"

"Yeah," I say. "I just hope MJ is, too."

"I know, it sucks she didn't get into Carnegie Mellon," Carly says. "She was really set on that school."

"We'll just have to make sure we cheer her up tonight," Ada says.

"Definitely," Carly says. "Jayson's bringing some of his wrestling teammates, so that should liven things up."

Ada and I exchange a glance. "Does MJ know they're coming?" Ada asks.

"No, but she won't mind," Carly says. "She said her mom made enough food to feed a small army."

"Oookay," Ada says, but she doesn't sound convinced.

"Hey. Thanks for coming early to help," MJ says.

"It's no problem," I say. "Love the eye makeup. It really brings out your eyes."

She seems happily surprised by the compliment, her eyes widening as her cheeks tinge the palest of pinks.

"Thanks," she says.

"See, I told you!" Carly says. "I've been telling her she should accentuate her eyes. That sweater and makeup combo really works!"

"I'm glad something does," MJ says in a tone that makes it hard to know if it's a joke or not.

Ada gives her a quick hug. "C'mon, MJ, everything's going to be okay in the end. Their loss, not yours."

"Hey there, girls," Mr. McKay says, coming down the stairs. "I hear congratulations are in order."

A pained look flits across MJ's face, but it's gone in an instant.

"Well, for these two," Carly says. "I'm with MJ. I didn't get into my first choice."

I hope we can change the subject, because it's obviously a sore topic for MJ and Carly.

"Aren't you and Mom supposed to be leaving for the movie?" MJ says to her dad, shooting him a pointed look.

"Yes, we are," Mr. McKay says, checking his watch. "Hurry up, Christine, or we'll miss all the previews!" he calls up the stairs.

"Where should we put our coats?" I ask.

"Up in my room. Second door on the right," MJ says. "Just throw them on my bed. I'll be in the kitchen."

"I'll take yours," I tell Ada and Carly, and once they've handed them over I head up to MJ's bedroom.

Mrs. McKay is just coming out of her room as I round the top of the stairs.

"Hello, Dara," she says, greeting me with a big smile. "Congratulations on getting into . . . Where was it now? Harvard?"

"Hopkins," I say.

"Right—that's terrific!" she says. "I hope this party cheers up MJ. She's been down about getting rejected from CMU."

"We'll do our best to make sure she has a good time," I assure her.

"Thanks," she says.

"Christine!" Mr. McKay calls up the stairs again.

"Better run," Mrs. McKay says. "Have fun!"

I continue to MJ's room to put the coats on the bed. I've been to MJ's house, but I've never been up in her room before. She's got cool framed artwork of vintage Nintendo controllers on the wall. There are clothes strewn all over the floor, which I tiptoe around to get to her bed. She's also got a bulletin board that's covered with pictures of her cat, Pascal, looking funny and adorable, and of the track team. I look closer and there are some hilarious pictures of her and Will doing nerdy things when they were younger. I smile, looking at little nerd boy Will.

After dumping the coats, I head back down to the kitchen. Mr. and Mrs. McKay have left for the movie, and MJ, Carly, and Ada are putting sandwiches out on a platter.

"What can I do?" I ask.

"There are some bowls over there on the counter. Can you put out chips?"

"Sure. What smells so amazing?"

"Mom made lasagna," MJ says. "It's in the oven heating up."

"There is seriously a ton of food," Ada says. "This is going to be awesome."

"Jayson's bringing some friends from the wrestling team," Carly says.

"How many?" MJ asks.

"I don't know," Carly says. "Does it matter?"

"I guess not." MJ bites her lip. "It's just . . . my parents weren't too thrilled about going out while I had a party, and this was just supposed to be a chill thing."

"Don't worry," Carly says. "I'll tell Jayson to keep them all in line."

"It'll be fun," Ada says, trying to be encouraging.

"All I can think about is the college applications I have to get done," MJ says. "It's like I have to start over. Figure out where I want to go. And I can't really improve my grades and SAT score at this point but—"

"You're third in the class right now!" Carly exclaims. "How much better can your grades get?"

"Seriously, MJ," I say. "It was just one school. I know it's the one you really wanted to go to, but—"

"There are lots of other great schools," MJ says. "Yeah, yeah, I know. I've been getting enough of that from my family."

"Sorry," I say.

"It's okay. I shouldn't have snapped at you."

She takes a bowl out of the fridge. "I've been wondering if I should completely rewrite my essay before I do the other applications," she says. "Writing isn't my strong point. I wish I could just send a series of elegant algorithms."

"I can look it over for you if you want. The writing, not the algorithms. I wouldn't be much help with those," I say. Then, wondering if I've overstepped, I add: "I mean, only if you think it would help."

MJ removes the plastic wrap from the bowl. "That would be great," she says. "I'll let you know when I've actually written the thing."

We've got pretty much everything set up by the time the doorbell rings and the first people arrive. It's a slow trickle at first.

"I hope this party isn't a total bust," MJ says to Ada and me quietly. "Although this week has been the worst, so it wouldn't surprise me."

"It won't be," I say. "People are always late."

"Yeah, Will's not here yet and he lives next door!" Ada points out.

I surreptitiously send a text to Will.

Get over here! MJ's freaking out that the party will be a bust.

He texts me back right away. On my way! Can't wait to see a certain someone.

Me: Who might that be, I wonder?

He sends back a kissy emoji.

That's when Jayson and his teammates arrive. Jayson comes

over, puts his arm around Carly, and says, "Hey, babe." He surveys the room.

"Man, I hope this party picks up," Jayson says. "It's kind of underwhelming right now."

"Jayson!" Carly says. "Don't let MJ hear you. She's already down enough."

Ada rolls her eyes at me, and I glance around quickly to locate MJ. I don't see her, so I hope she's well out of earshot.

There are already about forty people here by the time Will finally makes his appearance. When I see him looking adorable in his red Stanford sweatshirt, my heart rate beats out a stronger rhythm, like it always seems to since I realized I liked him as more than a friend.

Our eyes meet across the room, and he flashes me a smile. He saunters over to where we're standing.

"What's up?" he says.

"Took you long enough to get here," Carly says. "You live next door."

"Carly, you have no idea how long it takes for me to style this Jewfro," Will says, running his hand through his curls, which just makes them stick up even more. He looks hilarious and cute at the same time.

"Where is MJ anyway?" he adds, looking around.

"I think she's in the kitchen," Carly says. She looks over to where two of Jayson's wrestling team buddies are getting a little out of hand. "Jayson, let's go reel in your boys before they break something. That's the last thing MJ needs."

They walk away, and Will takes a step closer to me. "Hey," he says quietly, so no one else will hear, quickly looking me up and down in a way that makes me feel warm all over. "You look . . . great."

"Thanks," I say, smiling. "You don't look so bad yourself. Stanford red really suits you."

"College suits you," he says with a grin.

He leans down to whisper in my ear: "I'm counting down the seconds until I can figure out how to be alone with you tonight."

His breath in my ear sends shivers down my spine. "Me too," I say softly.

I want to keep our relationship a secret, but right now I can't help wishing we were somewhere else.

"Hold that thought," he says. "I'm gonna check that MJ's okay."

"I'll be waiting," I say. "Me and the veggie chips."

He smiles back at me over his shoulder. "Save me some."

I will. Maybe. If he's lucky.

MJ

I'm trying to be upbeat, but the unspoken pity I see in the eyes of my friends who *did* get into their first-choice college is more than I can take.

Then I overhear Jayson Trantor saying my party is underwhelming.

Everything I do seems to turn to crap. I can't even throw a decent party.

I go into the kitchen and pretend that I've got something to do, just so I don't have to deal with people.

"Hey, MJ," Will says, coming in to grab some lasagna and a drink. "What are you doing hiding in the kitchen?"

"You know, just making sure there's enough for people to eat and drink," I say.

Will looks at all the food on the counter. "I don't think you need to worry," he says with a grin.

"Seriously, Will. Do you think . . . are people having a good time?"

He puts his arm around me. "MJ, relax. Everyone's having a *great* time."

"Except for Jayson Trantor," I mutter.

"Why do you care so much what Trantor thinks?" Will says,

moving to start piling food onto a plate. "Your real friends are having a great time."

I swallow my bitter reply and mutter, "Yeah, I guess."

"So come on, let's go!" he says, pushing me toward the kitchen door.

"Okay, I'm going! I'm going!"

He lifts his hand from my shoulder and raises it in the air in surrender. "Fine! As long as you promise to enjoy your own party."

"I solemnly promise to try my hardest to enjoy my own party," I say. "Satisfied?"

He grins. "I will be as soon as I eat your mom's lasagna," he says with a wink, before heading back out to the family room.

I take a deep breath, plaster on a smile, and follow him.

Things have picked up since I went to hide in the kitchen. More people have arrived, and it's actually starting to feel like a real party—crowded and noisy.

"Hey, who wants to play Cards Against Humanity?" Amir asks. "You have it, MJ, right?"

"Of course!" I say. "The original and a bunch of expansion packs."

I get them out of the game cupboard under the TV.

"Count me in," Will says.

"Me too!" Dara says.

We end up with twelve people sitting around the coffee table, on the sofa, and on the floor, involved in a raucous and totally inappropriate game.

"Hey, MJ, are there any more tortilla chips?" Tony Ortega asks. "Everyone tells me the guac is amazing, and I didn't think you'd appreciate me sticking my finger in to try it."

"Please don't," Dara says. "The average hand carries over one hundred and fifty species of bacteria."

"Meet Dara: our living database of barf-worthy biological facts," Will says.

She makes a face at him.

"Guys, don't freak out, there are more chips!" I say, getting up and heading to the kitchen to find them in the pantry with Tony close on my heels.

"Thanks," he says when I refill the bowl, then he dunks one into the guac. "They were right. This stuff is great." He helps himself to some more. "Good party."

"Thanks," I say. "Hey, why don't you take the chips and guac into the family room with you?"

"You don't have to ask me twice," he says, grabbing the bowls and carrying them out. As he goes out of the kitchen door, more people come in to get food.

I know I told Will I'd try, but honestly, it's just exhausting out there. So I slip upstairs to my room so I can get a few minutes alone. But I forgot that everyone's been putting their coats on my bed, so there's nowhere to sit. Instead, I go to Zack's room and throw myself on his.

Even though I can hear the noise of the party, sitting up here in the dark is calming. The streetlight casts a faint glow from the window, highlighting Zack's pride and joy, his cryptocurrency rig. I glare at it. After winning the right to use it while Zack's away, I've been messing around on it—working on things I thought would help when I got to Carnegie Mellon. So much for that idea. Hopefully I'll get into somewhere else, but I can't help wondering and worrying that it wasn't just a numbers game that made them turn me down; that it was something the matter with *me*, something that's going to make all the other schools turn me down, too.

MJ, stop obsessing about it! Suck it up and enjoy your own party.

I can hear my brother's voice in my head as clearly as if he were standing here. I glance over at the nightstand, where he has a framed picture of Pascal. His friend Melissa took it when she was doing photography freshman year of high school and put it in one of those ridiculous heart-shaped frames because she said Zack loves Pascal more than anyone else.

Seeing Pascal's picture reminds me of the CatCam. I wonder if anyone else is complaining about the party. I start to open the app and then hesitate. Is it too creepy to use it to spy on my friends downstairs?

It's my party, I think as I open it and start watching and listening to what's going on in my absence.

DARA

The game of Cards Against Humanity is getting more epic by the minute.

"My face hurts from laughing," Ada says.

"Mine too!" I say, and start giggling again. "Owwww. It hurts." I reach for my Diet Coke and realize it's empty. "Does anyone want anything from the kitchen?" I ask, taking deep breaths.

"I'm good," Ada says.

"I need more of Mrs. McKay's lasagna," Will says, grabbing his plate and standing up. "It's crazy good."

He follows me into the kitchen and starts spooning more lasagna onto his plate. I realize the ice bucket is almost empty, so I go to the freezer to fill it up. I'm pouring my Diet Coke when Will's arms slide around my waist. "I've been waiting to do this all night," he whispers in my ear, then he nuzzles my neck, sending tingles down my spine.

I'm proud of myself for not spilling as I finish pouring, put down the glass, and turn to face him.

"Hi there," I say. Then I notice the red sauce on my sleeve. "Hey, you got lasagna on my sweatshirt!"

"Sorry," he says, brushing it off with his fingers. Then he

looks down at me and gives me a slow grin. "Guess what? We're alone in the kitchen."

"For now," I say, nervously looking around his arm to the swinging door that leads to the family room.

His head lowers. "Be quick, then," he says with a smile.

I laugh, but before I finish, his lips are on mine. I melt into him, standing on tiptoes, my limbs buzzing.

"Um, you're blocking the lasagna . . ."

Startled, I step back. Will looks sheepish, but I turn from him.

Carly and Jayson are standing there. Jayson is grinning from ear to ear. Carly is staring at us. She looks shocked.

"Since when have you two been a thing?" she asks.

Will glances down at me, and I keep my eyes away from his, hoping he just stays quiet.

"Since the summer," Will says. "We worked together at camp. The rest, as they say, is history."

I close my eyes. Seriously, Will? Fury wells up in me.

"No way," Carly exclaims. "How did you manage to keep it a secret for this long?"

"Keep what a secret?" I see Amir come from behind. "Hey, can you two move? We need more popcorn."

"Carly and I caught these two making out," Jayson says. "Apparently they've been at it since the summer."

Amir's eyes widen and he turns to stare at us. "*Dara and Will?* For real?"

Will confirms it with a nod.

Amir's eyes narrow. "*Dude.* How could you hold out on me like that?"

Will shrugs and Amir just stares at him.

"I don't get it," Carly asks. "Why didn't you want people to know you're dating?"

"Lots of reasons," I say, because I don't trust what Will might say. "Because there's enough pressure with college, and us being so close in GPA in the valedictorian race, and everyone speculating about who is going to end up on top. *This.*" I gesture to what's happening right here in the kitchen this exact moment.

"Yeah. We hadn't been dating that long when school started," Will adds.

"I can't believe you guys have been in a relationship and I didn't even know!" Amir complains. "How did I not pick up on it? I see you together every day!"

Even though I'm mad that we seem to suddenly have gone public, whether I like it or not, I can't help feeling a little secret amusement at Amir's bewilderment.

"Sam, Ada! MJ! Tony!" Amir calls into the family room. "Did you know Dara and Will have been dating since the summer?"

"I didn't," Sam shouts back.

"Me neither," Ada says.

"Nope!" Tony says.

"Come on, Dara," Will says, finally realizing that I'm freaked out by this. "Let's go talk."

"Did MJ know?" Sam asks as we emerge from the kitchen.

"No," Will says.

"Okay, now I don't feel so bad that you didn't tell me," Sam says. "I mean, if you didn't tell *MJ* . . ."

"Where *is* MJ, anyway?" Ada asks, looking around. "I haven't seen her for a while."

"I don't know," Tony says. "I haven't seen her since she got more chips."

"We're going to go out and get some air," Will says, pulling me toward the front door.

"Don't we need our coats?" I say, glancing up the stairs. "It's cold out. I can't get sick. If I do, I can't ride on the ambulance, and I've got a bunch of shifts lined up for over winter break."

I'm rambling.

"It'll be fine," Will says softly. "Come on."

The cold air is actually refreshing after being in MJ's crowded, heated family room.

Will pulls me into the shadows outside the garage and awkwardly shifts from foot to foot.

I stuff my hands in my hoodie pocket and stare, waiting for him to explain what that was back there.

"I'm sorry that happened," he says. "I really didn't mean it to."

I blink at him. "Will, we've been not telling people about us for months and you just told everyone without asking me."

"Dara, we got caught." Frustration is tingeing the edge of his words, but it just feels like he's being stubborn here.

"Yeah, but why did you tell them everything?"

"Because I'm not going to lie on top of keeping a secret! Look, I get why this started as a secret, but it's been months. We're in a relationship, just admit it."

"I know that! I just . . . ugh. This valedictorian thing is still there. It's just hanging there and I want to be known for being smart—not for being the girl who beat her boyfriend to valedictorian."

"What if I beat you?" Will throws back.

"Not going to happen," I snap. My fists are clenched, and I force them open. I bounce up and down on my toes to get warmer.

"Okay, look, I'm sorry. But it was time. We got caught. Now we can just date and continue our academic war," Will says, taking a tentative step toward me. He looks down at his feet, and then meets my gaze. "Besides . . . I love you."

"I know," I say slowly.

His eyes fix on me, warm and hopeful. I'm still mad, but it's true I was just as into that kiss as Will was, and we couldn't really deny it. Besides, if I'm being honest, deep down, something loosens inside me. Like I can finally just let go. I sigh. "Okay, fine, you're forgiven. And . . . I love you, too."

"Yes!" Will does a little victory jump.

I roll my eyes at him. "You're still not going to beat me," I say.

"We'll seeeee," Will says, taking another step closer to me.

I arch an eyebrow at him and he flashes a grin back before sweeping me up in a hug. He spins me around, shouting, "I love Dara Simons," over and over again until I'm dizzy and my laughter echoes through the night air.

MJ

I didn't realize how cool it would be to be able to see and hear my friends without them knowing. The camera is pointing toward the sofa, which must be the last place any of us checked in on Pascal. I pan the camera across the room to the windows, where some friends from Robotics Club are chilling. There's a lot of background noise, but I can just about hear them. Tony has left the Cards Against Humanity game and is speculating if Boris the BotBeast can beat Karla the Killer.

Slowly, I pan back to the sofa, where it looks like the game is on hold, and Amir, Sam, Ada, and a few others are talking about their plans for winter break.

"Um, you're blocking the lasagna . . ." I hear Jayson say. It sounds like it's coming from the left of the sofa, so I pan the camera toward the kitchen door.

"Since when have you two been a thing?" Carly asks.

Wait—who's a thing?

The answer is too muffled for me to hear.

"No way," Carly exclaims. "How did you manage to keep it a secret for this long?"

Meanwhile, Amir has gotten up from the sofa, and he taps

on Jayson's shoulder because he and Carly are blocking the doorway.

"Keep what a secret?" he asks. "Hey, can you two move? We need more popcorn."

"Carly and I caught these two making out," Jayson tells him. "Apparently they've been at it since the summer."

Who has been together since the summer?

"*Dara and Will? For real?*" Amir says.

A cold wave crashes over me, freezing my brain.

Will has been dating *Dara* since the *summer*? He never said a word to me about it!

How could it have been going on for so long without me knowing? Why didn't Will tell me?

I think back to the end of the summer, when Will was always so weirdly busy or MIA and he said it was because of him having to retake the SAT.

Was Dara the *real* reason?

He *lied* to me?

I feel so betrayed. I thought we were friends. Best friends. We've always been straight with each other.

But I find out from the stupid CatCam that he's been keeping this huge secret for months?

Anger starts building in my stomach, spreading, even as I try to breathe through it.

"Did MJ know?" Sam asks as I see Will and Dara emerge from the kitchen. He's holding her hand. Dara looks uncomfortable, and I wonder what that's all about. She was here helping me set up and I had no idea that she's been dating Will the whole time. I'm suddenly furious with her, too.

"No," Will says.

Maybe I don't know my best friend as well as I thought I did.

"Okay, now I don't feel so bad that you didn't tell me," I hear Sam tell Will. "I mean, if you didn't tell *MJ* . . ."

"Where *is* MJ, anyway?" Ada asks, looking around. "I haven't seen her for a while."

I'm here watching you. Listening to you. Finding out that my best friend has been keeping a secret from me. He's been lying *to me.*

I hear him say that he and Dara are going outside or something.

I flop on Zack's bed, stunned. The last thing I feel like doing is going back downstairs to the party, but my friends have started noticing my absence.

With a sigh, I sit up and as I walk down the stairs, I make myself inhale and exhale a deep breath with each step. By the time I get to the bottom of the stairs, I've swallowed my feelings and forced myself to smile.

"Hey, MJ, there you are! Did you know Will and Dara were a thing?" Sam asks as soon as I walk into the living room.

"What? For real?" I say, like I haven't already heard the news. "Since when?"

"The summer," Ada tells me. "I don't understand how they've been able to keep it secret from *everybody*."

"Yeah, even Rumor Has It!" Tony says. "And they know *everything* that goes on at GHS."

"I can't believe Will never told us," Amir says, shaking his head.

It's getting harder and harder to hold it together and keep the smile plastered on my face. I can't go upstairs again because I just came down, so I pick up some empty soda cans and take them into the kitchen to put in the recycling.

"MJ, are you okay?"

I jump and turn around.

"Sorry," Sam says. "I didn't mean to startle you." He looks into my eyes, a concerned frown on his face. "It's just . . . you seem . . . upset."

Guess I'm doing a terrible job at this.

"I'm fine," I say. "It's just been a long week."

"Yeah, I bet," he says. "It was really amazing of you to have this party, despite . . . well, you know."

"You came, and I bet you'd rather be at home playing *Warcraft III*."

"You know me too well," he says, smiling. "Come on, leave the recycling and let's hang. I promise to stay to help you clean up."

Sam's right. I might as well try to make the best of what remains of this party.

By the time my parents come home at eleven thirty, the party is over. Everyone's gone, except for Sam and Ada, who are helping me with the last of the cleanup. Carly left with Jayson, and Dara left with Will, who said he'd drive her home, even though he lives next door.

"How was it?" Mom asks, her eyes searching my face.

I lie because I don't want to get into it. That I feel worse than before the party. That I'm mad at my best friend and he has no idea. He never even came to talk to me after.

"Fun." Well, except for the fact that I found out my best friend has been lying to me since the end of the summer.

"We're just heading out," Sam says. "Thanks for the party. We had a great time."

"Yes, thanks, Mr. and Mrs. McKay," Ada chimes in.

"It was our pleasure," Mom says.

"Thanks for helping me clean up," I tell them.

"It was nothing," Ada says. "It was a really good party. And the food was amazing!"

"Drive home safely," Dad says.

"I will," Sam says, smiling at me.

Ada gives me a hug. "Hang in there," she whispers, before heading out with Sam.

That leaves me alone with Mom and Dad, who, judging by their expectant expressions, are excited for a full recap of the party.

I just can't.

"I'm going up to bed," I say, turning to head out of the kitchen. "Everything's pretty much cleaned up. Whatever isn't I'll get in the morning."

Mom stops me, placing her hand on my arm. "Wait, MJ. Tell us how it went."

"It was fine," I say.

"That's it? Fine?" Dad asks, exchanging a glance with Mom.

"I'm tired, okay?" I say, trying not to snap. "I'll tell you more in the morning."

"If you're sure you're okay," Mom says, stroking my hair and giving me a kiss good night.

"Yep!" I say, pulling away and escaping up the stairs.

I change into my pj's and wash all the stupid makeup off my face. Pascal is on my bed, still traumatized from so many people in the house.

"I feel you, buddy," I say, flinging myself on the bed next to him. I try to bring him in for a hug, but he swats at me with his paw and squirms away, jumping down from the bed and making himself a nest in one of the piles of clothing littering my bedroom floor. Even my *cat* is ditching me.

The anger that I've been forcing myself to suppress all night refuses to be contained any longer. Every time I think about Will lying to me, telling me that he was too busy to hang out with me when he was really hanging out with Dara, it feels like my chest is about to explode.

And Dara—I thought we were getting to be better friends this year. We've been doing more together. But all this time she's been secretly seeing Will? *My* best friend.

Ugh. I'm never going to be able to sleep. I might as well do something else to keep my mind off it.

At first I go to YouTube and watch some funny virtual reality videos. Then it suggests movie bloopers, so I watch some of those. Then it recommends this ridiculous video that puts Nicolas Cage into, like, every movie he's never been in. Seeing his face on Captain Kirk from *Star Trek* has me laughing so hard, I forget I'm mad for a second. But then it all comes rushing back.

So I go looking for how someone made the video to keep from thinking of everything that's gone wrong in my life, and I fall down a spiral reading about them. I start to wonder if I can make my own because it seems like a cool project. I watch a bunch more, and then search for programs on GitHub. I didn't realize I could also fake a digital voice, without that much input data to make it happen.

I'm reaching for my phone to text Will because we'd have a blast doing this together when I remember again. I'm mad at him.

Why did he lie to me?

Friends don't do that.

Why? Why?

Ugh, I can't even think straight because Will and Dara keep invading my thoughts.

I'm about to give up and make a probably futile attempt to get to sleep, when suddenly it strikes me: I don't need Will.

I can make a video without him. Or maybe he and Dara want to be the star of my video. The idea makes me laugh out loud, and I'm suddenly energized by my own joke. It'll be my very private revenge for him not being honest with me.

I've got hours of CatCam footage from tonight I can use. Between that and Instagram I should have enough input data, but there's probably too much ambient noise on the CatCam footage to use for the voice generator.

Then I realize there's a solution. It depends on which of them has more video on Instagram.

I search through each of their profiles and find there's way more material on Dara's than there is on Will's. *Thank you, Dara, for making your life an open book!* There's a video of her at homecoming, being silly with Ada, and a bunch of others of the two of them going back to the beginning of the school year. There's also a video of Dara at the Dairy Barn on Will's profile, from last summer when they were both counselors at Camp Terabyte. I vaguely remember seeing it at the time he posted it. Then it seemed like normal joking around between friends, but now that I know that's around the time when they started dating, I'm able to pick up clues I missed.

And for months, Will didn't bother to tell me. It makes me mad all over again.

I poke my head out into the hallway. My parents' light is off, and they've got to be deep into sleep. As quietly as I can, I creep to Zack's bedroom. After closing the door, I take a seat at his desk and boot up his rig. I need the kind of computer resources he used for mining cryptocurrency to make this video.

I'm up practically all night scraping video and photos from Dara's social media accounts. This is going to be great.

PART FOUR

DECEMBER
NOW

WILL

Hey, I know you don't want to talk to me.

I found something in the video.

It's fake.

I can prove it.

When I get the text from Dara on the Friday night break begins, I read it with mixed emotions. Part of me wonders if this is just another lie.

But the other part, the one that still thinks what we had was real, clings to the words in her text.

That part wins. *I hope I don't end up regretting it*, I think as I press call.

"Will!" she exclaims. "Hi."

"So what's this evidence you say you found?"

She tells me how her mom's fiancé, Ted, was over with his kids for dinner, and they were talking about the video.

"You know how Ted is an engineer at the TV station?" she asks.

"Yeah . . . What's that got to do with it?"

"Will, have you heard of deepfakes?"

"Sure—there's a bunch of subreddits devoted to them. You can put people's faces on other faces."

"Yeah, I found that," she says. "There are also ways to create voice fakes. And it looks like that's how someone made that video of me accusing you of cheating."

"Oookay," I say. "But what's the proof you said you found?"

There's silence on the other end of the phone, then Dara laughs bitterly. "I should have known you wouldn't actually *believe* me. That you'd want the proof."

"Come on, Dara, do you blame me?" I ask her. "Joyner has the College Board looking into this. They're probably going to notify Stanford. I might have to take the SAT *again* to prove I didn't cheat. Or Stanford might just take back my spot."

"I just wish that . . ." There's what seems like a forever pause, then she sighs. "Whatever, you want proof. So Ted has all this TV station software that he used to slow the video down and Saffron noticed that I don't blink at all in the video. Not a single time. The average human blinks fifteen to twenty times a minute. That's proof number one that something's not right."

"Blinking, that's what you've got?" I say. "I mean, that's weird, but I don't know. Doesn't seem like much."

"I mean, there's other stuff," she says. "Do you remember changing my ringtone?"

"Um, vaguely? I changed it from the theme song of that stupid TV show Sadie liked to the *Wonder Woman* theme song."

"Right. And do you remember *when* you did that?"

"Not exactly—near the end of the summer?"

"Yes—when we went to the Dairy Barn for the first time after Carnival Day."

Now I remember. It was the day Caleb broke his arm on the Slip 'N Slide and Dara splinted it before he went to the ER. The day I realized I wanted to be more than friends.

"Okay, yeah."

"Right. Now do you remember what I was wearing at MJ's party?"

"What is this, a quiz?"

"Trust me, it's all part of it," Dara says.

Trust me. That's a big ask from her after everything that's happened. But I think back to MJ's party. To how cute Dara looked right before I kissed her in the kitchen . . .

"That College sweatshirt?" I say.

"Yes!" Dara exclaims. "And I'm wearing that sweatshirt in the video."

"Okay. But what does that prove?"

"I'm going to send you links to two videos that I've uploaded and set to private. The first one I took at the slowest Ted's editing software allowed. The second one is of it speeded up a little bit, but not to normal speed. Pay extra attention around second twenty-six," she says.

"But—"

"Just watch it, okay?"

She hangs up on me, and a few seconds later I get an email with the links.

Sighing, I get up, grab my laptop off my desk, and then follow Dara's instructions. I catch some other sound at the point she tells me when I watch the first link, but I can't figure out what it is.

Then I play the second one and listen to it. Wait . . . is that? No, it can't be. I rewind to just before second twenty-six and listen closely. It's definitely that theme song Dara had as her ringtone when we first started dating.

But . . . I changed the ringtone months before her mom gave her the sweatshirt.

I play the video again. The lack of blinking. The ringtone. The sweatshirt. It's enough weirdness to make me wonder.

I dial her back. "It's the ringtone. I'd already changed it by the time you got the sweatshirt!"

"A-plus," she says. "So . . . now do you believe me? Do you finally believe I never said those things about you?"

"I mean, maybe?" I say. I'm not sure what to do with this info. Like, okay, so if she's right, then where did this video come from?

"Come on, Will, can't you just admit that I was telling the truth? This is the proof we both need to clear our names!"

"I *do* believe you," I say slowly. "It's just weird. Because there's this video. And it's you in it saying stuff."

"Yeah, but I've never been like that in real life and you know it," Dara says, her voice clipped with anger. "Or at least you should. I mean . . . until the other day, you loved me. So you can see why I'm pissed you believe that's me."

"Come on, Dara, you can't blame me! What if there had been a video of me saying that the only reason you got to be number one in the class was because you'd cheated your way through high school?"

There's silence on the other end.

"I . . . want to think that while I might have jumped to the wrong conclusion about you when I first watched the video, I would have been able to remember what I know about you to at least have *some* doubt that it was real," she says. "Especially if you *told me* that you never actually said it. Especially since I loved you."

She's right. I was willing to throw away everything I've known about her for the last four years, and especially the last few months, because of one video that now I find out was faked.

I had some doubt, because the Dara I thought I knew would never do that, but I didn't let myself listen to it. I let myself be persuaded by what I saw, and the fact that everyone else believed it, too. Well, except for Ada. But still . . .

"But you don't know that's what you'd do in that situation, though," I say. "Not really. It happened to me, not to you."

"Wow, Will. Seriously? This didn't just happen to you. It happened to both of us," Dara says. "Sure, it's affecting you more, but it's still affecting me, too. I've been getting the cold shoulder from people I thought were my friends. Amir and Sam have totally shut me out. MJ avoids even looking at me, and we're in the same English class." There's a pause and I hear her inhale. "And how do you think I feel knowing what this is doing to you?"

I've been so wrapped up in what's been happening to me and convinced that my anger at Dara was justified that I never really stopped to think about her.

"I'm . . . sorry," I say. "You're right. And I guess I do believe you."

"Gee, thanks, Will."

What does she want from me? "I said I was sorry, Dara. It's hard to get my head around all this, okay?"

"Yeah, okay."

She's definitely still mad.

"So . . . what's the next step now that we have this proof? Do we go to Joyner with this? Maybe then he'll help shut down the College Board investigation."

"That, and we should to try to figure out who made the video," she says.

"How?"

"I don't know yet. Let me think."

"How about we get together tomorrow to see if we can figure it out? You know, two heads are better than one."

Dara hesitates a second too long before replying. "I can't do it tomorrow," she says. "I volunteered to be the EMT at the senior center holiday party and then we have family plans for Christmas Eve. And Sunday is Christmas."

"So what about Monday?" I ask, even though I wish it were sooner. "Say at, like, eleven?"

"Okay," Dara says. "I'll see you then."

Right away, I send a group text to Amir, Sam, and MJ.

Me: Hey, I just talked to Dara. That video of her accusing me is a deepfake.

Amir: For real?

Me: Yeah, for real.

MJ: How do you know it's a deepfake?

Me: Long story, tell you later.

Sam: Crap. We've been pretty awful to her.

Me: Yeah, I know. Especially me.

Me: Just cut her some slack, okay?

Mom and Sadie are watching a movie in the living room, so I head downstairs, hope bubbling up inside me for the first time since Rumor Has It posted that video. I tell them what Dara found out, and have to explain what deepfakes are.

"So you're telling me that people can make a video of anyone saying anything they want, even if the words never came out of their mouth?" Mom asks.

"As long as they have enough material to train the algorithm in the artificial neural network," I say.

"Yeah, right, okay," Sadie says. "Can you explain that in non-nerd?"

"Fine. So, like, because Dara had so many videos and selfies on Instagram, there was enough stuff to help the algorithm learn how to make a convincing video of her."

"That's terrifying," Mom says.

"It's like the technology that lets you do Face Swap on Snapchat, but different," I say.

"Why didn't you just say that in the first place?" Sadie says. "But how did they get her to say all that stuff?"

"I don't know," I admit. "I forgot to ask Dara about that. We're getting together on Monday to try to see if we can find clues that might help us figure out who made it."

"Why would anyone do this to you?" Mom says. "Have you made any enemies at school? Who would want to mess with your life this way?"

"No clue," I say with a sigh. "That's what we're going to try to figure out on Monday. To be honest, it's making me a little paranoid to think there's someone at school who hates me that much and I have no idea who it is."

"I'm going to email your principal," Mom says. "He needs to notify the College Board of these latest developments. And we should let your father know."

"Yeah, okay. But . . . do you think he's going to go in and threaten to sue everyone again?" I ask. "I just want my record cleared and everything to go back to how it was before, not some lawsuit that makes it all drag on forever."

"All we can do is try to tell him that," Mom says. "There are no guarantees that he'll actually listen. But he's your dad, so we have to let him know what's going on. I can call him if you want."

"No, it's okay, I will." I don't have much hope that Dad will listen, but I go back up to my room to call him anyway.

When Dad picks up, it sounds like he's out at a restaurant. Guess he and Katelyn are living it up out in Aspen. "What's up, Will? It's kind of a bad time."

"We've got proof that video where Dara accuses me of cheating was faked," I say.

It takes him a second to catch up. "Proof? What proof?"

"I'll explain when it's a better time for you," I say. "It's easier if you can see the video while I'm explaining, and it has to be in a place where you can hear well."

"Okay, I'll call you tomorrow. I won't be home until late tonight, and we're two hours behind you."

"And, Dad—promise me you won't go into school threatening to sue people, okay?"

"I want to see what this proof is before I make any promises," he says. "Talk to you tomorrow."

He hangs up, and I wonder why I'm still disappointed that he wouldn't listen to what I want, when it's what he's been doing my entire life.

It feels like ants are marching in the pit of my stomach when I ring Dara's doorbell on Monday morning.

The front door opens and she's standing there, without the smile I got so used to seeing from her when we got together.

"Hey," she says. "Thanks for coming."

"Hey." I shift from one foot to the other. "Thanks for not punching me in the face."

"I have to admit, the thought did cross my mind," she says, a half smile quirking her lips. Standing aside to let me in, she tells me: "I've got everything set up in the living room so we can look at the video on the big screen."

I follow her in there, and we sit on opposite sides of the couch. God, this is so awkward.

"Did you have a good Christmas?" I ask her.

"Yeah," she says. "Ted brought Saffron and Carson over for dinner after they'd spent Christmas Eve and morning with their mom. It was . . . fun. We played board games, watched movies, and almost ate ourselves to death."

"So . . . are you ready to watch this for the hundred thousandth time?"

"More like the millionth," she says, pushing play.

Her face is larger than life on the big screen TV. Now that I know the video is a fake, I notice little things I didn't before. Not just how Dara doesn't blink, but how her lips move slightly differently than they really do.

When I tell her that, her eyes meet mine, and her determination is plain to see. "It's like, once you start to pick up on it, the more stuff you see that's wrong. It's just . . . scary. It shouldn't be so easy to make people believe things that aren't true."

I nod. "If we can narrow down where we think the footage

was taken, maybe we can figure out who made this. Watch it again?"

Sighing, Dara leans forward and pushes play.

Fake Dara starts talking, spreading the SAT lie, and suddenly it strikes me.

"Hold on . . . you said your mom gave you that sweatshirt Thanksgiving weekend, right?"

She pauses the video. "Yeah. I wore it to the homecoming game and then to MJ's party."

"Are you sure you didn't wear it any other time before the video came out?"

"No . . . I didn't," Dara says slowly. "The video came out pretty soon after MJ's party. And remember, you got lasagna on it when we were in the kitchen?"

"Oh yeah," I say, vaguely remembering that we also talked about this the other day. "Ada took some video of us at the homecoming game and posted it on Instagram," I add. "Remember, we were worried about it being too obvious that we liked each other when we went to get snacks?"

Dara looks at me wide-eyed. "Do you think it could be Ada? She's one of my best friends!"

"Not really," I admit. "It would be really weird if it were her, because she's one of the few people who raised any questions about the video. She didn't believe you would do something like that."

I swallow hard at the twinge of guilt I feel.

"If it *was* at MJ's, it would narrow down the list of people who could have made it," Dara says. "But I don't remember anyone taking video that night. Or posting it."

"I don't, either," I say. "Although I wasn't paying that much attention." I shrug at her and flash a small smile.

I'd hoped to make Dara smile back, but she tenses up and says, "We should stay focused on the video."

She's right. The best thing I can do right now is work with her to figure this out, so we can clear both of our names.

"Play it again," I say.

Focus on the problem at hand, Will. Focus on the problem.

Problem . . .

Problem . . .

Focus on the problem . . .

"Wait!" I exclaim, stopping the video. "It's a geometry problem!"

"Um . . . what?" Dara asks.

I can't help feeling the tiniest bit smug that I've figured this out before her.

"It's all about angles. Assuming it *was* taken at MJ's, if we draw a map of MJ's living room, and where you were sitting at various points during the party, we should be able to figure out where the person with the camera was."

Dara stares at me, and I see the moment she gets it.

"But that means . . . if the footage came from MJ's . . . it had to be someone who was there."

Which means it could be one of our friends. Or one of my

track teammates. Or someone from the wrestling team. I hope it's one of the wrestlers, because I can't face the thought of it being one of my friends or teammates.

"Let's make a map of MJ's living room," she says. "I'll go get some paper and a pen."

When she comes back, we try to remember everything we can about MJ's house and where everything was. Then we mark all the places Dara was during the party to figure out possible locations from where she might have been filmed.

"I think we can rule out the bathroom," I say. "Can I?" I reach for the paper and pen, my fingers touching hers as she hands it to me. I feel the familiar tingle and I try to catch her eye, but she looks away.

Focus on the problem, Will. Maybe if you solve this, it will solve other problems, too.

Or create new ones.

It only takes me fifteen minutes to do the triangulation. "Okay, this is weird. If my calculations are right, which I'm pretty sure they are, the most likely place for the camera is right here."

I point to the map, to the area where there's the TV and a bunch of bookshelves.

"So . . . wait . . . do you think . . . could the McKays have one of those spy cams?" Dara asks. "Because I don't remember anyone standing there and videoing me at all. I think I'd have noticed, don't you?"

"Yeah, probably. I never thought of a spy cam."

"Why would they have one, though?" Dara asks.

"I don't know. But if they did, it would have made it easier to make the video because they'd have a decent amount of footage of you. We were sitting on the sofa opposite for a while, playing Cards Against Humanity."

"True. But how could they get it from the McKays' spy cam unless . . ." She trails off.

I freeze. If the McKays have a spy cam, the only way someone could get that footage would be if they hacked it. To do that, they'd need to know it was there. Otherwise, it would have to be . . .

I shake my head. "No, MJ wouldn't. She's my best friend."

Hurt cuts across Dara's face.

Oh.

"Yeah, I know," I say. "Why didn't I say that when I watched that video of you?"

"I mean, I know that you saw me say it on the video, and that was very convincing. But . . ." She shrugs.

"I'm sorry," I say. "Really, I am."

She gives me a hint of a smile, then asks, "So how can we figure out if the McKays really *do* have a spy cam?"

"Easy. I'll see if MJ wants to hang out and game."

"Okay," Dara says, but she has a skeptical look on her face.

"What is it?" I ask.

"Will, what if it *is* MJ?" she asks.

"I don't know. I mean, she's my best friend. I don't know why she'd do this. But I'd have to know what gives."

"And I was your girlfriend," Dara says, getting up suddenly. "But I didn't get to explain anything."

I grab her hand and say, "Wait. Can we . . . talk?"

Dara shakes off my hand but sits back down on the sofa, as far away from me as she can possibly get.

"What exactly do you want to talk about?"

"Look, I'm sorry. I should have believed you wouldn't ever say something like that about me. I should have believed in the Dara I know."

"I know you're sorry. You've already said that. And as much as I want to, I can't blame you, at least not one hundred percent. I mean, it looked like you had the evidence right there."

"Do you think . . . I mean, can you forgive me enough to . . ."

She bites her lip. "To be together? Like we were before?"

I nod, my stomach starting to churn as I wait for her answer.

She studies me before saying, "It was such garbage that you didn't even try to talk to me. That you wouldn't listen. That hurt. And honestly, I don't know that I trust you the same way anymore. And I don't know how to be with you without that. I can't just go back, like none of this happened."

My heart feels like a lead weight in my chest. I don't really know what to say to that. How to change her mind, if I even can. "This sucks."

A sad look flits across her face. Then she gets up, which I assume means that I should leave. So I stand. "I'll keep you posted on what happens with MJ."

"Thanks," Dara says. "Then we can figure out next steps."

When we reach the front door, we stand there awkwardly, neither of us sure how to say goodbye now that we're . . . whatever we are now.

But then Dara takes a step toward me, and I hold her in my arms, inhaling her familiar scent.

"I miss you," I whisper.

"I miss you, too." She puts her head on my chest, and for a moment, I feel hope.

Then she sighs and pulls away.

"I'll see you," she says. "Good luck with MJ."

"Thanks, I'll need it," I say.

I have to find that camera.

RUMOR HAS IT

So, Panthers, did you get all the presents you wanted? Or did you get a lump of coal because you made the naughty list?

Some lucky Panther families jetted off to warmer climates. Don't you wish you did, too? I hear that Carly V bailed on school early for fun in the sun in Jamaica, Roberto K is going crazy in Cabo, Janine F is scuba diving in St. Croix, and Diane L is lazing on a beach in St. Lucia. Then there are the families who prefer a little more seasonal chill, like Petra G, who is off to ski in Bretton Woods, and Rick S, who is heading for Sugarbush.

What are *you* doing over winter break? Hope it's something fun, not having to read like five gazillion pages like Dr. Marino's poor APUSH students.

Whatever you're doing, make sure you're back for New Year's Eve. Amir H is throwing an epic end-of-the-year party. Miles C and Kelly G are both planning some firework-worthy parties of their own. I'll keep you posted with any other seasonal festivities that reach my ears.

Until next time . . . be sure to make the most of the last few days of this year, and if you can't be good, make sure someone emails me about it.

MJ

I've been freaking out ever since Will texted Sam, Amir, and me on Friday saying Dara had figured out the video I made was a deepfake. Thankfully, he doesn't know I made it—at least I hope not. I don't want him to find out.

When I saw that Rumor Has It posted it, I lost it. No one was supposed to see it. I was just mad because Will had been hiding things from me. I couldn't understand why he felt the need to keep his relationship with Dara a secret. He's dated before, but he always told me about it. I don't get what made this different.

Still, the video was supposed to just be for me, my private way of dealing with a situation that upset me. Watching it made me feel better, which is messed up, I know. But it seemed harmless. Thanks to Rumor Has It, it's all a giant mess.

Now he and Dara have figured out it's fake somehow. What if they're able to trace it back to me?

I was worried about Will being distant, but if he finds out that I'm the one behind the video, I can kiss his friendship goodbye. Dara's, too.

I couldn't figure out how Rumor Has It got it until I remembered that I forgot to log out of my school account in my rush to avoid answering Sam about going on a date. Yeah, I posted it to YouTube, but it was set to private. And I'm usually a freak about cybersecurity.

I'm such an idiot.

Even worse, I'm dead if that video is ever traced back to me.

The Tuesday morning after Christmas, I get a text from Will.

Hey, are you free to have your butt kicked in Mario Kart?

I breathe a sigh of relief. It's such a normal thing for him to say, my secret must still be safe.

Me: Sure, I'm always free to kick your butt in any and all video games.

Will: LMAO, see you in ten minutes.

When he turns up on the doorstep, we head into the living room, where I've already got everything fired up. I'm just about to sit on the sofa when he says, "Aren't you forgetting something?"

"What?" I ask.

"Duh! Chocolate milk."

"Two chocolate milks, coming right up," I say, although my stomach's been in knots for the past few days and I'm not sure I can handle chocolate milk.

I make two glasses, and then head back into the family room. Will isn't on the sofa, where I expect him to be waiting for me with a controller in hand.

He's over by the bookshelf with his phone out, and he seems to be taking a picture of . . . the CatCam. The shock makes my hands shake, and I spill one of the chocolate milks.

"What are you doing?" I ask, wiping my milky hand on my jeans. Now both my hand and my jeans are sticky and gross from the chocolate syrup, but I've got bigger problems.

Will turns around slowly, holding the phone up between us.

"Why are you filming me?" I ask, feeling my heart starting to race. "That's weird."

"Really, MJ? Isn't that kind of ironic coming from you?"

He knows.

"What do you mean? And stop it with the camera."

But he doesn't.

"Here's the thing, MJ," he says. "I told you Dara figured out the video was a fake. Turns out it's fake in so many ways."

"Really?" I say as nonchalantly as I can, sitting down on my hands to hide their trembling. "How? Will, can you turn off the video?"

He keeps filming. "Well, first off, Dara never blinks the entire time, which is, like, physically impossible," he says.

"Huh. That's weird."

"You know what else is weird? If you listen to it at half speed, you can hear a little bit of a ringtone Dara used to have on her phone—the theme song from *Gutter Girlz*."

"I used to watch that show," I say. "And you hated it so much."

"Exactly—which is why when Dara and I started dating last summer, I changed her ringtone to the *Wonder Woman* theme song." He's still holding up his phone and I'm about to ask him why when he continues: "But her mom didn't give her that sweatshirt until Thanksgiving. And she only wore it twice before the video came out—to the homecoming game and then to your party."

My heart drops and panic flushes along my skin. I force myself to take a deep breath. I just have to stay cool. "Oh my god, will you stop videoing me?"

"Why, does being on camera bother you?" He sounds weird. Sarcastic. "I know Dara didn't like it much."

Sarcastic and angry. *Really* angry.

"I can't talk to you with your phone in my face."

"I'm across the room, MJ," he says. "It's hardly in your face."

"I mean it, Will, turn it off!"

"I'll turn it off if you promise to answer my questions honestly," he says.

"Fine. I promise." *Lie.* But hey, Will lied to me. And if I want to keep him as my best friend, he can't find out it was me who made that video.

Will puts his phone in his pocket. "Okay, camera's off," he says.

"Good. Why are you acting so weird? What's with all these questions?"

"Here's the thing, MJ. There's a pretty good chance at least some of the video used to make the fake one of Dara accusing me was taken the night of your party, because of the sweatshirt she's wearing. And that got Dara and me thinking."

"Alert the press," I say, but Will doesn't even smile. Instead, he takes a piece of paper out of his pocket, and as he walks closer to me, he unfolds it. Then he holds it up so I can see it. The anxiety in my stomach tightens.

"Dara and I made a map of everywhere we could remember her being the night of your party. Then I worked out the angles to find where the camera might have been located to capture her."

I take the paper from him, my heart starting to beat so quickly I wonder if I'm having a heart attack.

"So when you went into the kitchen, I looked on the bookshelf, because I worked out that's the most likely place it could be, based on the angle in the video. And guess what? There's a spy cam here."

I try to swallow the panic that's creeping up my throat, making it hard to speak.

"God, Will, dramatic much? It's not a 'spy cam,'" I say, using air quotes. "It's a CatCam. We installed it so Zack could see Pascal while he's away at school."

That part, at least, is the truth.

"So it's linked to an app for viewing," Will says. "Huh. I bet you can move the camera around with it, too."

My stomach is churning. Will's eyes narrow on my face with cold fury—I've never seen him like this before.

"Tell me the truth, MJ. Did you make the video?"

"Really, Will?"

"I mean, all the evidence points to you," he says. "Still, I kept thinking, *Nah, it can't be MJ.* You're my best friend, and I couldn't for the life of me think of why you'd want to screw up my life like this."

"I wouldn't—"

"But then it hit me—you have a powerful enough computer to make a video like this at your house," he says. "From when Zack used to mine Bitcoin in high school. He showed me once when I was over here. Which means the only reason it couldn't be you is because we're friends."

Will takes a step closer and pins me with his gaze. "So tell me it wasn't you, MJ. Tell me that I'm wrong. That I'm the crap best friend here."

I want to lie, because I don't want to lose his friendship. But it's Will. Up until ten seconds ago, I've never lied to Will. Now suddenly it's a habit? No way.

Feeling like I'm about to jump out of a plane with no parachute, I say, "I did. But I didn't mean for anyone else to see it."

I feel both immediately better and instantly worse.

Will looks like I just sucker punched him, which I guess in a way I did.

"Why?" he asks, shaking his head in disbelief. "Why would you do that to me?"

Why? Guess it's my turn to be angry.

"Because I was pissed and hurt," I tell him. "You'd been seeing Dara for months and you never said a word. I knew something was weird at the end of the summer because you were being distant and—"

"No I wasn't!" he exclaims. "I was busy studying for the SAT. The one that the College Board is now investigating, thanks to you!"

"But you lied to me even after you'd taken it!" I say. "You kept being sketchy about why you were busy. When I found out you and Dara were dating and heard you'd been together since the summer, I knew that was the real reason. Why didn't you just tell me, Will? Why was it such a big secret? I thought we were best friends and then I find out you'd been lying to me for months and blowing me off. Do you know how much that hurt?"

"So you decided to ruin my life?" he asks. "Stanford could take back my acceptance because of you."

"You don't even want to go to Stanford!" I yell. "Not that you have the guts to actually tell your dad that. Maybe I did you a favor."

Will stares at me. "Are you serious, MJ? You think you did me a *favor*?"

I shrug and stare back.

"God, that's so messed up," Will says, looking like he doesn't recognize me.

I feel twitchy and desperate. I didn't mean for this to happen, and I don't know how to get Will to forgive me. What if he doesn't?

"Look, Will, I swear I never meant for that video to be seen by anyone except for me. I was upset that night, and I started working on it after everyone left."

His eyes are still stormy and he clearly doesn't believe me.

"I'm serious, Will. It was . . . like a fun AI challenge. I only did it to make myself feel better. Normally, I'd have made it with *you*, but you were kind of the problem."

"A fun AI challenge?" he says. "Are you for real?" Suddenly, a look of realization crosses his face. "Oh my god—no wonder you were defending me so fiercely when Ada asked if I'd cheated! You knew it was fake because you made it."

I cringe inside. "I told you, no one was ever supposed to see it!"

Will places his hands on his hips and raises a skeptical eyebrow. "Oh yeah? Well, that plan worked out great. So how did Rumor Has It get it?"

"I was watching it during study hall to make myself feel better and—"

"A video about me cheating on the SAT made you feel better?" Will bites out, his words short and clipped.

"It's messed up. I get it. But like I said, no one else was supposed to see it and—"

"You keep saying that, like it's supposed to make me feel better. Spoiler alert—it doesn't."

"I know," I say. "But I'm trying to tell you how I think it got out. So I was watching it, but that was the day Sam came over and asked me to the movies and . . . well, I forgot to log out of my account."

Will crosses his arms over his chest. "*You* forgot to log out of an account? MJ, the cybersecurity queen?"

"Yeah, I know. But I was freaking. How would *you* feel if *I* randomly asked you out? Wouldn't your head be spinning?"

That makes him pause.

"I guess . . ." he admits.

"Will, I lost it when Rumor Has It posted the video. As soon as I saw it, I logged into my YouTube account and realized that someone had changed the setting to public. I changed it back to private, but it was too late. They must have already downloaded the video as a backup plan."

Will raises an eyebrow. He's still not convinced.

"Can you imagine how guilty I've been feeling? Not only did the video I made get you in serious trouble, it caused you and Dara to break up," I say.

Will's shoulders slump as he looks down at his feet. "Yeah, it did. And I don't think she's ever going to forgive me for not believing her." He lifts his gaze to me. "And then when the evidence pointed to you, I told her that it couldn't be, because you're my best friend."

I didn't think it was possible to feel worse about everything than I already do, but it is. "So Dara thinks you believed me over her? Ouch." Looking into his eyes, I ask, "But my question is if *you'll* ever be willing to forgive *me*."

He fidgets with the string of his hoodie. "Why didn't you tell me you'd made it and it was a deepfake right away?" he asks. "If you had told me, I would have believed Dara when she told me that she never said it." He looks at me, his eyes sad. "We might not be in this stupid mess."

I don't know if he means him and Dara or him and me. All three of us, I guess.

"Yeah, but I thought it would go away. And I was afraid," I tell him. "Afraid that you'd hate me. That I'd end up losing my best friend." Swallowing the lump that's risen in my throat, I add, "And now it looks like that might happen anyway."

Will won't look me in the eye, and there's a lengthy and awkward silence. I wonder if this is really it, if I've caused the end of our long friendship.

The thought of not having Will in my life creates a great aching hole in my chest.

But then he meets my gaze. "Nah. You can't get rid of me that easily," he says. "I mean, you owe some serious groveling and all that. And I'm still mad. But I'm sure you'll make it up to me."

I feel a flicker of hope welling up. "I'll totally let you win at *Mario Kart* for the next ten years," I say, offering a small smile.

Will snorts. "You owe me so much more than that."

I nod. "Yeah, I know."

"But seriously, you have to tell Joyner right away."

"I can do that," I say. "We can do it right now if you want. Anything to get you out of trouble."

Will holds up his hand. "Wait. There's also another thing. You gotta help Dara and me figure out Rumor Has It's real identity."

"Done," I tell him. "I'm sick of their anonymous gossip."

"I know. I wish I could go back in time and tell the person that started Rumor Has It to just not," Will says.

"Yeah, but if people didn't love reading it so much, maybe the tradition wouldn't have carried on all these years. I mean, we always read it, right?"

I can tell it hurts Will to admit it, but he finally mutters, "Yeah, I guess. Even if it was to hate-read."

While I start writing the email to Joyner admitting I made the deepfake and explaining how and why, Will texts Dara to fill her in. I'm not sure what she texted back, but he goes outside to call her, and he's gone for a while. When he finally comes back, he says, "Well, she agreed to come to my house tomorrow, so we can work on figuring out who Rumor Has It is together."

"What did she say about me?" I can't stop myself from asking.

"Let's just say that it took some persuading for her to come," he says. "She's got good reason to be mad at both of us."

It's going to be seriously awkward tomorrow. But with the three of us working together, we've got to be able to figure this out.

Watch out, Rumor Has It. You're going down.

DARA

When I walk into Will's living room on Wednesday morning and see MJ sitting there, I actually grind my teeth. There's so much I want to say to her, but I force myself to hold it in—for now, at least.

She looks just as uncomfortable as I feel.

"Uh, hey, Dara," she says. "I just want to say I'm so sorry. I shouldn't have made that video. I just hope you know that I never planned to show it to anyone . . ." She trails off, biting her lip.

"Why would you make it if you weren't planning to show it to anyone?" I ask.

MJ plays with the strings of her COME TO THE MATH SIDE, WE HAVE π hoodie.

"Because it was a challenge," she says. "I wanted to see if I could create a realistic deepfake with a small data set. Most people use celebrities because obviously they have much bigger data sets to use for machine learning."

"Obviously," I say sarcastically.

She plows on, ignoring my tone. "I was mad the night of my party, so I decided to use you and Will to experiment with some new programs that don't require as much input. When

I looked at your social media accounts, you had the most video material for me to use," she explains, like I care about the how of this video more than the why. "That's why it was of you accusing Will rather than the other way around."

"Wait . . . is what you're saying that if I'd had more video than Dara on social media, you'd have a deepfake of me accusing *her*?" Will asks. He sounds completely dumbfounded by the idea.

"Um . . . yeah," MJ says, dipping her head to avoid eye contact. "But you didn't, so I knew I'd be able to get a more realistic deepfake if it was Dara doing the talking."

The thought that the only thing that saved me from being in Will's place was that I'd posted a few more videos on social media sends shivers down my spine.

"So I could have been the one facing investigation by the College Board instead of Will?" I ask.

MJ nods.

A fresh wave of anger hits me. "And you couldn't tell us any of this days ago? Like, the day Rumor Has It posted the video? That's so messed up, MJ!"

"Dara, I know you're pissed, but we've got to work together," Will reminds me. "We've all got reasons to be mad—me at MJ, MJ at me, and you at both of us. But how about we focus that anger on figuring out Rumor Has It's identity?" He looks from me to MJ, and then back to me. "They are the one we should all be mad at, because without that public post, none of this would have happened."

"Okay, sure," MJ says, giving me a tentative glance.

"Fine," I say with a sigh. "But just how exactly do you propose we do that?"

"Well, the video was set to private on YouTube," MJ says. She looks at me pleadingly. "I swear, Dara, I never meant for anyone to see it. There was no way Rumor Has It could have accessed it under normal circumstances. I think what happened is that I forgot to log out of my account in the library."

"Why would you watch it in school if you never meant for anyone to see it?" I ask.

MJ drops her gaze to the floor. "Because Will lied to me, kept secrets. We've never kept secrets. We're supposed to be best friends."

I glance over at Will, who is wearing a pained expression. Even though I'm still angry with both of them, I feel a twinge of something. Not guilt, exactly, but responsibility. Maybe trying to keep our relationship on the down low wasn't the best decision after all.

"And then Rumor Has It made that post saying I was upset and implying it was because I had some stupid crush on Will," MJ continues.

"That was bad," I say.

"It just makes me so mad when everyone acts like Will and I can't possibly be best friends. Like, just because we're a guy and a girl and straight," MJ says. "And it hurt that he seemed to be ditching me because he was dating you."

"I wasn't ditching you!" Will protests.

"You totally were!" MJ exclaims. "I know you might not have thought that, but face it, you hardly ever wanted to hang out, and you didn't trust me enough to tell me the real reason why. How is that not ditching me?"

"Okay, but you still haven't answered my question about why you were watching it in the library," I point out.

MJ bites her lip, like she's wrestling with something. "Because I was proud of having been able to create something that realistic. It gave me confidence that I'm good at what I do, even if Carnegie Mellon didn't want me and my best friend was lying to me."

"If you hadn't used Dara and me in that video, it would be much easier for me to appreciate your mad AI skills," Will says.

"I know," MJ says, looking up at Will. "But I swear it was just supposed to be for me, and it would have been if not for the whole Sam thing."

"So, wait . . ." I say slowly, thinking aloud. "That means Sam could have seen the video. Could he be Rumor Has It?"

"Sam?" Will exclaims. "No way! He's one of my boys. He wouldn't do that to me."

"That's what you said about MJ," I point out, with an apologetic glance at her, because I'm starting to understand that she feels pretty bad already.

"Ouch," Will says. "But yeah, you're right."

"Everyone's a suspect until they aren't," I say. "It could be pretty much anyone. But we have to start somewhere to try to narrow it down. Maybe with the people in the library with you that period?"

"But how do we know it wasn't someone who came in later and found me still logged in to my account? Someone who watched it and then emailed it to Rumor Has It?" MJ asks.

"We don't," Will says. "But Dara's right. We have to start somewhere, and it makes sense to start with whoever was in the library with you. If we clear all of them, then we start over and widen the net."

"Sounds like a plan," I say. "So, MJ, who was there besides you and Sam?"

"Ada. And Carly and Jayson," MJ says slowly. "Carlos Ruiz . . . Rosa Lang . . . Angie Blackmon . . . I can't remember who else."

"Let's map it," I suggest. "That might help you remember. It worked for Will and me when we were figuring out who was where at your party."

We sketch out a map of the media center and mark in where MJ remembers them sitting. It helps her remember a few other seniors.

"Joe Stotler . . . Jorge Burt . . . Ruthie Watson . . . That's all I can remember."

"Which computer were you using?" I ask MJ.

"I was here, and Ada was using the one there," MJ says, pointing to their respective locations. I mark them on the map.

"Could Carly or Jayson have seen what you were watching over your shoulder from where they were sitting?" Will asks.

"I didn't think so, but maybe?" MJ says.

"They were at your party. So were Ada and Sam," I say. "Maybe we should make a list of everyone who was at your party and see if anyone else was in both places."

By the time we've finished making and comparing the lists, there are only four people who are in the center of the Venn diagram: Ada, Sam, Carly, and Jayson.

"I can't remember if Ada left the library before me," MJ says. "If she did, we could rule her out. I think she did."

"But you're not one hundred percent sure?" Will asks.

MJ shakes her head.

"Then she stays on the suspect list," Will says.

"So do we start with the suspects?" I ask.

"What if we ask all of those in the library that day if they remember where the others were and when they left the library?" Will asks. "See if they come up with the same answers."

"It's a start," I say. "That might give us some other clues."

"Do we know if they're all around over break?" Will asks. "I know Sam's around."

"Ada is," I tell him. "No idea about Jayson or Carly."

"Carly left for Jamaica with her family on the twenty-second," MJ says. "But she's getting back in time for Amir's New Year's Eve party."

"Lucky her," I say with a sigh. I could really go for a week on a beach right about now.

"Jayson's got a seasonal job at Lord of the Fries in the mall," MJ continues.

"Maybe it's good Carly is away," I say. "If Jayson's home, we can ask him first, then see what Carly says."

"I'll invite Sam and Amir over to game tomorrow," Will says, picking up his phone to text them. "I can slip the question to Sam while he's here. And then I can hit the mall and talk to Jayson."

"And I'll talk to Carly when she gets back," MJ offers.

"Obviously I've got Ada," I say.

"Good," Will says. "We've got a plan. If it turns out not to be any of the people we check out first, we can divvy up the rest of the list."

It can't be Ada. She's my best friend. But Will thought MJ couldn't have, wouldn't have made that video, and it turns out she did. It's hard to know who I can trust right now. It's not a great feeling.

WILL

I invite Sam and Amir over for some gaming on Thursday, so I can casually drop the question.

"I've got Mountain Dew, and Sammy boy has his mom's homemade gingerbread," Amir says, and he comes bursting into the living room and drops everything on the coffee table. "So we're set for some serious gaming."

"Hand over the gingerbread," I say. "I could eat it all myself."

"Save some for me!" Sadie says from the doorway.

"Hey, stop eavesdropping!" I warn her.

"Why would I waste my time eavesdropping on you nerding out with your friends?" Sadie says with an eye roll so big I'm surprised her eyeballs don't pop out of her skull. "I just happened to be passing by on the way to the kitchen and heard the word *gingerbread.*"

"There's plenty," Sam says, holding the tin out to her.

"Why can't you be my brother?" Sadie tells him as she helps herself to a gingerbread reindeer with white-and-green icing. "You're so much nicer than Will!"

"You just don't know Sam well enough," Amir says. "He's secretly much more evil than Will."

"Not possible," Sadie says over her shoulder as she drifts out of the room.

What does Amir mean about Sam being more evil than me? It's just the usual trash talking between us when we get together, especially when we're gaming. Right?

We've been playing *Super Smash Bros.* for over an hour when Amir calls out: "Pause! Bathroom break!"

"Figures you pause when I'm beating you," I grumble as I stop the game.

"Total coincidence," Amir says, getting up and heading for the door.

Sam glances at me and laughs. "Right. Total coincidence."

"Hey, I've been wanting to ask you something," I say. "I know it sounds kind of random, but . . . do you remember the day you asked out MJ in the library?"

"Not if I can help it," Sam says, flopping back on the couch. "Thanks for bringing up a painful memory."

"Sorry," I say. "It's just . . . do you remember if she left the library before or after you did?"

Sam looks at me, puzzled. "Why do you want to know that?"

"Go with it for a second. Do you remember?"

His brow furrows. "I don't . . . Wait, I'm pretty sure MJ left first, because Ada and I walked out together." He gives me a sheepish look. "She was talking me off the ledge, because I figured I'd probably blown it with MJ forever."

"So you and Ada left together . . . Did you notice if Carly and Jayson were still there?"

"Yeah, they were still there," Sam says. "I stopped on the way out to ask Jayson if he'd watched the Nets game."

"So Jayson left after you?"

"I guess," Sam says. "Why?"

I hesitate, wondering if the fact that he and Ada left before Carly and Jayson is enough to clear the two of them from suspicion. I decide to risk it.

"I'm trying to figure out who Rumor Has It is," I say.

"You're trying to solve the insolvable mystery?" Amir asks, coming back to plunk himself on the sofa. "Why bother? You'll never figure it out—no one ever has."

"But we have clues," I tell him.

"Who is 'we'?" Sam asks.

"MJ, Dara, and me."

"So wait. Are you asking me questions . . . because you think it could be *me*?" Sam asks slowly. "You think that *I* would post a video of Dara accusing you of cheating?"

"Seriously, Will?" Amir says. "You thought *Sam* did it?"

"No, not really," I admit. "I know that you would never do that to me. But then I never thought that MJ would make a video like that, either, but she did."

"Hold up, hold up . . . did you just say *MJ* made that video?" Amir says, his eyes wide with shock. "Our girl MJ?"

I nod. "Yep."

"Shut up!" Sam says. "Why?"

"She was mad because I didn't tell her Dara and I were dating, and I kept bailing on hanging out for no reason," I explain.

"She wasn't the only one," Amir mutters. "I can't believe you held out on us like that."

"Yeah," Sam says. "But I wouldn't ever send something like that to Rumor Has It." He looks me straight in the eye. "And I swear to you, I'm not the one behind that website."

"I didn't really think you were," I say. "But we're starting with the suspects who were in the library that day with MJ and were also at her party."

"So . . . does this mean Sam and Ada are in the clear?" Amir asks. "Because they left the library before Jayson and Carly?"

"I think so," I say. "Dara's talking to Ada. You know, to double check everything."

"Wow," Sam says. "I hope you realize I'd never do that to you. Or to anyone."

"I know," I say. "But how do you think Dara feels? I was a total jerk to her. We all were."

"I guess we owe her an apology, huh?" Amir says.

"Big-time," Sam says. "So are you two back together?"

I shake my head. "I don't think she's ever going to really forgive me," I say with a sigh. "Ugh. I don't want to think about it. So I'm focusing on trying to figure out who is behind Rumor Has It."

"So how are you going to figure out if it's Jayson or Carly?" Amir asks.

"Are you guys free tomorrow? How do you feel about a trip to the mall?"

"Are you kidding? You want to go to *the mall* the week after Christmas?" Sam says. "With all the people returning the presents they don't want and fighting each other in the sales? It's like hardcore mode in *Call of Duty*. We'll never survive."

"Trust me, I'd much rather stay here and destroy you at *Call of Duty*, but MJ said Jayson is working at Lord of the Fries," I tell them. "And now that I know that Sam and Ada left before him and Carly, I want to ask him some questions."

"You realize Carly is his kind-of, sort-of girlfriend, right?" Amir says.

"Duh," I say.

"So is he going to answer you truthfully?" Amir asks.

Oh. I hadn't really thought about that. "But what am I supposed to do?"

"Why don't I ask him?" Sam says. "I was the one who talked to them in the library that day."

I run my fingers through my hair, thinking. "That's a good idea," I say finally. "It'll be less obvious."

"As long as you appreciate the depth of my friendship," Sam says. "Going to the mall with everyone and their mother. Man." Sam shakes his head.

"I do," I say. "But how do you think Jayson feels? He has to work there!"

"He deserves danger pay," Amir says. "But it's probably more like minimum wage."

I arrange to pick them both up the following morning. After they leave, I text MJ and Dara.

Me: Sam says he and Ada left the library together.

Me: BEFORE Jayson and Carly.

Me: Dara, did you talk to Ada yet?

Dara: Yup. I talked to her today, and she said she left with Sam.

Me: Yeah. So it's down to Jayson and Carly.

Me: Sam, Amir, and I are going to the mall tomorrow to talk to Jayson.

MJ: Do you think Jayson will tell the truth? I mean, he and Carly are dating.

Dara: That doesn't mean he won't throw her under the bus. Look at what happened with Will and me.

Me: Ouch.

MJ: Yeah, ouch, but also . . . true.

Me: Well, Sam said he'd ask Jayson, since he talked to them that day.

MJ: Good thinking. But if Jayson did it or knows that Carly did, I bet he'll lie.

Dara: Probably. But we gotta ask.

Me: Talk to you tomorrow.

Parking at the mall on Friday morning is insane. We're cut off like three times for parking spots by ruthless shoppers. Sam's right—this is hardcore mode and we're not even in the mall yet. After driving around for fifteen minutes, we finally get a space and head into the mall.

It's not much better inside. People rush past, smacking my legs with their shopping bags. "Jingle Bells" is blasting over the loudspeakers even though Christmas is over, like we haven't already had to listen to nonstop carols since before Thanksgiving.

"Promise me we're leaving as soon as we talk to Jayson," Sam says. "I'm having sensory overload."

"Deal," I say.

Lord of the Fries is hopping, even though it's not even lunchtime. Jayson looks frazzled.

We get in line, and when Jayson sees us, he smiles. "What's up? You crazy enough to come here during the post-holiday frenzy?"

"I know, right?" Sam says. "I don't know how you stand it, especially now."

"Yeah, I'd probably be yelling at customers half an hour into my shift," I say.

"Oh, I am," Jayson says. "But just in my head." He eyes the line forming behind us. "So what can I get you?"

"Three large fries," Sam says.

"Gotcha," Jayson says, turning to get them.

When he comes back and we're paying for the fries, Sam asks him, "Hey, Jayson, do you remember we were in the library the Monday before break? It was during study hall? You were sitting with Carly at the table near the computers, and as I was leaving with Ada, I asked you if you'd seen the Nets game the night before?"

Jayson looks confused. "Uh . . . yeah, I guess."

"Did you and Carly leave the library together?" Sam asks.

"What? Why do you want to know?"

Jayson sounds more curious than defensive.

"I just wondered, because I left my GHS Robotics hoodie there, and it hasn't turned up in Lost and Found, so I was wondering if you saw anyone take it," Sam says. I'm impressed with how quickly and easily he came up with that lie—then my paranoia kicks in. If he can lie this easily to Jayson, how do I know he's not lying to me?

Ugh. I remind myself that Ada confirmed she and Sam left together.

"I didn't see your sweatshirt," Jayson says. "But you should ask Carly when she gets back. I had to leave because I didn't want to be late to earth science again. Mr. Hardy threatened to give me detention if I was. And I can't get any more detention or Coach is going to bench me. But maybe Carly saw it."

"All right, thanks," Sam says. "Well, hang in there. See you at Amir's tomorrow night?"

"Yeah," Jayson grumbles. "Happy fricking New Year."

I laugh. "See you tomorrow, dude."

"Later, Jayson," Amir says.

We fight our way back through the mall while devouring fries and relinquish our parking spot to a big SUV with antler horns on the roof and a red nose on the grille.

"So," Amir says. "What now?"

"Do you believe him when he says he left first?" I ask.

"Yeah, why wouldn't we?" Sam asks.

"It should be easy enough to check with Mr. Hardy if Jayson really *was* under threat of detention," Amir adds.

"True," I said. "I guess we'll have to wait until tomorrow when Carly shows up to your party."

If it's not her, then we have to start working through the list of all the others who were in the library that day. And if they check out, then we'll have to start over.

Ugh. I can't wait to clear my name, so life can go back to normal.

Then I think about Dara.

Well, normal-*ish*, anyway.

RUMOR HAS IT

Good morning, Panthers! The clock is ticking down on this year . . . Less than twelve hours till we roll on into the next one. Was last year a good one for you, or are you in the hope-next-year-will-be-better camp?

Will H continues to sweat it out about Stanford, and there's still no word on the investigation by the College Board.

Did you catch the front-page article about Valentina V's dance talents in the *Greenpoint Gazette*? She's been performing the part of Clara in the Greenpoint Arts Center production of *The Nutcracker*. Brava, Valentina!

Life hasn't been so great for Agnes K, who fractured her ankle ice-skating on Monday. After surgery, she's got a bunch of titanium pins. Check out the pictures on her Instagram—they're crazy! She'll be on crutches when school starts again in January, which is a big disappointment for her and Panther girls' basketball, because she's been one of our team's high scorers. Heal fast, AK!

Who is heading to Amir H's party later? I'm told that it's the place for seniors to be tonight. For the rest of you, there are parties at Miles C's, Destiny M's, and Kelly G's.

I wonder whose party will spill the most titillating tea?

Wherever you're planning to ring in the New Year, be sure to send your scandalous snippets to rumorhasitghs@gmail.com.

And don't forget to check out the New Year's scandal roundup on Monday.

Happy New Year!

MJ

I spent most of my vacation doing college applications and gaming with Zack, who is home from college and being a total slob. Oh, and besides working more hours at my usual job, I did some babysitting, even though it meant having to deal with sugared-up, hyper little kids. I don't know how Will and Dara survived being camp counselors last summer.

Meanwhile, I've got a meeting with Joyner and my parents when school starts again hanging over my head all break. My parents said I couldn't go to Amir's party because I'm grounded. I begged them to change their minds.

"I have to be there!" I pleaded with them after Will told me Jayson's probably in the clear. "It's my job to talk to Carly!"

"If only you had a small device that fits in the palm of your hand that you spend way too much of your life glued to that might enable you to do just that . . ." Dad said.

My parents complain about me being snarky, but it's obviously an inherited trait.

"Dad, it's not a phone call or text kind of thing," I said. "I need to see her face when I talk to her. We need to know if she's telling the truth."

They didn't relent, though—at least not until Will's mom

called to talk to mine. I'm not sure what she said, but Mom called me downstairs afterward and said they'd agreed to give me a "very temporary hall pass" to go to Amir's.

"Don't blow it by getting into even more trouble," Dad added.

Like I would. It already feels like I'm grounded forever.

I take a break from working on college applications the morning of New Year's Eve to go for a run. I'm twitching on a sugar high from eating too many cookies and need to burn off some nervous energy.

I'm not supposed to hang out with Will because I'm grounded, but we agree to just happen to be out for runs at the same time so we "randomly" bump into each other at the corner.

"Well, fancy meeting you here!" he says.

"I know, right?" I say. "Total coincidence."

We take our usual route around the neighborhood.

"By the way, did you ever talk to Sam?" he asks, setting the pace. "You know, about the whole asking you out thing?"

"What? No." I match Will's stride and fall into the easy gait.

"That's cold."

"C'mon, Will, the next day Rumor Has It posted the video and everything blew up between you and Dara, so . . . Anyway, why are you asking?"

"Well, when I was asking him about that day in the library,

he said something about reminding him about painful memories."

"Oh," I say. "Now I feel bad."

"Don't feel bad," he says. "But one way or the other, maybe put the poor guy out of his misery."

"Fair enough," I say. "I'll talk to him tonight."

"And what are you going to tell him?" Will asks.

"I don't know," I admit. "I mean, maybe . . . if we went out as friends, just the two of us. Like as an experiment."

"And just see how it goes?"

"Yeah. You're a guy. Do you think he'd go for that?"

"I'm a guy, but I can't speak for Sam. Still, it's worth a try, right?"

"Guess so. I mean, Sam's cool. I just never really thought of him like that."

Our breath comes out in small clouds for a moment before Will says, "So, now that I've done my bit for true love—or not— what I really want to know is: Did Zack manage to dethrone you as the *Marvel vs. Capcom* queen?"

I flash him a grin. "No, Her Majesty still reigns supreme."

Will tries to bow while he's running and almost trips on a pothole. I grab his arm to steady him.

"I appreciate your fawning adoration, but try not to injure yourself before track season starts."

"Good plan," he says, falling in line with my stride again. "So, you psyched for Amir's party?"

"Yes and no," I say. "Psyched for the party—don't forget to

thank your mom for getting me sprung for the night. But I have feelings about the possibility that Rumor Has It might be Carly."

"I hear ya," Will says between breaths. "I can't decide if it's worse for it to be her or to find out it's *not* her."

"Of course it's better if it's not her," I say. "She's my friend. To think that she'd say all that stuff about me behind my back—"

"Is it behind your back if it's plastered all over that website?"

I throw him an exasperated glance. "Fine, that she'd post all that stuff about me . . . about all of us . . . for all of the world to see."

"True. But if it's not her, that means we have to start with the list of all the other people at the library. And that means it's going to take even longer to clear my name."

He's right. It feels like there aren't any great outcomes here.

"Ugh, I don't want to think about this now. I'm supposed to be *not* thinking about it."

"Fine, so what did you think of the latest episode of *BattleBots*?"

We spend the rest of the run talking about what we can take from how the robots were destroyed on *BattleBots* to apply to Karla the Killer. The county-wide competition is coming up in a few weeks, so we're still tinkering and fine-tuning her lethal talents.

"Race you to the stop sign," Will says when we're almost at the end of our three loops.

He starts sprinting right away, giving himself a head start. I try my best to catch up, but he beats me.

"You cheated," I grumble as I try to catch my breath. "How am I supposed to keep up with your giraffe legs when you give yourself a head start?"

"Just trying to keep you on your toes," he says, panting. "Come on, let's go chill for a while at my house."

"I'm not allowed to," I say. "I'm grounded, remember?"

"So I'll go in the front door and you sneak around the back. Your parents will still think you're out for a run."

"I knew there was a reason you're my best friend," I say.

He lets me in the back door, and we grab drinks before sprawling out on opposite ends of the sofa.

"How are the college applications going?" he asks.

"Okay, I guess," I say. "Though I've added three more schools to my list, because now I'm worried I won't get in anywhere."

"Come on, MJ," Will says. "You can't let the fact that one stupid-competitive school turned you down make you convinced you're going to be rejected everywhere."

"Easy for you to say," I tell him. "You got *in* to your stupid-competitive school."

"Don't remind me," he says. "But still. I know you're going to get in somewhere great."

"That's if Joyner doesn't expel me for making that video."

"They can't expel you for that. You weren't the one who posted it."

"I hope you're right," I say. "Anyway, I still have to figure out what to do for my essay. I want to rewrite it."

"So what's stopping you?" Will asks.

"I want it to be on something important, that will make someone who is bored to death from reading hundreds of essays a day pick mine out of the pile."

"Wish I could help, but I got nothing," Will says. "Although . . ."

"What?"

"Ever since this happened, I've been thinking about how I want to work in tech . . ."

"Duh."

"Yeah, I know. It's just . . . now I can't help wondering if I'd be doing good for the world by solving problems with tech or just helping to destroy it faster."

"Wow. That's deep," I say. "But . . . not all tech is bad, right? It depends on the application. I mean, look at all the good that AI is doing, like reading X-rays for disease as well as or better than radiologists. Or helping to lower manufacturing costs."

"Yeah, and putting people out of work," Will says. "Or making it easier for anyone to create a deepfake that could screw up someone's life or . . . I mean, on a bigger scale, think about how the same skills you used to make that video of Dara could be used to completely mess up . . . well, anything and everything."

"I guess," I admit. It never occurred to me to think about AI that way. I don't know why. But I get what Will's saying. "So are you planning to change your major or something?"

"No, I still want to study computer science. But now I'm wondering if I want to design games or focus on cyber-security instead."

"Whoa. White hat hacker Will," I say, adding a cheesy, "Channeling his inner evil for good."

"What? I'm not evil," he says. "I'll just have to *think* like a black hatter."

I poke him in the leg with my sneaker. "Will, I've known you forever. You definitely have inner evil. You tried to get me to eat Peeps made of Play-Doh!"

Will laughs. "Who could blame me? You were such a sucker for fake food!"

"So evil. I was afraid to eat Peeps for, like, *years* after that."

"Sorry, not sorry," he says. "Anyway, I guess what I'm trying to say is that since my life was almost completely derailed because of what this technology can do, it's made me think more about the implications of . . . Well, I realize now that I was so young and naive when I said tech is neutral and objective." He sighs. "No more thoughtless fanboying about how cool the latest tech advance is."

I burst out laughing. "*So young. Like, six weeks ago* younger."

I grin at him. "And I'll believe you'll stop fanboying about tech when I see it."

Will chuckles. "Okay, I'll still fanboy. But I'm trying to figure out what kind of person I want to be, too. Like what would you do if you got asked to work on a really exciting project from an AI point of view, but you knew it was going to be used for something bad?" He glances over at me. "I want to be a good person." He laughs ruefully. "Wow, could I sound more ridiculous?"

"You *are* a good person, Will," I say. "Even if when we were in kindergarten, you told me that *Star Wars* T-shirts were for boys."

"How many times can I apologize for that?" he asks. "Even I'm a victim of the patriarchy sometimes."

"I'll skip recounting all the ways it was still wrong," I tell him. "Because I like you."

"Noted," he says.

I realize that Will has been thinking about the long-term implications of the technology I used to make the deepfake video more than I have.

Maybe instead of spending so much time feeling sorry for myself because I didn't get into Carnegie Mellon, I should spend a little more time considering that.

Will is driving to Amir's, so I head over to his house when I'm dressed for the party. It feels good to be sprung from MJ Jail for a night.

"You look nice," Will says. "I like that shiny stuff you have on your lips."

"That *stuff* is called lip gloss. And thanks."

There are already cars parked down the street by the time we get to Amir's. I spot Jayson's truck as I'm getting out of the car.

"Looks like Carly's here," I tell Will. I feel a flash of nerves.

"You know what to do," he says. "Play it cool and let's see what happens. Remember, we don't know that it's Carly."

"Hey! About time you guys showed up!" Amir shouts when he spots us walking in the front door. He hands us each a pair of those crazy glasses shaped in the number of the New Year.

I put mine on, then look at Will, who has done the same. We both start cracking up.

"Well, it's definitely a look," I say.

"It goes with your lip gloss," Will says. "Maybe I should borrow it?"

I'm about to pull the lip gloss out of my bag because I know he will totally put it on, when I spot Carly and Jayson over by the window talking to Cara Smith and Arkady Morosov.

Dara is there with Ada, and they're talking to Tony Ortega. Well, it's more like Tony and Ada are involved in a super-animated conversation and Dara's watching with an amused smile. I wonder if Tony and Ada are finally going to act on the glaringly obvious thing they have going between them. About time if they do.

I glance over at Will and I feel a twinge of guilt, noting the look on his face when he sees Dara. It's so obvious he still has a thing for her. I guess I understand why she can't feel the same way about him anymore, but it's Will. He's such an awesome guy. I just . . . wish she could.

I head into the kitchen to fill a plate with nibbles, making sure to take some of Mrs. Hassan's baba ghanoush, which I know from experience is amazing.

Then I head back out to the living room, where some of the swim team is starting a dance-off. I'm glad I have food so no one can rope me in.

"Is that baba ghanoush?" Will says when he sees my plate.

As soon as I confirm it is, he grabs a pita chip off my plate and scoops up half the stuff I had on it.

"Hey, go forage for your own food!"

"But it always tastes better when I steal it from you!" he says with a grin.

I roll my eyes. "If you're going to eat all my food, you have to go get us more."

"Fine. You didn't get nearly enough anyway." Will takes off, shouting, "Coming through! Need more snacks!" while everyone in his way laughs.

I keep my eye on Carly, who is currently dragging a reluctant Jayson to the center of the room to dance with her. If she's dancing, she's going to get thirsty. Maybe I'll be able to catch her without Jayson if she goes to the kitchen to get a drink.

Will weaves his way back through the dancers, miraculously without spilling anything on his plate.

I steal some chips off his plate, just because.

"Oh, I see how it's gonna be," he says, moving his plate to his other side where I can't reach it.

"So do you think Ada and Tony are finally going to go for it?" he asks.

"If the way they're flirting is any indication, then yeah," I say.

"They've been flirting since the beginning of the school year," he says. "Talk about a slow burn."

Amir joins the dance-off, and I call out encouragement. Sam sidles over, a smile on his face. "My boy Amir has some moves, huh?"

"And you're surprised? He's been playing *Dance Dance Revolution* for as long as I can remember," Will says. "And he's been crazy into *Beat Saber* ever since he got the VR setup last year."

Then he gives me a meaningful look and says with absolutely no subtlety, "Oh, I need more chips thanks to you snarfing mine."

He heads back toward the kitchen. I can't help noticing that he detours to pass by Dara. She gives him a brief smile that I'm pretty sure only I notice, then continues her conversation. Poor Will.

But I've got my own stuff to deal with right now. "So, Sam, uh, about that day in the library . . ."

He dips his head so his hair shields his face, but it doesn't hide the flush rising from his neck.

"Forget it," he says. "I shouldn't have—"

"No. I won't forget it. I want to apologize for getting so freaked out. It just, you know, took me by surprise."

He raises his head, and his hopeful expression unnerves me, because I'm still not sure how I feel. "So I was thinking . . . what if we went to the movies, just the two of us, but as friends, and then we just, like, see what happens next?"

"Wow. I thought . . . Yeah, let's do that," he says. His smile is wide and genuine, lighting up his face.

I smile back at him, feeling a little fluttery.

Then I see Carly break away from the dance-off, heading for the kitchen. I look around for Will, but he must still be in the kitchen.

"Sam," I say, shoving my plate of food into his hands. "Carly just went into the kitchen. Can you hold this for me?"

"Yeah," he says. "Good luck. Is there anything I can do?"

"Come up with some reason to keep Jayson in here if you see him heading to the kitchen," I tell him. "I want to ask her when he's not there."

"Will do," Sam says, taking a chip and scooping up some of my baba ghanoush.

"Hey, leave some for me!" I call back to him as I navigate the dance floor obstacle course.

Tricia Searles, Jackie Bell, and Jermaine Kilworth are in the kitchen with Carly and Will helping themselves to snacks. Will gives me a you-got-this look.

"Carly! Happy New Year!" I exclaim. We hug each other. "How was your vacation?"

"Nice glasses," she says. "And it was amazing. A total blast. Lots of super-hot guys at our resort, too." Lowering her voice, she grins at Will and me. "Don't tell Jayson."

"My lips are sealed," I say, trying to figure out the best way to bring up the library. "Not sure about them." I nod my head toward Tricia, Jackie, and Jermaine.

"I heard nothing," Tricia calls over as she grabs soda from the fridge.

Jackie taps her lips with her forefinger. "I don't know, y'all. I bet Rumor Has It would *love* to hear that."

"So how was your break?" Carly asks me, ignoring the mention of Rumor Has It. "Do anything fun?"

"Not really," I say. "It's hard to have much fun when you're grounded. Babysat and worked. Played a lot of video games with Zack. Worked on rewriting my college essay. Snuck out to go running with Will. It definitely wasn't as much fun as hanging out on a beach in Jamaica surrounded by hot guys."

"I'll say," Will mutters heavily.

I flash him a let-me-handle-this look.

Jermaine, Tricia, and Jackie have gone back to rating all the snacks. I grab a pretzel and then ask, "So, Carly . . . I know this is kind of random, but can you remember being in the library during study hall Monday of last week? Like right before your hot-guy-a-thon?"

Carly raises an eyebrow. "You're not kidding about random," she says.

"Okay, but do you remember when we were all there? You were sitting at a table with Jayson, Ada and I were working on the computers, and Sam was sitting near the stacks?"

Her brow furrows. "I . . . think so?" She looks at me curiously.

"Did you leave before or after Jayson?"

There's a long pause that's emphasized by the party noise going on around it.

"I don't know. With him, I think."

Is she lying, or does she legit not remember?

"Are you sure?"

"Why?" Carly asks. "What's the big deal about when I left the library?"

I'm not sure what to say without coming out and confronting her. What if it wasn't Carly? Then again, I don't want to find out that Rumor Has It is a good friend. Someone I trusted.

That's how Will must have felt when he found the CatCam in my living room.

He's been standing there, snacking on chips, watching me handle it. But I guess he can't take it anymore, because he suddenly says, "Want to know about my break?" There's an obvious edge to his voice. "It's been as okay as it can be given that I've still got the College Board investigation hanging over my head."

Carly dips a carrot in the onion dip. "Yeah, that must be

super stressful." She munches on her carrot. "So . . . are you worried about losing your place at Stanford?"

"I was," he says. "But now that I can prove I didn't cheat, I'm pretty sure it's not going to happen."

Carly's eyes widen. "What do you mean?" She looks from Will to me.

"Hold up—you mean Dara lied about you?" Jackie asks. Everyone in the kitchen is now focused on this, not food.

"No, she never said any of it," Will says. "The video was a deepfake."

Carly stares at Will. "What do you mean *deepfake*?"

"He means that someone created a video of Dara saying things she never actually said," I tell her.

"Wait . . . so that video Rumor Has It posted was fake?" Jermaine says. "That's crazy."

"People can do that?" Tricia asks. Everyone gathers around the island in the middle of the kitchen, but the food is no longer the main attraction. They smell drama brewing.

"I'm . . . confused," Carly says. "How do you know the video was a deepfake, whatever that is?"

I exhale. Here goes nothing. "I know because I made it."

"No way!" Tricia exclaims.

"Hold up, hold up! *You* made that video?" Jermaine says.

"Savage!" Jackie says.

"Why would you do that?" Carly asks. "I thought you and Will were best friends. And he and Dara . . ." Her voice trails off as her eyes track from one of us to the other.

"Will and I *are* best friends," I say. "Why I did it is a whole long thing. All I care about now is clearing Will's name."

"And Dara's," Will adds.

I give him an apologetic glance. "And Dara's. I already told Joyner that I was the one who made the video," I say.

"But this whole thing never would have blown up the way it did if Rumor Has It hadn't posted it," Will says. He leans his elbows on the island, which to someone else might look like he's being casual, but I can tell he's tensed up like a tightly coiled spring, just ready to explode.

"I don't understand. What does any of this have to do with whether I left the library before or after Jayson?" Carly asks.

"Because there's something we haven't been able to figure out," I say.

"What's that?" Tricia asks.

"How Rumor Has It got the video," I say.

"Isn't that obvious?" Carly says. "Someone emailed it to them."

"But how did that someone get it? It was set to private on YouTube," I say.

"Did someone hack your account?" Jermaine asks.

"No," I say. "But I did forget to sign out of it that day in the library because I was in such a hurry to leave."

"So it could be anyone," Jackie says.

"It could," I say. "But I don't think so."

"To cut a long story short, we started with a list of four suspects," Will says. "And now we're down to one."

"Who's that?" Carly asks. "And what's that got to do with when I left the library?"

"Because the four suspects were you, Jayson, Ada, and Sam," I say. "Ada left the library before Sam."

Jackie, Trish, and Jermaine are looking from Carly to Will and me like they're watching a game of tennis.

"Sam stopped to talk to you and Jayson, and then he left," Will says. "So while you were checking out hot guys in Jamaica, we asked Jayson if you left the library together, and what do you think he said?"

"He said yes, of course," Carly says. "Because we did."

I stare at her. She's lying.

"So what does that mean?" Jermaine asks.

"Well, it's interesting," Will says. He's obviously trying to play it cool, but I know him well enough to catch the undercurrent of excitement in his voice. "Because that's not what Jayson told us. He said that Carly left after him."

"You're Rumor Has It, aren't you, Carly?" I say. "And you've been writing crap about Will and me, even though we're supposed to be friends."

"Wait, Carly is Rumor Has It?" Trish says, looking surprised.

"Keep up, Trish," Jackie says. "It's gotta be her."

"In what world?" Carly says. "Y'all are dreaming."

I look her in the eye. "The evidence points to you. Especially since you lied about leaving with Jayson."

"How do you know he isn't the one who's lying?" Carly says, tossing her head. "Why are you so convinced it's me?"

"That should be easy enough for Joyner to check," Will says. "Mr. Hardy can confirm—or not—Jayson's story."

"Ball's in your court, Carly," Jackie says.

"Oh my god, what is the matter with everyone? I'm not Rumor Has It!" Carly says, rolling her eyes.

"I don't know," Jermaine says. "There's a lot that points to you." He glares at her. "And if it is you . . . I wanna know why you'd write all that crap about me after Mykala and I broke up. Not funny."

"You're not listening!" Carly exclaims. "I. Am. Not. Rumor. Has. It." Then, turning to Will and me, she says, "Prove it," and walks out of the kitchen.

"Oh, don't worry, we will," I call after her.

I have a feeling this is going to be a very happy New Year— but not for Carly Vickers.

RUMOR HAS IT

Happy New Year, Panthers! How many of your resolutions have you managed to break so far?

But I know what you're here for. You want *all* the NYE dirt, and Rumor Has It never lets you down. Got your popcorn ready? Good. Let's get to it!

Destiny M's party was well attended, and we hear that several new couples are ringing in the New Year together, including Patricia K and Brenda L, Kim J and James P, and Aliysha B and Cameron F.

I hear Miles C has been grounded thanks to Skip L, who managed to back into Mrs. C's car while leaving Miles's party. I'm told Mr. C called Skip's parents and demanded that they pay for the damage. Not so happy New Year, Skip!

Meanwhile, over at Kelly G's, things got heated when Patty D started dancing with Lucas J . . . instead of her boyfriend, George S. He and Patty had a monstrous fight in the middle of the party, and it looked like the end of the year *and* their relationship. But don't worry, readers, by the time the ball dropped they were back together. (We got whiplash just watching it play out . . .)

Amir H's party had the best snacks and an inspired dance-off with some of the swim team. I'm happy to report that Ada T and Tony O finally locked lips. I hear it's about time, because they've been flirting for, like, the entire semester.

Amir's party also featured an unsolved mystery. Apparently rumors are flying around about who I am—as if any of you would ever be able to figure that out.

It's so cute how much you want to know.

But I'll never tell.

WILL

I pick up MJ and we drive to Greenpoint High early on the morning of our first day back, January 2, so we can meet with Joyner. MJ's got a second meeting with him and her parents later this afternoon. "To discuss my punishment," she says as we're driving to school. "On top of having been grounded at home. Ugh, it's been hanging over my head all break."

I know she's my best friend, but I'm having a hard time feeling *that* sorry for her. "MJ, we've *all* had bad things hanging over our heads," I say.

"Oh. Yeah. Sorry," MJ says.

"I hope he saves the worst punishment for Carly," I say. "But first we need to show him the reasons why we're convinced it's her."

Joyner welcomes us to his office and wishes us a happy New Year.

"So, tell me the new developments you alluded to in your email yesterday," he says.

We briefly go over how Dara figured out the video was a fake, and then MJ tells him about the conversation with Carly at Amir's party.

"So there were witnesses to this conversation?" Joyner asks.

"Yeah, Tricia Searles, Jackie Bell, and Jermaine Kilworth," I say.

"Leave it with me," Joyner says. "I'm going to call in the school resource officer and our IT director. We'll interview the witnesses to the conversation, and I'll check in with Mr. Hardy about Jayson being under threat of detention."

"So . . . can you tell the College Board to cancel the investigation?"

"Once we've concluded our internal inquiry, yes," Joyner says. Then, seeing the look of disappointment on my face, he adds, "As soon as I got the email from MJ over break, I emailed the College Board to inform them of the new developments and asked them to hold off on notifying Stanford."

I'm relieved, but at the same time, I realize that now the college decision might be back in my hands.

"I wonder how long his investigation is going to take," MJ says as we leave Joyner's office.

"No matter how fast it is, it can't be quick enough for me."

I want this over right now.

We're walking to our second-period class when we hear Tricia Searles being called to the office.

"And so it begins," MJ says.

"As long as it ends with my name being cleared."

Over the course of the morning, I hear Jermaine and Jackie paged to go to the office, too. Then, just before last period starts, the announcement comes: "Carly Vickers, please report to the office."

I want to be a fly on the wall of Joyner's office so badly.

Sadie and I are heading to the parking lot after school when we see Carly storming down the hallway.

"Thanks for nothing, Will! You just got me suspended!" she shouts at me. "Joyner said I might be expelled for breaking the district's internet use policy."

A kaleidoscope of emotions rushes through me: relief, vindication, anger so powerful that I can't speak.

"So you *are* Rumor Has It!" Sadie exclaims.

I manage to say, "You admitted it? To Joyner?"

"How could I deny it when they have security camera footage of me downloading MJ's video from the computer in the library?" Carly spits out.

I can't help the bitter laugh that explodes from me. "Kind of ironic that you got nailed by a video after you almost destroyed my life with one."

"How was I supposed to know that stupid video was a fake?" she says. She puts her hands on her hips. "Face it, Will. You thought it was real enough to break up with Dara!"

"I don't know," I say slowly. "But maybe before spreading it around, you could have, you know, checked to make sure it was true?"

"Oh, come on, Will! Don't be so stupid. Since when has

Rumor Has It ever done that? It's all about gossip." She pins me with angry but reddened eyes, making me wonder if she's been crying. "And you read it, just like everyone else. You just didn't like it when it was about you."

I feel the heat rushing to my face. Because she's right. I did read it. We all did, even if it was as haters.

"Wow, Carly," Sadie says, stepping into the space between Carly and me like a boss. "You almost ruin my brother's life, and now you're blaming *him*?" She shakes her head. "That's all kinds of messed up!"

Warmth spreads in my chest, seeing Sadie have my back. Guess she's the only one who is allowed to diss me.

Stunned into silence, Carly stares at us open-mouthed and then turns on her heel and stomps away.

"Thanks," I say.

"Whatever. She deserved it," Sadie says. "Come on, dork-face, drive me home."

The insult makes me feel like maybe, just maybe, my life might be getting back to normal again, and a smile spreads across my face.

I'm not smiling later that afternoon when MJ texts me to say her parents are out so she's sneaking over to tell me about the meeting with Joyner.

She flops into the beanbag chair in my room and groans. "It's good to escape from MJ Jail. I never thought I'd say this, but I'm so sick of looking at the four walls of my room."

"So are you going to tell me what happened?" I ask.

"Joyner suspended me for ten days," she says. "Obviously, my parents were not happy, especially since that's going to be on my record while I try to get into college for next year." She sighs.

"I'm sorry, MJ," I say, even though I'm not sure what I'm apologizing for. She made the stupid video, after all. But I believe her when she says she never planned for anyone to see it. I just wish she'd told me sooner.

"I'm sorry, too," she says. "For using you and Dara in that video. I should have used a celebrity, like everyone else does. Or Zack. Well, at least I know what I'm going to write my revised college essay about."

"What, your skills or the consequences?"

"Both. But also what all this has taught me about, I don't know . . . like how I have to think more about how something I make can be used for good—or bad. It's like we all get so excited about new technology and how it can make the world a better place, but we don't always think enough about what might happen if people with bad intentions use it."

"That sounds like a good essay."

"I hope so. Dara and Ada offered to help me revise it the night of my party. I don't know if they'll still be willing now." She picks a piece of fluff off the beanbag. "Not that I'd blame them. Especially Dara."

"If they don't, I will," I say.

"Aw, Will," MJ says. "You're the best."

"I know," I say with a grin. She rolls her eyes, but it's the first time she's smiled since she got here.

I still get mad every time I think about that video and how it messed with my future. But MJ's been a big part of my life too long for me to let it destroy our friendship.

Dad's been nagging Sadie and me to have that dinner with Katelyn ever since he got back from Aspen last week. I've been putting it off, because I've been trying to get the applications in for some other colleges. Midway through the second week after the New Year, I realize we can't put it off any longer.

"What about this Friday?" he says. "Although I'll have to check with Katelyn on that."

"Dad . . . can we just make it you, me, and Sadie? There's a lot we need to talk about, and it'll be difficult to do with . . . well, with someone else there."

There is silence on the other end of the line, except for the sound of my dad's breathing. I brace for the explosion, but it doesn't come.

"Okay, we can do it just the three of us," he finally says. "As long as we get a date for you to meet Katelyn on the calendar really soon."

Wait . . . did my dad get possessed by someone reasonable while he was in Aspen?

I just hope it holds up till Friday, whatever it is.

· · ·

When Mr. Joyner calls me down to the office on Thursday morning, my stomach turns over. What now?

"Will, have a seat," he says. I perch on the edge of the chair, my right leg moving in a nervous rhythm.

"I've got good news," Joyner says, smiling. "Given the additional information we provided them, the College Board has agreed to end the investigation."

The breath leaves my body, and I slump back into the seat. "For real? It's over?"

"For you, yes. For Carly Vickers? Not so much," Joyner says.

I dreamed about this moment when I was lying awake with worry over winter break and my future was so uncertain for reasons that had nothing to do with me. Now that I'm cleared, I realize it's time to take control of it. As much as I wish this all had never happened, it has helped me make some decisions. Now I just have to survive telling Dad about them.

When it's time to go meet Dad for dinner on Friday, I find Sadie buried in her bed.

"Hey, Sadie, we need to go."

"I can't," she says, lifting an ice pack off her forehead. "I've got a killer headache."

"Are you sure it's not just Dad-itis?" I ask her before I leave.

"No, it feels like someone is sticking a knife in my brain," she says, putting the ice pack back.

"Sounds fun. Have you told him yet?"

"No. You tell him. I don't want to even look at my phone, because it makes me dizzy."

I can't imagine having a headache that bad. Poor Sadie.

"Okay, I'll tell him why you couldn't make it." I turn to leave.

"Feel better," I say as I close her door, feeling sick to my stomach at the thought of talking to Dad about what I want to do.

Dad's made a reservation at one of his favorite restaurants, Le Mouton Blanc, downtown near the apartment he moved to when he and Mom split up. He's already sitting at a table for three when I get there.

"Where's Sadie?" he asks.

"She's not feeling well. She's got a really bad headache," I say.

"Well, as much as I miss seeing my girl, I'm glad it's given me some one-on-one time with my boy," Dad says, smiling. "Especially now we've got two things to celebrate—you getting into Stanford *and* the end of that whole fake video business."

My stomach flips at the mention of Stanford. I'm going to tell him tonight, but I'm not ready yet. So I deflect by asking him about his trip. He tells me how great the resort was and what an amazing time he and Katelyn had. I don't know if he means to do this, but he gives me the distinct impression he's having a much better time being a part-time dad than he ever had being a full-time one.

It takes a while before he finally says, "So I'm glad your name has been cleared. I'm still mad that your principal risked your future by notifying the College Board."

"He was doing his job," I say, even though I wasn't so happy about it at the time. "The good news is that everyone now knows I didn't cheat, and word seems to have gotten around even without Rumor Has It."

"I always believed that," Dad says, like everything that he said before break never happened. My hands clench on my knees under the table. *Really, Dad?* I take a deep breath—this dinner is going to suck no matter what. Might as well start the honesty early.

"No, actually, you didn't," I say. "You said you wanted to take me at my word, but you saw the video."

"We'll have to agree to disagree on that," Dad says. "I have a different recollection."

"I can't agree to disagree. Because I know what you said. And agreeing to disagree is like telling me the truth doesn't matter."

"Any updates since we last spoke?" Dad says, deflecting, like I'm starting to realize he tends to do. I wonder how Sadie picked up on this before I did. Maybe because I was so busy trying to avoid his disappointment.

"Well, you know MJ got suspended, right?"

"Which she deserved," Dad says.

"I guess. But I still feel bad about it. She never meant the video to get out."

Dad shakes his head. "Will, you need to toughen up, otherwise you'll never make it in business."

"It's not being soft, Dad. She's my best friend."

"Your best friend who nearly ruined your future," he says, like I didn't already know it.

I start tapping my fork to keep my hands from clenching. "Not intentionally," I say. "No one would have even known it existed if Carly hadn't posted it. And as if we needed any more proof that Carly was Rumor Has It, there haven't been any more posts since she was suspended."

"Good," Dad says, nodding his head in approval. "So now you can focus on Stanford and your future." He grabs a bread roll, rips it in half, and then takes a bite.

Here it is. The point where I have to tell my dad how I really feel about Stanford. How going through all this has made me think about the future I almost lost, and what I want that future to be.

So I take a deep breath to summon up more courage and say, "Actually, Dad, I need to talk to you about that."

"About what?" He offers me the breadbasket, and I take a roll but set it on my plate.

"About Stanford. I'm not sure I actually want to go there. I'm applying to some other schools with good computer science majors. Schools that also have programs for cyber-security, which is what I think I really want to do now."

Dad chokes on the piece of roll he just bit off. I wait with a growing sense of dread as he coughs it out and then takes a sip of water.

"What do you mean you don't want to go to Stanford?" he says. "It's one of the top schools in the country."

"I know it's one of the top schools in the country, Dad," I say. "But I'm thinking that . . ." I trail off, seeing the thunderous expression on his face, but I force myself to finish what I started. "I want to explore some of the other schools that offer good cybersecurity programs to see if they might be a better fit. For me. For what I want do with *my life*."

"A better fit? Come on, Will, this is your future we're talking about. You got into *Stanford*. Do you know how many kids are at home crying because they didn't?"

"Yeah, I know. I'm really lucky that they accepted me—"

"It wasn't luck," Dad says. "You worked hard, you're on the track team, and you've got a lot going for you. They're lucky to have you."

"A lot going for me including a dad who is an alum and donates money."

"Is *that* what all this is about?" Dad says. "You wanting to make your own way instead of following the footsteps of your old man?"

"Partly," I say. "If I'm as smart as you always tell me I am, I should be able to succeed even if I choose to go somewhere else."

Dad emits a loud snort of disgust. His disappointment in me is evident.

"When you get out into the real world, you'll realize how important it is to use every advantage you've got in order to succeed," he says. "You'll be grateful for having had the benefit of my connections."

"You're probably right but—"

"You know I'm right," he says. "So why aren't you listening to me?"

Now is when I'd usually give in and do what my dad wants me to do. But I'm tired of being interrupted. I'm tired of always being told what I should do, without him ever asking me what it is that *I* want.

I need my dad to hear me. *Really* hear me.

"I could ask you the same thing," I say. "Why aren't you listening to *me*? Why don't you *ever* listen to me?"

"Did your mother put you up to this?" Dad says, shaking his head. "She's been putting ideas in your head, hasn't she?"

That's the final straw. I throw my napkin on the table and stand up. "I'm out of here," I tell him. "This isn't about Mom. Why do you always assume it's Mom speaking whenever I disagree with you? Huh? Why do you always have to make everything about you and Mom? I get it, you guys hate each other, but stop putting Sadie and me in the middle."

"Will, lower your—"

"Do you think I'm incapable of deciding anything for myself?" I fold my arms across my chest. "This is about *me*, and what *I* want for *my* life. Why can't you understand that?"

Dad stares at me, dumbfounded. I can't read the expression on his face. I don't know if he's mad that I'm rebelling against being his clone, or embarrassed because I'm making a scene in his favorite restaurant.

I turn on my heel and walk away, because I'm beyond done, ignoring his shout of "Will, get back here!" as I exit the restaurant.

I drive around for a few hours, and when I get home, Mom tells me Dad's called like five times wanting to know where I am. He's called my cell and texted me, too, but I've ignored it all because finally standing up to him was exhausting.

"I think you should call him," Mom says.

"I'll call him tomorrow," I say. "I've had enough for one night."

"I hear you, but he was different when he called," Mom says. "Can you believe he actually asked my advice for how to talk it through with you?"

I stare at her. "Seriously? Dad asked *you* for advice?"

She nods. "It surprised me as much as it did you. Maybe even more." She comes over and gives me a hug, then pushes back the irritating bit of hair that always falls across my forehead. "Give him a chance to apologize," Mom says. "It's a big deal coming from him."

"Apologize? Let's not get crazy, Mom. He's never apologized."

"All the more reason to call him back. Maybe he will this time."

"I'll think about it. But not till I've had more time to cool down," I say.

"I know you and Sadie have been avoiding meeting Katelyn, but I think that she might be a good influence on Dad," Mom says. "He said she encouraged him to talk to me about you. To actually make the effort to parent together, even though we're divorced."

"I should have known it wasn't something Dad would come up with on his own," I say.

"Do you come up with all of your best ideas on your own, Will?" Mom asks.

Ouch. She's good. Now I know where Sadie gets it.

I avoid dealing with the Dad issue all weekend. We had a Saturday session for the Robotics Club, doing our final tune-ups for Karla the Killer bot ahead of next weekend's Bot Battle Extravaganza. Then, on Sunday morning, I get a text from MJ:

MJ: Will, I'm SOOOOOO BOOOOOOORED!

MJ: Being grounded sucks.

MJ: My parents went out to run errands.

MJ: Sneak over and keep me company for an hour so I don't start talking to the walls.

MJ: PLEASE, I'M BEGGING.

Me: There's always Pascal.

MJ: I always talk to Pascal. But while he's undoubtedly the cutest cat in the entire universe, he isn't the best conversationalist.

Me: Good to know I'm better at something than Pascal.

MJ: Does that mean you're coming over??????

Me: Sneaking out the back as we speak.

Then I wonder why I'm sneaking. It's not *me* who's grounded.

"Hey, Mom, I'm heading out for a bit," I shout upstairs, not waiting for an answer.

MJ almost knocks me over with the hug she gives me when she opens the door. Even Pascal, who is usually pretty stand-offish, comes to wind himself around my leg, purring loudly.

"Thanks for coming," she says. "Go into the living room, I'll get the snacks."

I nod and head for the couch.

"At least my parents said I can go to the bot battle competition next weekend, even though I'm still grounded," MJ says when she comes in carrying a tray. She hands me a glass of chocolate milk, wedges the bowl of popcorn between us, and picks up her controller. "I mean, I know I'm supposed to be locked up here until I see the error of my ways and stuff, but if they didn't let me go, it would have been war."

"Yeah, that would have sucked, big-time," I say. "You put so much into Karla the Killer."

"Too right," she says. "Come on, let's play. I'm warning you, I've got a lot of pent-up feelings to get out, so I plan to smash you to smithereens."

"Like you could," I say.

She can. It's humiliating.

"Are you even trying?" she says, putting down her controller between games. "What is with you today?"

"The usual, just my dad," I say. Then I tell her about what happened with Dad on Friday and me walking out on him.

"You walked out *before* eating dinner at Le Mouton Blanc?" she says. "What is the matter with you?"

I throw her a dirty look, and she realizes I'm not in the mood for joking about it.

"Okay, okay," she says. "Listen, I'm glad you finally told him. I mean, it's your life, right?"

"Yeah," I say. "And it's weird, I feel bad that things are awkward between Dad and me, but I've been getting this feeling of . . . I don't know, rightness, while doing the applications for other schools. Like I'm finally taking my life into my own hands."

"Or as much into your own hands when people you've never met are deciding whether to admit you," MJ mutters.

"You know what I mean, though, right?"

"Yeah, I do," she admits.

Then I tell her how Dad called Mom and they had a civil conversation.

"Shut up!" she says. "Gary and Stephanie? No way!"

"I know!" I grab a few kernels of popcorn. "It's, like, too good to be true. What if I call him and he's the same my-way-or-the-highway Dad, not the Gary that called Mom?"

"I think you should give him a chance," MJ says. "I mean, what have you got to lose?"

• • •

Later, I'm back in my room, texting Dad.

Me: Hey, Dad. Mom said you called on Friday.

Dad: Yeah. Can we talk?

Me: Not tonight. I'm too tired. There's a lot going on.

Dad: Okay. Want to meet at Buddy's sometime this week? Just you and me?

Me: Yeah, okay. How about Thursday?

Dad: Thursday works.

Dad: And, Will . . . I love you.

My thumbs hover about my phone. I can't help wondering if an alien is occupying my dad's body. But I type: Love you, too, Dad.

I meet Dad at Buddy's at five thirty on Thursday, and it feels like I'm kind of on repeat. He does the usual talk-about-sports thing until we sit down. I'm eyeing him warily, wondering if this dinner is really going to be so different from the last one.

As we order, my stomach starts to churn with hunger and nerves.

"I wanted to say I'm sorry, Will," Dad says. "I shouldn't have brought up your mother when you were trying to tell me how you feel about college."

I stare at him. Did my dad really just apologize? Like, actually?

He leans forward. "Talk to me," Dad says. "I'm listening."

I'm not convinced this will end well, but Dad says he's listening, and now that I've started letting this out, there's no point trying to stuff it back in.

"I'm just not sure Stanford is the place for me," I tell him. "I've never had much of a chance to check out other options because you've been telling me I'm going there since practically the day I was born."

"I think it was the day after," Dad says, with the ghost of a smile. "That's when I got that onesie."

"Exactly," I say. "It's like it was already decided, no matter what I might want." I look him in the eye. "All I'm saying is that I want to apply to some other places so I have choices. Then I can decide which school is the best fit for me." I muster a smile. "Who knows, maybe it'll end up being Stanford after all."

Dad rubs his forehead; then his eyes, which everyone always tells me are so like my own, meet mine. "I can't say I'm happy about this, or that I think it's the right decision," he says slowly. "But if it's what you really want, then you should do it."

"Really?" I say, wondering if I'm in some alternate universe, because my dad is actually being reasonable.

"Yeah, really," Dad says. "But promise me you won't give up on Stanford just because I went there, okay?"

"I won't," I say. "At least if I decide to go there after exploring other options, it'll be because *I* really think it's the best place for me, not because you told me it is."

"Makes sense," Dad says. "I don't want to lie and say I won't be disappointed if you don't go there, but as two very intelligent women keep reminding me, it's your life, and you have to make your own decisions about how you're going to live it." He flashes a small smile. "Besides, there's always Sadie. Maybe she'll want to be a Cardinal."

"Maybe," I say, smiling back but resolving to warn Sadie before she starts applying to college.

For the first time in a long time, pretty much since the divorce, I actually really enjoy having dinner with my dad. He doesn't go off about Mom, and when we're talking about other stuff, he actually listens to what I've got to say, instead of telling me what I should be thinking instead.

It makes me feel hopeful. Maybe I don't have to force myself to be Dad's clone to get his approval. Maybe I can make him proud of me just by being myself.

DARA

Three weeks after Amir's party, there's a hearing at the school board about Carly getting expelled. We didn't know about it in advance, but that night, Mr. Joyner sends out an email to the entire Greenpoint High School community.

I'm writing to let you know the results of the investigation into the posting of a deepfake video involving serious allegations of academic dishonesty from a school computer to the gossip website Rumor-Has-It.com.

This website has caused pain and disruption to our school community since its inception. But this latest episode was the proverbial straw that broke this administration's back.

After lengthy interviews with all the parties involved and review of footage from our security cameras, we were able to prove, without a reasonable doubt, who the culprit is beind Rumor Has It. The student was first suspended and, after a hearing at this evening's school board meeting, has been expelled from Greenpoint High School.

I get a text from Ada before I've even finished reading it.

Ada: Did you see Joyner's email?!!!

Me: Yeah. I kind of expected it after what Will said about her being caught on the library security cameras.

Ada: Maybe I'm imagining things, but I swear GHS seems more chill without Rumor Has It stirring things up all the time.

Me: Totally.

Ada: Do you think Carly being expelled means the end of Rumor Has It?

Me: I hope so. I don't want anyone else to have to go through what Will and I went through.

Me: But I've overheard some people complaining how much they miss it.

Ada: Ugh! No way!

Me: Maybe I'd miss it, too, if Carly hadn't made Will and me the subject of so many posts.

Me: If she hadn't shared that video with the world.

Ada: Yeah, I guess. So . . . on a totally different subject . . . are you coming to the Bot Battle Extravaganza tomorrow?

Me: Wouldn't miss it! Ted is coming with. The geek runs strong in that one.

Ada: Well, at least you have that in common. 😊

Ada: Does that mean you're feeling better about him marrying your mom?

Me: Yeah. I'm getting more used to the idea.

Me: It still brings up, you know, FEELINGS sometimes. About my dad.

Ada: That's natural.

Me: But it's going to be kind of cool to have siblings.

Me: And the most important thing? My mom is so much happier.

Ada: It's good to see you happy again, too.

Me: 😄 ♡

"So, Dara, are you ready to watch some bot battle action?" Ted asks as we pull into the parking lot where the Bot Battle Extravaganza is being held.

"What's not to love about robots trying to destroy each other?" I say. "Better they destroy each other than try to control us."

"This thing you went through with the deepfake really does make you think, huh?" he says as we're getting out of the car.

I nod as we walk toward the building. "Ever since it happened, I've been thinking about all the other ways someone with enough computer power can mess up people's lives. It's . . . scary."

"It is, and in so many different ways: personal, legal, economic, political," Ted says. "And on that cheerful note, let's go enjoy some robot destruction—instead of worrying about our own."

"Sounds like a plan," I say, smiling at him. Maybe it's because I'm more interested in fixing the human body rather than tinkering with robot ones, but that sounds like a lot more fun.

Karla the Killer really does kill it. After a few hours of heats with a lot of repairs in between, she's in a final battle with Data the Destroyer from Roosevelt High.

"Come on, Karla!" I shout as the teams put both of them in the ring. "You can do it!"

Ada looks over to where we're sitting and gives me a thumbs-up. I catch Will's eye and he smiles. We're at this weird place now where we're kind of friends, but it's awkward sometimes. Part of me remembers how much fun we had together, but I know it would never be the same.

Ted is practically bouncing out of his seat with excitement. "Let's do it, Greenpoint!" he shouts. "It's time to decimate Data the Destroyer!"

"Whoa, Ted!" I say. "Does my mom know about this bloodthirsty side of you?"

"The good thing about robots is that they don't have any blood," he says. "Well, unless one of them shatters and a flying part injures an actual person." He smiles at me. "Luckily, I happen to know that there's a really smart EMT in attendance."

The buzzer goes, and the Roosevelt Data bot, which looks like a crab with wheels instead of legs and sharp projections instead of claws, moves across the ring while Karla comes rolling toward it with her hammer raised. She manages to get in a good smash, and the GHS fans go wild.

But then Data the Destroyer manages to flip her. "Karla!" Ted shouts. "Right yourself!"

Data goes in for another attack, but just as he's about to reach Karla, she flips back over and raises her hammer. Before Data can change course, Karla smashes him right in the middle. He tries to reverse away before she can smash him again, but she's damaged his gears and she basically pounds him to an electronic pulp.

"And the winner of this year's county-wide Bot Battle Extravaganza is . . . Karla the Killer from Greenpoint High School!" says the announcer. "Congratulations to all of our contestants! Thanks to our audience for coming out. We'll see you next year!"

Not me. I'll be premed at Johns Hopkins. It's strange to think that everything will keep carrying on the way it has while I'm not here. Except for all the things that will be different by this time next year: I'll have a stepdad and stepsiblings, and they'll be living in our house when I come home. I'll be sharing a room with Saffron, since I'm not going to be there most of the time. It's weird to think about giving up part of what's always been my space.

We head down to congratulate the GHS team.

"Congrats! You did it!" I exclaim, giving Ada a big hug first, and then congratulating Amir and Sam. I give MJ a small high five.

Then there's Will standing in front of me. We give each other an awkward hug.

"Hey, we're all going to the Dairy Barn after this," he says. "You should come."

"Are you sure?" I ask. "Isn't it, like, a team thing?"

"Come, Dara!" MJ says. "It's the only fun thing I'm allowed to do for another two weeks."

"You're still grounded?" I ask.

"Yeah. If I didn't have Zack's rig to keep me busy, I'd go crazy."

"As long as you're not busy making more fake videos of me," I say, only half joking.

"Nah," she says. "We're good. I'm sticking to famous people for now."

"Stay away from the dark side, MJ!" Amir says.

"Well, I came with Ted," I say, glancing over my shoulder at him. "So . . ."

"Go, have some fun, you deserve it!" Ted says. "Congratulations, kids. Very impressive work."

"Okay, Dairy Barn," I say, grinning at my friends' victory.

I ride to the Dairy Barn with Ada and MJ, and the guys go in Amir's car.

MJ got video of Data the Destroyer's death throes, and she keeps playing it.

"Oh my god, MJ, I'm as proud of Karla as you are, but can you stop?" Ada says, plugging her phone into the stereo.

"I don't think I can ever watch this enough," MJ says. "It's . . . victory."

It's weird to be back at the Dairy Barn. I haven't been here since that day Will and I came after camp; the day things between us kind of began. It's like we've come full circle, and we're back to just being (sort of) friends again, all in a space of six months. I've spent way too much time doing the what-ifs of Will and me: What if we hadn't been a secret, what if Will had told MJ before her party, what if she'd been accepted at Carnegie Mellon so she wasn't in such a bad mood the night of her party, what if MJ hadn't forgotten to log out of her account, what if Carly hadn't been in the library when she did?

But it's a waste of time to wonder. Things happened the way they did, and now we're all figuring out the new normal.

Like hanging out with a group of friends that includes Will, and working things out so it's not awkward.

He and I are the first two to get our ice creams, so we go grab a table for everyone.

"So how are things?" I ask him. "Your dad must be happy that there's no more threat of losing your place at Stanford."

"Oh, he is," Will says. "But he wasn't so happy that I've decided to apply to other schools."

"Wow, you decided to do that? And you told him? That's huge!"

"It was huge," Will says. "And at first it didn't go well. But then he surprised me by actually listening."

"I'm not going to pretend I understand why you wouldn't want to go to Stanford having gotten in," I confess. "But I'm happy that your dad was understanding."

"So the great Dara Simons admits she doesn't understand something," Will says, smiling. "Good to know that Wonder Woman has at least one flaw."

"You'll be happy to know that's still my ringtone," I tell him.

"I *am* happy—ecstatically happy. If you'd changed it back, we couldn't remain friends." He gives me a tentative smile. "We are still friends, right?"

I hesitate a moment, then nod.

"What do you think would have happened with us if Carly hadn't . . ." Will trails off, as if afraid to say the words out loud.

"But she did," I say as gently as I can. "So we're going to be friends."

"Guess so." He grins. "Well, the good news is that I won't have any mixed feelings about beating you for valedictorian," he says.

"It's cute you still think you can."

"It's cute he still thinks he can what?" Amir asks, coming to join us with a serious-looking sundae.

"Beat me for valedictorian," I say.

Amir laughs. "He'll be lucky if he's salutatorian," he says. "MJ's not far behind him, and she's on the warpath."

I glance over to where MJ is still in line. She and Sam are laughing, and there's something about the way they're looking at each other . . .

"What's up with MJ and Sam?" I ask. "They a thing now?"

Will and Amir look at each other and they're both grinning. "I hope so. About time," Will says.

"Yeah, poor Sammy's been crushing on MJ since sophomore year," Amir adds.

"So are they, like, dating?" I ask.

"From what MJ says, they're doing stuff together as friends, and seeing where it leads," Will says. "Okay, they're coming over now, so . . ."

"William, have you been talking about me?" MJ says as she slides into a seat holding a waffle cone. "You've got that guilty look you always get when you've been talking smack about me and then you shut up the minute I get there."

She really *does* know Will.

"Oh, just talking about how I'm going to beat both you and Dara to be valedictorian," Will says.

I snort. "Yeah, right."

"Will, you realize I'm only two-tenths of a point behind you and closing fast, right?" MJ points out.

"I'm sooooo scared," Will says.

"You'd better be," MJ says. "Being grounded, I don't have a whole lot left to do besides study."

"I'll make bets with both of you," Will says. "If I beat Dara for valedictorian, she has to buy me a sundae and vice versa, and if MJ beats me for salutatorian, I have to buy her ice cream."

MJ and I exchange a glance.

"You're on," MJ says.

Will looks at me. "What about you, Dara?"

I stick out my hand. "I'm in."

We do a three-way shake and settle down to eat our ice creams.

I don't know which of us will win—although I'm betting on me. One thing I do know: We're all glad Rumor Has It won't be there to write about it.

RUMOR HAS IT

Surprise! I'm BAAAACK! Just in time for all the summer fun. Did you miss me?

Hope you didn't think that just because Carly V got expelled, I would disappear. Rumor Has It cannot be destroyed. I am forever.

Booted out of school, second semester senior year: That has to hurt, right, Carly?

Hey, did you know there are security cameras all around school? Carly did, because she posted about other students being busted after having their candid camera moment. Unfortunately, she forgot about them when it came to causing trouble of her own.

Before we break for summer, let's catch up on what's been going down since my predecessor's humiliating departure from our hallowed high school halls.

Patty D ended up dumping George S for Lucas J after all. It caused a major splash at Marilena S's graduation pool party.

It wasn't all betrayal and breakups at Marilena's, though. Love was in the air for Nick P and Sean M, who were cozying up poolside.

Happy news for Ms. Johnson—she's engaged . . . to *Mr. Hardy*!

That romance slipped under the Rumor Has It radar during our unscheduled break in coverage of GHS gossip. Congrats to the happy couple.

But I know why you're all here. Did Will H pull off the greatest heist in Greenpoint history and steal the valedictorian spot from Dara S?

That would be a no. Dara is this year's valedictorian.

Will also wasn't able to steal back Dara's heart.

In a surprise twist, MJ M beat out Will for salutatorian by .03 of a GPA point. Crazy, huh?

It really was the closest competition for the top spot in GHS history. I'm told Will had to buy both Dara and MJ ice cream. Something about a bet.

Well, I'm off to enjoy my summer vacation. Be good, Panthers. And if you can't be good, be interesting!

I'll be here waiting in eager anticipation to spill it all.

ACKNOWLEDGMENTS

Maya Angelou wrote: "You may encounter many defeats, but you must not be defeated." Reader, this book was born of defeat. I worked on a different book for a year, writing, rewriting from scratch, again and again. By the time my beloved editor, Jody Corbett, told me that we should start over with a new idea, I hated that book so much it was a relief. Well, mostly . . . I did allow myself a one-day pity party to feel very, *very* sorry for myself, because those were legitimate feelings after having worked so hard and failed. But then I got up the next morning and started brainstorming new ideas, and I'm proud of the result.

So firstly, thanks to Jody and David Levithan for telling me to start over, because it gave me the opportunity to write a much better book. As always, Jody took my mess of ideas and helped me shape them into a book. I am truly grateful to work with her.

Thank you to the Scholastic team for getting this book out into the world: Josh Berlowitz; Maeve Norton, whose amazing design blew me away; Erin Berger; Elisabeth Ferrari; Rachel Feld; Shannon Pender; Lizette Serrano; Emily Heddleson; Danielle Yadao; Mariclaire Jastremsky; Anna Swenson; Ann Marie Wong; Robin Hoffman; and the entire sales team.

Jennifer Laughran is the best agent ever. She helps to keep me sane in an industry that is anything but.

One of the best parts about writing books is that it gives me the opportunity to speak to really interesting people for research. Any mistakes are all mine.

Thank you to Connecticut State's Attorney Richard J. Colangelo Jr. for putting me in touch with Inspector Mark C. Sinise of the Stamford/Norwalk office. Being able to visit the Technical Investigation Unit of Southwest Connecticut was a highlight of my research, and I integrated some of what I learned there into the novel.

My sincere and grateful thanks to Alexander Bein, who gave me insight into qualifying as an EMT while still in high school. Thanks also Natalie Medico of the Greenwich EMS 911 Explorer Post and my Greenwich BJJ pal Jeff Brown for answering my questions. Readers of *Backlash* might remember a Dr. Delman. Well, David Delman, MD, is a real-life doctor—and friend—who continues to be extremely generous and patient about answering all my ER questions.

Thank you to Diane Morello for putting me in contact with her colleague Whit Andrews. Whit was incredibly helpful in helping me flesh out my rudimentary ideas with plot points that actually made sense.

I'm so proud of my children, Josh and Amie, for continuing to promote the love of books in their respective careers.

Hank, you are my rock. Thank you for knowing when to let me vent, when to remind me of which stages of neuroses are part of every book process, and when to just give me a hug and hand me another square of dark chocolate. There's nothing fake about my love for you.

Finally, I am ever grateful for you, dear readers. Here's a deep truth: Your emails and letters give me the courage to keep writing when the going gets tough.

ABOUT THE AUTHOR

Sarah Darer Littman is the critically acclaimed author of *Backlash*; *Want to Go Private?*; *Anything But Okay*; *In Case You Missed It*; *Life, After*; and *Purge*. She is also an award-winning news columnist and teaches writing at Western Connecticut State University and with the Yale Writers' Workshop. Sarah lives in Connecticut with her family, in a house that never seems to have enough bookshelves. You can visit her online at sarahdarerlittman.com.